Homecoming

SALLY TYLER HAYES

D0544531

*All the characters in this book have no existence outside the imagination
of the author, and have no relation whatsoever to anyone bearing the same
name or names. They are not even distantly inspired by any individual
known or unknown to the author, and all the incidents are
pure invention.*

*First published in Great Britain 1996
Silhouette Books, Eton House, 18-24 Paradise Road,
Richmond, Surrey TW9 1SR*

© Teresa Hill 1996

ISBN 0 373 07700 9

18-9610

*Printed and bound in Great Britain
by Mackays of Chatham PLC, Chatham*

Another novel by Sally Tyler Hayes

Silhouette Sensation®

Our Child?

I am blessed in having the most wonderful mother in the world. She's kind, caring, generous with her time, her support and her love.

Mum,
I don't say it enough, but I hope you'll always know that I love you very much.

Daddy,
I love you, too. And I'm so glad you are a reader and that you turned me into a reader. Special thanks for those Saturdays we spent at the used bookshop in Lexington picking out bags full of books to take home. Maybe someday I'll write you a Western.

I wish you both a long, happy, healthy retirement.

Prologue

Allison Jennings sat pale, still and dry-eyed in the lawyer's office while he quickly and ruthlessly stripped away everything she had left.

Even herself.

Or at least everything she'd ever known and believed about herself.

And he did it all with a self-righteous anger that she simply didn't understand.

She had just turned eighteen, and she'd just lost her parents in a train derailment. That had been hard enough, but this? This was like something out of "The Twilight Zone." She kept waiting for the funny theme music to play. Glancing up, she saw that the lawyer was glaring at her.

He had to be wrong. There was no other explanation. The lawyer must be wrong. But ... what if he wasn't?

She gripped her trembling hands tightly together in her lap and tried not to even think about the possibility. It would be even worse than the accident she'd had at age thirteen, when her whole past had disappeared. But she'd had her parents then, to help her get through the traumatic experience.

They had filled in all the missing pieces of her past, going into long, vivid detail about all the birthday parties, Christmases and family vacations. They hadn't had a lot of money, but they'd had a wealth of love. And slowly, as they meticulously filled in memory after memory of their lives together, she'd come to believe the things they said. She'd reconstructed the days and the years in her own mind, until she couldn't quite tell whether she actually remembered them or not.

And what had it really mattered, anyway? They'd been her parents. They'd loved her, and they'd remembered. That had been enough.

But now?

Oh, God, now?

Her stomach rolled. She pictured her mother and father in her mind as they had left on the train for an anniversary trip to Chicago. They had looked so happy, and so very much in love. She'd never see them that way again. She'd never be able to ask them about the unbelievable story this lawyer had told her. She could never ask them to come here and set him straight.

She looked up at him now, gathered what little energy and courage she had left, then told the coldhearted stranger, "There's a mistake."

Allison had come here yesterday, to this Indiana town where she and her parents had supposedly lived before her accident—before she lost her memory. She'd hoped it would spark some recollection in her mind, give her some new memories of her parents to help her through the years she now faced without them.

It hit her now, as never before during this whole nightmare, that she was totally and absolutely alone in the world. She had some cousins somewhere in this town, and an uncle, she thought. But she had no memory of them. She and her parents had moved away shortly after her accident, and they had never returned. Bad memories, her mother had told her, and never elaborated. Allison hadn't pushed the issue, but now she wished she had. Because then she wouldn't be so alone right now.

Among her parents' possessions, she'd found a business card for this attorney in Indiana, along with a scribbled note in her father's handwriting about a will. She was certain that her parents had left what little they had to her, as their only child. She would need it, if she was to have even a hope of starting college this fall.

So, she'd come here, because eight years ago her parents had made out a will with their lawyer who'd now become her accuser.

"There's no mistake," he said, his tone strident. "I'm tempted to have you locked up."

"Me?" she cried. "For what?"

"Impersonating someone may not necessarily be a crime," the lawyer bellowed at her, "but coming in here and attempting to steal what doesn't rightfully belong to you certainly is!"

"My parents just died," she said, her voice breaking. "And I'm their daughter, their only daughter. I'm Allison Jennings."

The lawyer moved in for the kill. "I've known Libby and Randy Jennings for years. I handled the closing on their first home, twenty years ago. I was their friend. And to think, now that they're dead, some conniving little phony would try to take advantage of them this way... It sickens me!"

She didn't know what to say. She just sat there with an awful feeling of impending doom. Still, she'd lost her parents. She had no one now. What could possibly be worse than that?

"Why?" she said at last. "Why do you think I'm lying?"

"Because Allison Jennings is dead," he told her. "She's been dead for five years."

Chapter 1

Seven Years Later

Federal Prosecutor Jack MacAlister's latest case had brought him here, to the wrong side of Chicago, on a cold, snowy evening, in search of a runaway shelter called Hope House. The weather had even the most hardened street kids scrambling for cover. Hope House, among other things, had a reputation for not skimping on the heat or the blankets, and for serving the best shelter food in the city.

Word on the street was that it also had a new director, not much older than the kids herself, one who'd been out there on the streets in the not-so-distant past. She didn't hassle kids who didn't want a hassle, she helped the ones who were willing to accept help, and she cared for them all.

MacAlister had to admire that particular quality in anyone who dealt with so many hopeless cases. Caring was a very dangerous thing. Too much of it would eat a person alive. Too little, and a person couldn't do the job the way it needed to be done.

He struggled with that himself.

He walked past the converted Victorian house that held the staff offices and those of the foundation that ran the shelter. Next door was an old parochial school, which now served as the runaway shelter, among other things. He brushed the snow out of his hair and off the lapels of his heavy overcoat, feeling more than a little uncomfortable while next to him kids in jeans, sweatshirts and lightweight coats stood shivering in the cold in the lengthening lines to get inside.

Jack MacAlister had never wanted for anything in his entire life, and he worried that these kids always would.

He tried hard not to look at their faces, not when he might well see them again all too soon, under different circumstances. Shooting victims, drug overdoses, kids who belonged on elementary school playgrounds rather than the morgue—he saw too many of them, too often, to look these kids in the eye. It was hard enough to do his job in the U.S. Attorney's office without recognizing the face of the next kid who didn't make it.

MacAlister stopped at the desk and asked one of the kids huddled in the entranceway, one he hoped was a regular, where he could find Allison Jennings. The kid wore torn jeans, high-tops that failed to keep out the snow and a windbreaker. MacAlister received nothing from him but an insolent stare.

"She works here," he said, realizing the problem immediately. Kids on the street didn't want to be found until they were ready, and this one must have thought he was looking for a runaway. "Allison Jennings."

"Don't mean nothin' to me, man."

MacAlister shrugged and went on inside. The heat was pumping full blast, and it felt good. He took off his coat and threw it over his arm.

The halls were overflowing with kids in lines snaking through the hallways, and the noise level was deafening. MacAlister asked two more kids about Allison Jennings before he hit on someone who knew her.

"You mean A.J.?" a skinny, baby-faced boy who might have been fourteen, with the big brown eyes and skin the color of watered-down chocolate milk, said from across the hall.

"She runs the place," he said, not knowing whether the lady used her initials or not.

"And her real name's Allison?" The kid seemed to find that incredibly amusing.

Actually, from what MacAlister had been able to find out, Allison Jennings wasn't her real name at all. In fact, he was betting on that. Now all he had to do was find her and convince her it was time to figure out what her real name was. If he was right, she was the woman who was going to help him keep a kidnapper in jail, where he belonged.

"You know her?" MacAlister asked the boy, trying not to figure out what had made him turn to the streets.

Drugs? Alcohol? A parent who used him as a punching bag—or worse? Kids didn't end up this way on a whim, or because their parents wouldn't let them stay out past midnight.

"Everybody knows A.J.," the kid informed him.

"Know where I can find her?"

"Who are you? Her daddy?" the kid said, his wiseass streak coming out. After all, it wouldn't do for him to be seen being too friendly with anyone over the age of twenty, especially someone who was clearly in a position of authority.

The other kids were staring and starting to laugh. One with a particularly smart mouth had started chanting, "Al-li-son," drawling it out in a sing-song kind of voice.

"You have a problem, Skippy?" a slip of a girl in jeans and a sweatshirt demanded as she stepped into the hallway ahead of them.

"Al-li-son," he taunted her again. "That yo' real name, A.J.?"

"What if it is, Skippy?" she snapped back at him. "Oh, of course, that's not your real name, is it? You want me to tell everybody what it is?"

The kid threw up his hands in a theatrical gesture of surrender and turned away. The other kids expressed some interest in Skippy's real name, but they didn't get anything out of the girl.

"Good," she said, nudging Skippy with her elbow as she made her way down the hallway. "Then you can call me A.J., and we'll leave it at that."

It wasn't until she was standing a foot away from MacAlister that he realized she wasn't a teenager. She looked the part—the worn jeans, the Bears sweatshirt with the sleeves pushed up to her elbows, the thinness that it couldn't hide, the white-blond hair clipped short around her face. No, her appearance never would have given her away. It was the air of authority about her that did, the voice that was obviously used to giving orders and to being obeyed. And it was the challenge that was so clearly visible in the look she threw his way.

"If you're with the fire marshal's office, I don't even want to hear about it," she said, no apology whatsoever in her surprisingly husky voice.

MacAlister decided silence was the best policy while he determined how to handle this. He had a badge in his pocket. The fire marshal would, as well. He wondered if he could get away with flashing it under that cute little turned-up nose of hers, maybe intimidate her into coming somewhere away from this zoo where they could talk in peace and privacy.

He wondered if anyone intimidated her. Now that he thought about it, he hoped not. He needed her to be tough as nails, because he was going to ask her to do something very unpleasant. And, surprisingly, his conscience came to life in that moment, as he looked at her, standing in the midst of these lost kids.

Had she truly been one of them once? He didn't like to think about that, because he knew what living on the streets did to kids, knew the risks they took and the lengths to which they went in order to stay alive.

"Well? Are you?" she said, looking up at him. If she stood on tiptoe, she might come up to his chin. And she did an amazing job of trying to be intimidating, in spite of the fact that she was a foot shorter than he.

He thought longingly of the badge, and of subterfuge.

No way, MacAlister, he told himself. The lady didn't take crap from anybody. She wasn't going to start with him.

"Am I what?" he asked, as innocently as he could.

"In case you haven't noticed," she said impatiently, "my hotel's booked solid tonight. I have work to do. Are you with the fire marshal's office or not?"

"Why don't we go upstairs and talk about it?" he suggested, deciding that a little evasion was the best tactic available to him now. Cupping her elbow in his right hand, he propelled her in the direction from which she'd come. "You do have an office, don't you, A.J.?"

At first, he didn't think she was going to come with him. But he had the distinct impression that she didn't like him touching her, and in trying to break away from his light touch, she took several steps in the right direction, took even more when he kept coming after her.

"This had better be good," she told him threateningly as they made their way down the hallway, through the steadily filling gymnasium and up the back stairs.

A.J. led him down a narrow hallway, then turned and headed through an old-fashioned smoked-glass door that was a bleary shade of watered-down green. Once inside, she took a seat behind the desk and left him to struggle to find room between the chairs pushed against the back wall and the front of her desk.

"Nice closet," he said, wondering if she ever smiled and what she'd look like if she did. He had an inexcusable and unexplainable urge to tease her and see if he could find out.

"You came out on a night like this to bad-mouth my office?" she said as he tried to guess her age. The woman for whom he was searching would be twenty-four in the spring—if, by some miracle, she was still alive. It was probably foolish to think that she was, but then, MacAlister didn't have any angles left.

"What kind of a bureaucrat are you?" she demanded when he didn't answer her right away.

"A cold one. It's supposed to be ten below tonight," he said, watching in satisfaction as her lips twitched into some semblance of a smile. And it was nice. He saw a definite possibility that a full-blown smile would do magical things to that face of hers.

She caught him staring, and quickly looked away.

Amazingly, he felt something close to fascination with her. Obviously, she was a woman to be reckoned with. Obviously, he wasn't going to be able to bully her, which he would have done if he thought it would work and work quickly. He'd have to try something else.

She cared, he reminded himself. She cared about the kids. She'd understand what he was trying to do, and she would help him. Because, ultimately, she'd be helping the kids, keeping them safe from the piece of scum he had parked in jail and awaiting a trial MacAlister couldn't afford to lose.

Surely she would understand that.

"Wait a minute," she said, suddenly serious. "Has something happened to one of my kids?"

"No," he reassured her, then told himself to stop baiting her and get on with it.

The "alleged" kidnapper, entrusted to him by the United States of America, had finally gotten a public defender who wasn't as green as grass in the springtime, and the guy was making noises about actually setting a trial date.

Jack MacAlister couldn't let the case actually go to trial, because he'd never win. After all, he had no evidence. It was a miracle he'd managed to keep the guy in jail for this long. If he asked for one more continuance, the judge would laugh him out of court for sure. And there was no way he was letting the guy out while he tried to build a stronger case. So here he was.

"Well," she said. "You wanted to talk. So talk."

"You are Allison Jennings?" he asked.

At the sound of the name from his lips, she sank back in the chair and sagged downward, for just an instant. She blinked, twice, slowly and deliberately, as if she couldn't believe she was hearing such a question from him.

And then she was back, the seemingly invincible tiger, protecting her hopeless cases with a vengeance.

"A.J.," she insisted.

"But you're not sure about that, are you?" he said, seeing no more reason to beat around the bush.

She took his retort like a slap in the face, and he winced at the pain he'd obviously caused her.

Prosecuting wasn't easy, particularly in a case as ugly as his current one. People got hurt. Innocent people. All in the name of justice.

It hurt to gather the necessary evidence, to get the testimony needed for a conviction, to convince people to relive their worst nightmares in front of the good people in the jury box and whoever else happened to be in court that day, whoever might turn on the TV that night or pick up the newspaper the next morning.

But he did it, because it was his job. Because he believed in what he did and because he saw the greater good that sometimes came of it, no matter who was hurt in the process called justice. Still, momentarily at least, he was ashamed.

He had a surprising urge to reach out to her again, to offer some kind of nonverbal apology, if she'd let him. But he quickly remembered the way she'd drawn herself away from his touch only moments before, when he hadn't yet given her a real reason to dislike him.

MacAlister felt a little better when her chin came up again, that perky little nose of hers tilting regally into the air. She folded her arms across her chest and leaned over the desk.

"Before we talk about who I am, I think it's time you told me who in hell you are and what you're doing here."

He reached inside his jacket, drew out his ID and flicked it open for her to see. Then, in a rare attack of conscience, he wished, for her sake, that the biggest problem she had on a night like this *was* the fire marshal.

"Jack MacAlister," he said. "U.S. Attorney's office."

"And exactly what do you want from me, *Jack?*"

He couldn't help but laugh at the disdain she managed to instill into her pronunciation of his first name. And no one called him Jack.

"I'm looking for someone," he said.

"Would you like to give me a name? A description? Or do we get to play twenty questions for another five minutes?"

"Annie," he said, watching for some flicker of emotion, and finding it—in spades.

"I don't know anyone named Annie."

He held up his hands to silence her. "That's not what I asked."

"Then what? We don't have a runner named Annie at the moment, and even if we did, none of them use their real names out here. Surely you know that."

He was losing his patience, and that wouldn't do. She deserved better than that. But he'd been in court all day, been hounded by one too many of the high-priced lawyers who spent their lives proving the theory that money could buy anything for their clients.

And he did feel guilty about this.

He was going to hurt this girl, and he didn't like doing that. But it was necessary, and he would do it, because he didn't see any other way to keep that animal in jail.

"You didn't let me finish," he said, searching for the nonthreatening, noncensuring tone that he'd use with a recalcitrant judge. "I'm not asking if you've seen anyone named Annie or if you know anyone by that name. I want to know if you are Annie. Annie McKay."

She was obviously puzzled by that, which didn't fit at all with the situation as he understood it.

"There's a Carolyn McKay who's the executive director of the foundation that oversees the runaway shelter," she offered, obviously trying to read him as carefully as he'd try to read a potential witness to assess his credibility. "And her mother, Grace McKay, who volunteers here. Maybe you should start with them."

"Oh, hell," he muttered as the truth hit him, and he looked away. He should have talked to Drew Delaney with the FBI before he came down here. Now he'd stumbled into something quite sticky, and he didn't know how to get out of it.

"What do you mean, 'Oh, hell'?"

He had the feeling that people didn't often surprise A.J., and that when it happened she didn't like it one bit.

Well, neither did Jack MacAlister, and he'd just gotten a rotten little surprise himself. Now he'd just have to make it work in his favor, especially since it was too late to backtrack. She was suspicious now. And it wouldn't take her long to figure things out. He might as well be the one to explain it to her. Maybe she'd think he was on her side.

"They didn't tell you?" he said, knowing damned well that they hadn't.

"Tell me what?"

Drew was going to kill him, once Drew found out what he'd done. He was stuck now. He couldn't stop. He couldn't back down. This woman sitting before him wouldn't let him—and that would be the only excuse he had when Drew came after him. "The girl's full name. They didn't even tell you that?"

"The Annie you're looking for is *Annie McKay?*" she said, and he watched as the knowledge hit her. "And Grace McKay...and Carolyn McKay..."

"Her mother and her sister," he interjected.

She didn't say anything for a moment, just sat there, still as a statue. This time, her face gave nothing away; it was her utter stillness that betrayed her. He had the feeling that he'd shocked her.

"I'm going to kill them," she said finally. "They knew I didn't want to see either one of them, and Nick sent me over here so I could work with them both?"

He didn't blame her for being mad, even as he couldn't blame either one of those women for wanting to get to know her better. It had to be torture for them to know about her, but not know her true identity.

Grace and Carolyn McKay were searching for a little girl they hadn't seen in nearly eleven years, and they had reason to believe that Allison Jennings—A.J., as she insisted on being called—could be that girl.

MacAlister had reason to believe that the man he had in jail was the one who'd kidnapped Annie McKay nearly eleven years ago.

And if, by some miracle, A.J. was Annie, she might be his only hope of getting the man convicted. He'd exhausted every other lead he had, found none of the physical evidence he needed to tie the man to the crimes. His only eyewitness was a frightened seven-year-old girl whose testimony would never hold up in court.

He was banking on the possibility that, nearly eleven years ago, the woman in front of him had been another frightened little girl, pulled into a car and sucked into a nightmare by the criminal he had stewing in a jail cell. And he wanted her to remember that, wanted her to talk about it in open court and in front of what would no doubt be a media circus. To say he could understand her reluctance would have been an understatement. But he couldn't walk away from this. He couldn't let her off the hook. Too many people—like that little seven-year-old girl—were counting on him.

MacAlister looked up at the woman sitting across from him. It wasn't cold in this tiny office of hers, but she was rubbing her hands up and down her crossed arms in a futile effort at warming them. He picked up on the fine trembling of her body, the look of pure fear in his eyes.

"I can't help you," she said, standing and making her way around the desk, coming to a halt when he didn't rise and get out of her way so that she could leave the office.

"You have to," he said, ready to plead his case. "You may be the only one who can. I need to find Annie McKay. Otherwise, I don't have a prayer of winning in court."

"I don't have time for this now," she told him when her first refusal got her nowhere with him. "It's cold as hell out there tonight, and I don't want to find some kid frozen solid in some alley in the morning. I don't have time."

"Make time."

"Make time?" The words nearly exploded from her. "Who the hell do you think you are, meddling in my life like this? What gives you the right to do that?"

He didn't have an answer for her.

"You come in here, sticking your nose into what's left of my life. You've obviously been talking to the FBI about me, maybe even Nick. He was my therapist, for God's sake. You don't have a right to know anything I said to him in those sessions."

"You don't have any rights, because you haven't been accused of any crime," he told her, his cynicism shining through. "In this country, we only offer real legal protection to the criminals."

"Now we're going to have Civics 101?" she said. "I don't believe you. Get out!"

He considered his options, didn't like any of them, but decided on retreat. He'd thrown her a nasty surprise, and he could understand that she would need some time to get used to what she'd just learned.

Telling himself there'd be other days, he rose to his feet.

"Get out," she repeated.

"For now," he said, not adding the obvious—that he'd be back.

Chapter 2

A.J. slammed the door behind him and locked it, then leaned against the edge of her desk, when she wasn't sure her legs could hold her anymore and she was certain no one could see her give in to that particular weakness.

She couldn't afford to be weak. It was a luxury she hadn't allowed herself in years.

"You are Allison Jennings?" he'd said so coolly. *"But you're not sure about that, are you?"*

She wanted to scream at the nerve of the man. Who in hell did he think he was, butting into her life like this? And why would a federal prosecutor care what her name was? Or whether that was her real name?

She wished for a minute that she'd let him stay long enough to find out why he was so interested in her, but he'd thrown her off-balance by telling her the missing girl's last name.

McKay. Annie McKay.

She'd been working here at Hope House, coordinating its programs for runaways, for almost two months now. She and Carolyn had struck up a friendship of sorts. A.J. respected her for the work she did here. And A.J. hadn't found the woman to be nearly as intimidating as she'd feared.

After all, Carolyn McKay, the director of the foundation that ran the shelter, was beautifully elegant, polished, well dressed and self-assured. What could A.J. possibly have in common with her? Yet they had found common ground. The work, the battle against the twisted maze of the all-powerful bureaucracy, the kids who all too often seemed to have no reason to hope. But, obviously, Carolyn McKay had sought her out, because Carolyn thought A.J. was her long-lost sister.

And Grace McKay's deceit hurt just as much. Carolyn's mother had started volunteering at the shelter a couple of weeks ago. She made the most incredible homemade breads and pies. The kids were crazy about them. She liked to hum off-key, liked to show off her pictures of her little boy, Billy, and tell stories about him to anyone who'd sit still long enough to listen.

A.J. had found herself drawn to this wonderfully nononsense, down-to-earth woman who clearly knew what it was to struggle and to overcome. Life obviously hadn't been easy for Grace McKay, but it hadn't worn her down the way it did so many people who knew what it was to have real problems. Surely that was why A.J. liked the woman so much, because A.J. had struggled so much herself with so many things she simply couldn't change, regardless of how hard she tried.

And to think that all the time she'd been working here, these two women had been so kind to her, so interested in getting to know her and in being a friend to her, because . . .

She shook her head back and forth. It made her more than a little sick to her stomach. She hated subterfuge. Hated half-truths and omissions. Most of all, she hated lies.

She'd been lied to her whole life, at least all of it that she could remember.

And the only way she'd found to cope with that was to simply not trust anyone anymore, except her friend, mentor and long-ago therapist, Dr. Nick Garrett. And judging by the things Jack MacAlister knew about her past, A.J. had misplaced her trust in Nick, as well. Because he was the only person she'd ever told about the time she'd spent with the Jenningses, and the lies she'd lived.

Surely Nick's betrayal proved she shouldn't count on anyone, shouldn't trust anyone, shouldn't lean on anyone, except herself.

It was safer that way.

Carolyn McKay, her so-called parents, her friend Nick, this hotshot prosecutor who thought he could just storm into her life and turn it inside out—it didn't matter what they needed from her.

Because she didn't have anything to give them.

She saved it all for her kids. Everything she had to give went to them. When it came to these kids, she held nothing back.

Jack MacAlister would just have to understand that. All of the others would, too.

She couldn't be the one to give Annie McKay back to them. Her past was a giant void, a black hole of sorts, and nothing was ever going to convince her to climb back into that emptiness.

Five minutes later, after she'd calmed herself, but before she lost her nerve, A.J. stood outside Carolyn McKay's office.

It was late, and with the snow coming down so hard, she was surprised to find Carolyn still here. At the moment, she was on the phone with someone, and A.J. stood in the doorway, waiting for her to finish.

She couldn't help but remember that day a few months ago when she'd walked into this office and met Carolyn and Drew Delaney for the first time. He'd been introduced as her fiancé, but A.J. had since learned that he also happened to be an FBI agent, working in the Bureau's division of missing and abducted children. She wondered if Drew had anything to do with this ridiculous assumption that she could be Carolyn's long-lost sister.

Looking back on that first day now, she realized she'd known even then that something funny was going on. Carolyn McKay had been very emotional. She'd been wiping tears from her eyes, and Drew had said they'd just gotten some very good news—something about a family matter that he hadn't explained further to A.J.

But now she knew. She'd just shown up at their door looking for a job at the runaway shelter affiliated with Hope House—all thanks to her friend Nick, who'd recommended her for the job at the shelter. When she thought about him sending her here to take this job, for Carolyn and her mother to watch her, to wait and hope for some sign that she could be their Annie—she wanted to scream at the injustice of it all.

She'd trusted Nick, despite her misgivings about trusting anyone. And he'd betrayed her.

She remembered when this whole ridiculous mess had started. Nick had come to her weeks ago, when she returned from a conference on runaways in Philadelphia, and told her a preposterous story about how he thought he'd figured out who she was, that she had a family waiting for her and he'd somehow stumbled upon them.

A.J. had stopped him right there. She hadn't been interested in the least. Nick had a hard time understanding that, but it was all very simple to her. A.J. didn't know much about the girl he thought she used to be, except for the fact that she was blond, had blue eyes and had disappeared nearly eleven years ago, never to be heard from again.

She'd been presumed dead, but then, in a bizarre break, the FBI had managed to find a link between the girl's kidnapping and the abduction of a little girl named Sara Parker a few months before in one of the neighboring states.

Sara Parker was one of the lucky ones. She had escaped and made it home safe to her parents. They had caught the man they thought had snatched her, and for some reason A.J. had never explored and had no desire to check out now, Nick thought A.J. might be the first little girl the man had kidnapped—Annie.

He'd told her an outlandish story about something she'd said to him years ago under hypnosis that stuck in his mind, about something that had clicked when Sara Parker's kidnapper was arrested and he heard Annie's sister talking on the evening news. But A.J. simply hadn't been interested in hearing about it. Nick hadn't even told her the girl's last name, and she hadn't asked. She hadn't sought any details, and had refused to take any sort of tests that might confirm or deny whether she actually was this girl.

A.J. had lost her identity twice in her life now—once after she sustained some kind of head injury, nearly eleven years ago, and again when the two people she'd believed to be her parents had died and she'd learned that she wasn't their daughter.

Surely that was enough. She wouldn't lose herself again.

She'd put her life back together again, and it suited her just fine. The past was simply that—the past. Anything she found out about that past would only hurt her. And because she could not change it, could not go back and regain the years she'd lost, she saw no reason to explore whatever was back there.

And even if she'd been interested in solving the mystery of her past, she would never have dug into her own background for something like this. A little girl kidnapped, separated from her parents at a very young age, probably

molested in ways she didn't want to imagine—who needed
the kind of grief that came from experiences like that?

Certainly not A.J.

She looked up, startled by the sound of a voice calling to
her. She'd been totally lost somewhere inside herself, and
now Carolyn McKay was off the phone.

"I need to talk to you," A.J. said, not waiting to be in-
vited inside the office tucked away high in the corner of the
old Victorian house.

"Of course," Carolyn, ever the gracious lady, replied.
"Come in and have a seat."

As usual, she was impeccably dressed in a pair of tai-
lored slacks, a soft, dark-colored sweater, her long, dark
hair swept back in an elegant knot on top of her head.

A.J. looked at her own clothing and regarded her casual
outfit with a rueful smile. If she did have a sister, she
couldn't imagine her being anything like Carolyn McKay.
And she damned Jack MacAlister, her buddy Nick and
anyone else she could think of for making her even wonder, even wish for the briefest of moments that she might
have a sister somewhere out there waiting to find her, the
way the McKays wanted and waited for their Annie.

She'd been ready to blast away at Carolyn with all the
anger she'd bottled up inside her since Jack MacAlister
crossed her path and showed her how these people she'd
come to know and like had been lying to her ever since she
came here. Yet now that she was here, now that she was
ready to get this all out in the open, she found it difficult.

She didn't think she could do this calmly, as it needed to
be done. If she didn't, she was going to show Carolyn
McKay just how much this upset her, and she didn't care to
reveal that much about herself to anyone.

A.J. decided to change her mind about having a seat, because now that she was here, she didn't feel that steady on
her feet. She looked down at her hands, knotted together in
her lap, worrying over themselves. She willed them to be

still, then looked up into Carolyn McKay's elegantly beautiful face.

Unbidden came the image of her own face. A chin that was too angular, cheekbones that were too narrow, a nose with a little upward tilt to the tip. Her dishwater-blond hair was cropped short. She was too thin, always had been, but it had become more of a problem after her time on the streets, and she always had to struggle to maintain her weight. When she didn't, it always showed on her face first, making her look even more like a teenager than she normally did.

She was a totally unremarkable woman, while Carolyn McKay was the exact opposite. Again she wondered how anyone could think they were sisters. Obviously it was merely a combination of desperation and wishful thinking on their part. She had no such delusions. When she was done, neither would Carolyn McKay.

"You should have told me," A.J. said simply, working hard to keep her tone even, her voice relatively quiet, when what she wanted was to rant and rave. "You had no right to bring me here under false pretenses, then watch me the way I've noticed you and your mother watching me, without telling me why you were doing this."

Carolyn was clearly uncomfortable, but she didn't say anything at first.

"You had no right," A.J. continued, her control slipping further with every agonizing word.

Why was it so hard? she wondered. This woman didn't mean anything to her. The job did, but she could find another one. She was good at what she did, and there were plenty of runaway shelters in the city of Chicago. She didn't even have to stay in Chicago. She could go anywhere she wanted, and . . . Dammit, her hands were shaking again.

"You lied to me," she said. In her book, that was the greatest sin of all.

"We didn't mean to," Carolyn replied, reaching her hand across the gleaming surface of the dark wooden desk, toward the spot where A.J.'s hands rested on the outer edge. "Please believe that. We were desperate to see you, to talk to you, to have any sort of connection to you. Surely you—"

A.J. snatched her hand away, no doubt looking like some wounded animal in Carolyn McKay's eyes. And A.J. didn't care for weakness, especially a weakness in herself that was displayed for anyone to see.

"You had no right," she repeated, standing up to leave. She'd said her piece. The rest, the details, it was all inconsequential. She was getting out of here.

"Wait," Carolyn said, coming around the desk to stand between her and the doorway.

A.J. backed up against the desk and looked longingly at the door. She should have moved faster. Don't beg me, she thought. Don't ask me for things I simply don't have to give.

"Please don't go," Carolyn said. "Please. Let me try to explain."

It was A.J.'s turn to be silent. What could she say? What kind of sound could she get past her throat, considering how tight it was at this moment.

"We never meant to hurt you." Carolyn told her.

Then who had? Wouldn't the Jenningses have told her much the same thing? *We never wanted to hurt you, Allison.* She could just imagine.

"No matter what you intended, that's what you've done."

"Try to understand, please," Carolyn said. "We've waited so long. We'd given up, and when Drew received that call from—"

"From my therapist?" That was the worst betrayal of all. "Surely you've heard of doctor-patient confidentiality. Surely you understand that he had no right to tell you about me."

"He cares for you very much," Carolyn said.

A.J. opened her mouth to say something to that, then thought better of it.

Nick cared for her? She'd known that, of course, although she'd carefully avoided giving him any opportunity in which he might fully explain to her exactly how much he cared.

She didn't have much to do with men, and Nick knew that. He had to realize that she wasn't at all interested in changing that fact. Yet he'd remained her friend, even after he realized that was all he could ever be to her.

Still, he did care for her, and she supposed that explained why he'd done this—because he thought he was helping her. Well, she would just have to set him straight about that notion. She might not know her own name, might not have any idea who she was or what had happened to her all those years ago, but she was more than capable of making her own decisions now. Nick would have to respect that.

A.J. looked up, startled, then realized she'd been lost in thought. "I'm not here to discuss Nick with you."

"Of course," Carolyn said, obviously uncomfortable. "Could I just tell you about Annie?"

"I'm not your sister," she stated quite firmly, knowing she couldn't allow this to go on. "I'm sure you'd like to believe that she's still alive. I hope for your sake that she is, but I'm not her. And that's something you and your mother are going to have to accept."

Determined to escape this time, she once again turned toward the door, praying that Carolyn would get out of her way.

The woman looked heartbroken, and A.J. tried not to notice that. When she still didn't move, A.J. added, "I can't help you."

"Couldn't you let us help you?" Carolyn put her hand on A.J.'s arm as she said it.

A.J. felt the touch like a burn, felt a funny little flutter in her stomach, then pulled away, unsure what to make of her reaction.

She would figure it out later, when she was alone and she had managed to calm herself. There was a way to handle this, and she would find it. She'd handle Jack MacAlister and his unreasonable demands, as well. And she would not let either of these people force her to do anything she didn't want to do.

"I don't need your help," she told Carolyn. "I don't need anyone's help. I was fine before you and your mother and that man Jack MacAlister ever showed up. And I'd thank the three of you for leaving me alone from now on."

"Jack MacAlister?" Carolyn asked, genuinely puzzled. "The prosecutor?"

"Yes, the prosecutor." She didn't want to explain any more of this. She didn't owe Carolyn McKay anything. "He was just downstairs, and he seems to know a great deal about my life that he has no business knowing. And that makes me very angry."

"I'm sorry," Carolyn said again, and suddenly A.J. was ashamed of herself, as well.

She worked with runaways, and she'd seen more than her share of parents desperate to find their missing children. Unfortunately, their desperation often had a way of blinding them to reality, of robbing them of all their common sense at the time when they most needed it.

Hope was at once a very fragile and a very powerful thing. Taking away someone's hope, especially that of a parent whose child was missing, was the cruelest thing she could imagine. Yet at times it was necessary. Surely this was one of those times.

She was relieved when Ricky Davis, one of the shelter workers, stuck his head around the side of the blocked door.

"Found you," he said to A.J.

"What's going on?" she asked.

"I thought you'd want to know. It's in the single digits outside already, feels colder than that with the wind blowing the way it is, and Trini still hasn't come in."

A.J. glanced at her watch. It was nearly seven, and Trini had been on the streets long enough to know that on a night like this, every shelter in the city would be full to overflowing. She should have come in by now.

Hell, she shouldn't be on the streets at all. She was fourteen years old, and seven months pregnant.

"I'll be down in a second, Ricky. And thanks for coming to find me."

He disappeared around the side of the door. A.J. had no choice but to turn back and deal with Carolyn.

"I suppose I need to find another job," she said.

"You don't have to decide anything tonight," Carolyn told her. "And please don't let this situation keep you from doing your job. You're very good at it, and the kids . . . they need you."

"One of them needs me right now," she said.

Outside, in the cold and the snow, Jack MacAlister sat inside his dark sedan with the heater running full blast. He'd just finished a very unpleasant phone call to FBI agent Drew Delaney when he saw A.J. come outside and get into a rather worn-looking van with the Hope House logo on the side.

He'd been waiting in front of Hope House, trying to decide what to do, berating himself for handling the situation badly and making his apologies to Drew, when he saw her.

Where in the world was A.J. going on a night like this? he wondered. He knew from Drew that her job at the shelter was a live-in position; she had a room somewhere in the old house. So what would she be doing out by herself on such a horrible night.

The snow was falling in golf-ball-size flakes, coming down so thickly it was hard to see ten feet in front of the car.

The wind was howling, as it almost always did in Chicago. The streets had been slick when he drove over here; they'd have grown worse in the hour he spent arguing with A.J. and then sitting in the car trying to figure out how to salvage something of the situation.

He waited while she started the van, then came out to scrape the snow off the windows. Then she climbed back inside and took off into the cold and the snow.

As the van's taillights flashed red in the distance, then disappeared off to the right, he made his decision. He was going to follow her. And when she arrived at wherever her destination was, he was going to make her sit still long enough to hear him out.

He'd bungled his first attempt badly; he couldn't afford to screw up the second. Waiting would only give her time to grow more angry at him, more determined to avoid him. And he couldn't let her do that, because he had to know if she was Annie McKay.

Chapter 3

A.J. huddled in her red wool coat and banged her fist against the van's heater. She was afraid it had picked to-night to turn temperamental on her once again—tonight, when it was supposed to be well below freezing and one of the shelter regulars was missing.

Paused at a stoplight, with the van just managing to idle strongly enough to keep from dying in the cold, A.J. rubbed her gloved hands together and watched the way each breath turned to a stream of white when she exhaled. If it was that cold *inside* the old van, outside must be horrible.

She looked up into the spill of light coming down from a lamppost, watched the thick puffs of white floating to the ground and felt her sense of desperation grow. Trini had no idea what it was like on the streets of Chicago in winter; she hadn't been here long enough. It was already February, and the city hadn't yet seen its first major storm. The season, so far, had been impossibly mild, leading many of the newer kids to believe that they could make it outside. This would be the storm that convinced them they were wrong.

A.J. hoped all of them would survive to learn the lesson. She was particularly worried about Trini, a fourteen-year-old girl from somewhere in Alabama who was about seven months pregnant. The girl had yet to see a doctor. More than likely she wouldn't go until the day she delivered.

A.J. had told them all yesterday about the coming snowstorm and warned them to get inside early. All the shelters would be overcrowded tonight. Some would be turning kids away, and with the windchill the way it was, they'd have a hard time making it from one shelter to another if the first one they tried was full.

A.J. had tried several of Trini's known hangouts, with no luck. She'd telephoned three of the closest shelters before she left Hope House—no one had seen Trini tonight. Her street family, two fifteen-year-old girls and an older boy, hadn't seen her since around noon. But they claimed she'd been feeling fine at that time.

A car behind A.J. honked. She looked up and noticed that the light had turned green. When she pressed on the accelerator, the van made a coughing, hiccuping noise, then died on her. She shifted into neutral and tried to start it. No luck. It just churned. Behind her, the car honked again, then swung around her and through the intersection. She was deep into the South Side, three or four miles from Hope House, which wasn't in the best of neighborhoods itself.

Instinctively she started looking around for a pay phone, though she seriously doubted she'd find one that was operable in this area. She cranked the ignition again.

Ricky and a couple of the other staff members hadn't wanted her to come out alone on a night like this, and normally she would have listened to them. But the shelter was packed. They never had enough hands on a normal night, let alone a night like this one. She couldn't ask one of them to come with her, when she knew how much work there was to be done at the shelter.

And she'd wanted to be alone. She hadn't wanted to talk to anyone. No doubt the whole place knew about Jack MacAlister coming to visit her tonight. She didn't think they knew why he'd come, but they definitely wanted to know something about his visit. A.J. had no intention of telling them, and she didn't want to play twenty questions, either.

So a few hours spent in the van, even if the heater didn't work, hadn't seemed so bad. The engine, however, was another story.

Outside, the snow was coming down in sheets, and the wind was howling. Ten below, they'd predicted. People froze to death in this kind of weather.

And Trini was out there somewhere.

A.J. looked up and down the now deserted streets. There was a pool hall two blocks west of here. She was sure of that. She'd lived on these streets herself at one time. She could make it that far, and use their phone.

She looked around the inside of the van, checking for anything of value that she could stuff in her pockets and take with her. The van was old enough and worn enough that it might still be here when someone made it out to get it tomorrow, but she wouldn't take any chances.

As she turned back to the door, it opened from the outside. The cold wind blasted inside, making her gasp as it hit her cool skin. The snow flurries streamed inside, as well, for a moment, then cleared enough for her to see an all-too-familiar face scowling at her.

"What the hell do you think you're doing out here on a night like this?" Jack MacAlister growled at her.

Dumbfounded by the sight of him here, by the knowledge that he must have been following her—what else would he be doing here on a night like this?—she didn't say anything at first. Obviously he was very angry. But why? She couldn't imagine.

She wasn't anything to him, except a potential witness. And surely he didn't make a habit out of following potential witnesses around in the middle of blinding snow-storms.

Not that it mattered in the least to her what he did with his witnesses or his time. But, thinking of herself and of Trini, she realized he might be just what she needed. After all, he was here, and if she couldn't change that fact, she might as well take advantage of it.

"Do you have a car?" she said, thinking that he would have a wonderful car, one with a heater that blasted bless-edly warm air even on a night like this, one with the best snow tires money could buy, one that wouldn't dare die on him in the middle of a cold, snowy night in one of the most dangerous neighborhoods in the city.

She would put up with anything to be warm again, even an evening in the company of Jack MacAlister.

"A car?" He frowned, as if he couldn't possibly have heard her correctly. "No, I have Rudolph and the rest of the reindeer pulling my sleigh. I thought we'd make better time in the snow that way. I guess you did notice it's snowing like hell tonight."

"Nearby?" she dared to ask. After all, if he could make jokes on a night like this, so could she. And she could al-most feel the heat even now.

"The sleigh?" he said, proving the depths of his imper-tinence. "Right behind you."

A.J. grabbed her flashlight, her keys, then checked the doors to make sure they were locked.

"Wishful thinking," he told her, locking the one on the driver's side for her.

"What if it is?" She stepped out of the van. It was a long way down, and when her feet finally hit the slushy mess on the streets, they nearly slid out from under her. They would have, if Jack MacAlister hadn't been so close, so quick and so surprisingly strong.

He braced himself with his shoulder against the door of the van, then grabbed her around the waist. Granted, there wasn't much else he could have done to save her from going down in the mess of ice and snow, but when he caught her to him with one hand, she found herself flush against his body.

He hadn't bothered to button his coat, and now both sides of it came around her, shielding her from the wind and the blowing snow, enveloping her in the incredible heat coming off his body. His coat left her warm, the wind muffled slightly, blocking the sight of everything but a crisp white dress shirt, a striped tie now pulled loose, a strong jawline in need of a shave, eyes the color of the lake on a dark winter night staring down at her. He was big and strong and solid, thoroughly male, absolutely threatening to her even as she wished she could stay right here and soak up a bit more of his warmth.

Shaken as she hadn't been in years, A.J. shoved hard against his chest and found some breathing room for herself. She sucked in the night air—it was so cold it burned all the way down into her lungs—and that was enough to clear her head and to steady her.

MacAlister was breathing hard himself. Those dark, dark eyes of his narrowed as his gaze bored into her own, told her that he was searching for some meaning to the way she had just reacted.

A.J. looked away. Let him wonder what had just happened between them. Let him figure it out for himself if he could.

"Is that all you're taking with you?" he said, glancing at the flashlight that had somehow remained in her right hand during the whole mess.

She nodded and turned toward his car. MacAlister's hand slid into the crook of her arm, gripping it tightly.

"It's at least half ice out here," he said, seeming to dare her to pull away from him.

She willed herself not to do so. She could do that if she really tried. She could free herself from his hold, if she absolutely had to, and that knowledge alone kept her from fighting against him.

The car was maybe ten feet away. She measured the distance carefully in footsteps, meticulously counting them down in her head. Six more to go. Then five. Surely she could endure the touch of a man's hands for that long.

He'd left the car running, and the heater was hard at work. She'd been so cold outside that the heat actually burned when it hit her chilled skin.

She huddled in the warmth while he climbed inside, closed the door and put on his seat belt. When he didn't say anything, she dared to look over at him.

"Nice sleigh," she said.

MacAlister looked as if he were ready to explode. "Do you have any idea how dangerous it is out here for a woman alone? And on a night like this? Especially in that piece of junk you were driving?"

"I used to live on these streets, MacAlister. There's nothing you could tell me about them."

"Then you ought to know better than to be out on a night like this. What would you have done if I hadn't—"

"Been following me?"

"Yes, if I hadn't been following you, what would you have done?"

She gave him points for not even trying to deny it, then shook off that thought. Surely she wasn't coming to admire the man?

"I would have walked to the pool hall two blocks over, and hoped it was open," she replied.

Clearly he was aghast at that idea.

"It's not such a bad place," she told him.

"They'd slit your throat for the price of a cup of coffee around here," he said.

She doubted that, though she didn't carry a purse for that very reason. She had a little cash, a few coins and her keys in the pocket of her jeans. She had no need to carry anything else.

She also didn't need this man following her. Didn't need him lecturing her or reminding her of the dangers surrounding her and the kids out here. But she did need someone to help her find Trini before it was too late.

Did she dare ask this man to help her? She caught her breath at the thought, and remembered all too clearly what it had felt like to be caught up against those broad shoulders of his, the flat stomach, the powerful arm muscles.

He was entirely too big, too strong, too threatening to her. He towered over her, making her feel absolutely inconsequential next to him. Except for the fact that he was a federal prosecutor and a very determined man, she knew nothing about him. Alarm bells were going off inside her head. Just not the usual ones.

A.J. blinked twice, as if she couldn't quite believe what she was seeing and thinking and feeling—that she was alone in the dark and the cold with a stranger who'd burst into her life not four hours ago and turned it all upside down. And what was she doing? She was remembering all too well what it had felt like to be caught up against him. She opened her eyes once again, looked just to her left to see him sitting beside her, watching and waiting. But for what? What did he want from her?

A.J. shook her head in wonder. It had been a strange night indeed, and it wasn't over yet.

Much as she hated to admit it, she needed help. Trini needed help. And he was the only one here. That made the decision much easier.

She didn't ask why he'd been following her or what he'd intended to do once he caught up with her. She didn't need to. Jack MacAlister was obviously a man who didn't know how to take no for an answer. She'd just have to enlighten him about a few things—namely, her stubbornness—later.

For now, she was in the unenviable position of needing his help.

"I'm betting that if you don't have anything better to do on a night like this than to follow me around, you have time to help me with something," she said, sinking into the leather of her seat.

"Help you with something?" he said.

"Yes." Why was that so hard for him to understand? "I've got a missing kid out here somewhere. I was looking for her when the van gave out."

"You have one kid who didn't happen to show up at the shelter, and that sent you out alone in that piece of junk on a night like this?"

She didn't bat an eyelash.

"Lady, are you nuts?"

"Does it matter?" she said.

He looked thunderous at that. Curiously, she wasn't afraid of him. Not exactly, anyway. She didn't fear him physically, though his size made her uncomfortable. She had the distinct impression that it would be difficult to convince Jack MacAlister that he'd have to try his case without her help. She didn't think she'd be able to get rid of him soon enough to save her hard-won peace of mind.

"Look, MacAlister," she said, "you said it yourself. It's ten below tonight, snowing like crazy. Someone will likely freeze to death out here before morning, and I'm going to make damn sure it's not one of my kids. You can either help me or let me off at that pool hall on Jefferson. Of course, if someone slits my throat there, it would just make more work for you in the end, right? You might have to prosecute the guy."

She had to fight with all she had in her not to smile at the scowl that spread across his face at the thought. Maybe she had pushed him too far. But why should it be so irresistible to her to torment him this way? She felt something that bordered on shame for enjoying butting heads with him this way.

"What do you want to do?" she said, in as non-confrontational a tone as she could manage.

He didn't say anything for a minute, but that didn't make her nervous. There was no way he was going to put her out on the street tonight. She was certain of that.

"You're not the only one who wants something," he said, still thinking about that precious case of his.

"You son of a—"

"Hey," he jumped in, looking a bit wounded. "I'm one of the good guys, remember?"

"I'm looking for a fourteen-year-old who's seven months pregnant, and you're so worried about getting what you want that you're trying to bribe me now?" she challenged. "I'm worried about one of the kids . . ."

"Lady, what do you think this is about, my ego? This bastard I'm about to turn back out onto the streets kidnapped a seven-year-old girl nearly four months ago. We think over the past ten years he snatched four others, none of whom have ever been seen or heard from again. So don't make me out to be the bad guy here."

She felt a definite twinge of conscience at that, and she wished with all her might that he hadn't told her about the missing children. Not that it mattered. She couldn't help him. But then, he didn't have to know that right this minute.

"What do you want from me?" she asked, prepared to bargain.

"Fifteen minutes of your time."

"After we find Trini," she said.

"Of course."

"Done. Now drive," she demanded. She could do that—just listen to him—for Trini's sake. But she wasn't going to do anything else.

They drove for hours in silence. The snow continued to fall, the wind to howl. On the streets, the stuff turned to slush first, then a dangerous sheet of ice.

MacAlister still couldn't believe A.J. had gone out alone in this storm. He couldn't believe she relied on that beat-up van for transportation, or that she didn't even have a car phone in it—for her own safety.

They used his to call the shelter, where they learned that no one had seen Trini, then called three other shelters with similar results. Shortly after 2:00 a.m., about a mile from Hope House, when he was getting ready to tell her they'd have to give up—the streets were too much of a mess, and visibility was a joke—they spotted something moving in the mass of white and shadows on the ground near an abandoned building.

"Stay here," he warned her, thinking that it might be nothing more than something blowing in the fierce wind or that it might be something much worse.

He grabbed her flashlight and climbed out of the car. The night was eerily quiet, save for the howl of the wind. It was as if the whole city were inside and asleep tonight.

He was amazed at A.J.'s determination. She was doing all this for one kid, he thought. Would she do it for any one of the kids who passed through the shelter? he wondered. Surely not. She couldn't afford to care that much about them all. She'd never last in this business if she did. A person could take only so many disappointments and still go on.

In order to do his job properly, he had learned to protect himself. He wondered who protected the woman sitting in his car tonight, wondered what would have happened to her if he hadn't decided to follow her into the snow. He didn't like the image that brought to mind at all.

Up ahead, the shadow moved again. A cautious man by nature, he watched his back, his sides, and the huddled figure in front of him. It moaned. Either that, or something caught the wind just right.

MacAlister brought the light up toward what he thought was a head. A gloved hand motioned helplessly, and another moan came to him through the darkness.

He knelt beside the figure, brushed away the snow, moved the tattered rag wrapped around the face, then cursed with all the breath he had left in his body.

He'd expected a bum, a wino, the weathered, well-lined face of a drunk who lived on the streets, but he found the smooth, unlined features of an adolescent. She rolled over stiffly at his urging. A small, rounded mass at her stomach confirmed his suspicion.

"Trini?" he said.

She looked confused—dazed, actually. He wondered if it was the cold, or something else. At that moment, she went stiff in his arms, her face scrunching up in pain.

Damn, A.J. was right. She'd been certain the girl knew better than to get caught outside on a night like tonight, sure that something had to be wrong with her to keep her from coming in out of the cold.

Scooping the girl up in his arms, he carried her back to the car.

Unless he was mistaken, Trini was in labor.

It was nearly five in the morning when Trini gave birth by cesarean section to a three-and-a-half-pound baby boy with a sluggish heartbeat and irregular breathing. Still, considering the way his mother lived during her pregnancy, her age, her poor nutrition and his early arrival into the world, the doctors thought the baby was in pretty good shape.

Through the glass enclosure in which the baby lay, MacAlister watched its tiny arms and legs flail about, watched the way its chest heaved up and down with every breath. The baby's face was nearly covered by the light blue cap that adorned a head that seemed too big for the frail body to support.

He didn't want to think about what would have happened to the baby, or his childlike mother, if they'd been left in the snow, couldn't imagine how the woman standing beside him handled the enormous responsibility she'd taken on to see that "her kids" were safe.

One woman couldn't do that. The job was simply too big, the potential for heartbreak perilously close at all times.

He couldn't begin to understand how A.J. managed to do so, hated the idea that he was going to add to her burden. Standing here beside him in the hallway, she seemed incredibly fragile. He knew what she'd been through in the not-too-distant past—parts of it, at least. She couldn't possibly be all that fragile and still have survived on the streets.

Yet she seemed just that tonight, fragile, a little lost, maybe even defeated. He read the pain in her stance, her one shoulder against the wall, her head bowed, her arms curled in around herself, and he thought about going to her and trying to comfort her in some small way. But he wasn't sure she would welcome that from him, and he doubted she wanted anyone to see her the way she was right now. So, though he turned back to the baby, his thoughts stayed with A.J.

How had she done it, he wondered? She could so easily have ended up like Trini, half-frozen in the snow.

A.J. had managed to come so far from that. Drew had told him that she had gone to Northwestern on scholarship, finishing in three years at the top of her class with a degree in counseling. And she'd stood her ground with him tonight in a way that some of the attorneys he'd faced in court would envy.

But she couldn't do that much longer. It was nearly dawn. He knew she was exhausted and emotionally drained. What in the world was he going to do with her?

He had an absurd idea to take her home with him, feed her, let her soak in his whirlpool for a while, then put her to bed and dare her to get up before dark tonight. His place had more than enough room. He'd bet his last dollar that if he took her back to Hope House, she wouldn't sleep until tonight, and the hot water would be long gone by the time she got there.

Put that way, it almost sounded like his civic duty to take her home with him.

But it wasn't a sense of duty that was pushing him on right now. She reminded him of someone, someone he had loved a long time ago. Someone he had lost.

He hadn't thought of Miranda in years, hadn't felt guilty over her death in so long. But she'd been a lot like A.J., taking the weight of the world on her shoulders, and she hadn't been strong enough to manage that task. No one would have been. He only wished someone had convinced her of that sooner. He wished he'd been the one who made her see that she couldn't be everything to everyone, that others' problems were not her own, that she was only human, that she had her limitations.

Miranda had found her own limits the hard way—she'd taken her own life.

Someday, A.J., would find her own limits. He wondered what would happen when she did.

After visiting Trini, A.J. stood in the hallway and looked at Jack MacAlister, beyond the swinging doors. Why he was still here, she couldn't say. Couldn't imagine. Surely he wasn't going to demand his fifteen minutes of her time tonight—or rather this morning. It was nearly dawn, after all.

He shouldn't be here. She hadn't asked him to stay, had repeatedly pointed out to him that there was nothing to keep him here. Yet here he was.

A.J. shook her head in anger and in wonder as she felt something curiously close to need for him, this stranger who'd barreled into her life, helped her save Trini and the baby, yet come so close to destroying her hard-won peace of mind.

How could she need a man like that? She didn't even know what to do with that particular feeling. Especially now that her energy was waning low, her hope, her enthusiasm and her drive, coming close to deserting her.

Tonight, when he caught her to him outside the van, when his coat flared around her and the heat of his body flamed toward her, she'd imagined what it would be like to let go of all her problems, all the kids' problems that became her own, and let him shoulder them all for just a while.

He could carry the load; she'd felt the strength in him. And she would be able to rest. Just for a little while.

It was an incredible thought for her, the woman who leaned on no one, needed no one, trusted no one except herself.

It was the hour, she told herself. Nothing but that dangerous, vulnerable window of time between the darkest of the night and the breaking of day. Everyone hit a low point right there, in that hour or so before dawn. It didn't mean anything.

Jack MacAlister might have charged into her life today, leaving chaos in his wake, but he would be gone tomorrow. Her kids, her work, would still be here, and she would forget him, no doubt as easily as he would forget her.

Chapter 4

She must have fallen asleep, the movement of the car lulling her into a false sense of security. Her world had turned all warm and cozy, her exhaustion taking over when she should have remained alert and aware.

With her eyes still closed, her brain caught in that instant of emerging from a deep, deep sleep, she experienced the sensation of movement very different from that of the car. The cold penetrated her dreamless sleep for an instant, then was gone. Voices followed, laughing, joking voices.

Groggily she opened her eyes, then squeezed them shut as the light, blinding at first, invaded.

"Take it easy," a smooth, deep voice coaxed. It was a little rough, husky and strangely familiar. It sent shivers up her spine, and not the kind caused by the cold.

The voice snapped her out of the awful lethargy that had invaded her body. When she opened her eyes again, the light wasn't nearly as bright, and she discovered she was in Jack MacAlister's arms. Either that, or she was dreaming.

"Almost there," he said.

She watched his lips move, felt the raspy, stubble-covered skin of his jaw against her forehead as he turned his face toward her as he spoke.

Doors swung open—elevator doors, her brain registered—and he started walking down the hallway, carrying her as he went.

She wasn't dreaming.

A.J. pushed with all her might against the broad chest her head had been leaning against only moments before. She caught him unawares, and she suspected that was the only reason she managed to break away from him, because he was very strong. She landed on her feet, but off-balance enough that she fell hard against the wall.

He cursed, putting out his hand to steady her. She made a ridiculously large effort to evade his touch, surely making a fool of herself all over again.

As she stood with her back to the wall, she saw that he was watching her, dissecting her, digging into the heart of her and trying to find out what was inside her.

What did he see? Some pitiful woman huddled against the wall—all because he had reached out to steady her. And this when he'd already had his hands all over her while he carried her from the car.

She swallowed hard at the thought of being in his arms, being held against his big, hard, thoroughly male body, remembered the slightly rough feel of his jaw against her forehead, the sound of his voice so close to her ear.

Clearly she had made a fool of herself in front of him. Her cheeks burned at the thought.

"Are you all right?" he said.

She ignored his question and tried to get her bearings. She couldn't help but stare at him, standing in the hallway in his big wool coat, the very end of his tie hanging out of one of his pockets, his shirt open at the collar, his perfect hair actually out of place right now. He had a very rumpled look about him—as if he'd been out all night.

Which, of course, he had.

With her.

Even under the most innocent of circumstances, it seemed much too intimate a thing to be with him this early in the morning, after having spent the whole night together.

A.J. didn't spend the night with men. She didn't spend time with them at all, unless it was through work. And she liked it that way. She was comfortable with that, and she saw no reason to change it. She didn't have to explain or justify her feelings to Jack MacAlister or anyone else.

"Where are we?" she asked. "And what do you think you're doing?"

The last thing she remembered was the two of them in the hospital parking lot. She'd come out of Trini's room; she hadn't been able to hide the fact that she was quite upset, but she hadn't told him anything, either. She'd intended to catch the El or a bus or something to get her back to Hope House, where she had a mountain of work waiting for her, but he wouldn't hear of that. He'd insisted on driving her back to the shelter, and she'd been too tired to argue.

That had been a mistake. She should have made good her escape when she had the chance.

She glanced at her watch—6:55 a.m., nearly an hour after she'd come out of Trini's room. She'd lost an hour with this man. Anything could have happened in an hour.

He was calmly pressing numbers on a keypad at the door across the hall. She heard a beeping sound, then watched as he opened the door.

"My place," he said, gesturing for her to precede him through the doorway.

In another lifetime, maybe.

A.J. sometimes wondered if there would be another lifetime for her. If she might show up back on earth at some point as a normal, well-adjusted, happy woman. If she might stay out all night with a man like him and walk into his apartment at this hour with no worries, no fears about what might happen inside.

There were times when she couldn't help but wonder about her chances for a normal life, times when she saw a man and a woman together, so caught up in each other, so obviously comfortable with one another, so happy together.

But, though she'd wondered, she'd never done anything about it. She'd never pushed herself to see just how much she could take from a man without fear taking over. Was it because she'd never found a man who was worth taking such risks for? Because she'd never been so tempted?

She suddenly found it hard to breathe.

"A.J.?" he said.

She didn't budge as she tried to pick up the threads of the conversation. "I asked you a question," she said, with as much indignation as she could muster.

"And I answered. We're at my place."

"Why?"

"Because you promised me fifteen minutes of your time as soon as we took care of Trini."

She couldn't believe this. Just when she'd decided he might be a nice guy. Dangerous, but with a nice streak in there somewhere. After all, without him she didn't think she ever would have found Trini. And now it seemed he was only in this for what he wanted—a victory in this precious case of his.

"MacAlister, I'm dead on my feet," she protested. "So are you."

"Which is why I'm prepared to be reasonable about this. I want some food, a shower, and about four hours' sleep, not necessarily in that order. I thought you might appreciate the same thing."

"Here?" she said, stunned. No way was she staying here alone with him.

"There, for me—" he pointed to the left, then to the right "—and over there for you. Two bedrooms, two baths, down that hallway. I'll wake you up around one o'clock. We'll order some lunch, and we can have our talk."

She was speechless, and feeling something close to panic. She didn't even want to be in the same room with him, and he wanted her to stay here in his apartment, sleep here, shower here and eat here, with him? And he thought this was being reasonable? The whole idea scared her to death. Of course, her pride wouldn't let him see that. She'd already made it painfully obvious to him that she was scared to have him even touch her. And she was trying desperately to figure out exactly what he meant by the suggestion that she stay here.

Nothing, she told herself. It meant absolutely nothing. Looking down at her old jeans, her wrinkled sweatshirt, knowing she had a wrung-out, dog-tired look about her, she understood this had nothing to do with any sort of sexual urge he might have. Still, she couldn't help but feel uneasy.

He was flat-out gorgeous. Tall, broad, strong...sexy, she supposed, though she wasn't an expert on that subject. She certainly didn't spend her time gazing at strange men and cataloging their assets. Still, there was something about him that left her uneasy... as a woman. How long had it been since she'd thought of herself as a woman and been aware of someone else as a man? Truly, she couldn't remember the last time that had happened.

A.J. had never felt comfortable around men. It had to do with the fact that she'd lost the first thirteen years of her life. Those feelings stemmed from that lost period of time, and it didn't take a genius to figure out why.

Obviously, something had happened to her then, something that made her uncomfortable around men. And she'd never gone out of her way to figure out all the horrible details. Why would she? Why would anyone?

It was there. It had happened. It was a fact of her life. She could not change it. Nor did she have to dwell on it.

It was buried deep inside her, and she saw no reason to dig up all that grief.

She'd dealt with the fact that she was uncomfortable with men quite effectively by staying away from them, except on a professional level.

Why should this be any different? she asked herself. Why did he have to make this different? After all, Jack Mac-Alister was simply working. Of course, he'd also asked her to spend the night at his apartment.

He might simply be offering her a kindness, but that was hard to accept. They were strangers. Surely he didn't bring exhausted women to his apartment on a regular basis and offer them a place to sleep, shower and eat. True, A.J. knew little about men, but she doubted that many of them behaved this way.

Could it be pity? Did she detect the slightest hint of that in him? She wasn't sure. He had to know, from the way she'd behaved at the hospital, that she was fighting with all she had to hold herself together right now. She'd been certain that she'd lost Trini for good, and the baby, as well. And she would have—without his help. So she supposed that meant she owed him . . . something. But what in the world did he want from her?

Whatever it was, he would simply have to understand— she didn't have it to give. There were probably thousands of women in this city who would have no hang-ups about giving him whatever he wanted. After all, *she* was nothing to him except his last hope for this case. Surely he wasn't looking at her as a woman. Surely he wasn't responding to her as a woman.

"Hey, don't make a big deal out of this," he said casually as he shrugged out of his expensive coat and threw it across the back of what had to be a very expensive leather chair. His suit jacket, also very expensive, followed.

A.J. swallowed hard, wondering what he was going to remove next. "I have a bed," she pointed out. "My own bed, at Hope House, and that's where I'm going."

"Power's out," he informed her, with just enough glee that she wondered for a minute if he was lying. "Not here, of course, but all over the South Side. It was on the car radio. Water main busted. The repair crew cut some sort of cable in their haste to stop the leak. It's crazy down there."

"Then they'll need me even more at the shelter," she said, ticking off in her head the things that would have to be done, thanks to this complication.

"You're dead on your feet," he said. "You told me so yourself. That place was packed last night, it'll be a zoo this morning. You won't get a bit of sleep if you go back there now."

She'd taken a step backward, putting her just outside the doorway, but now she paused. What he said was absolutely true. She wouldn't sleep. The place would be a zoo, and everyone would want to know all about Trini and the baby. She wasn't sure she was up to recounting the tale for anyone. They'd want to know how the baby was, what his chances were, how he looked, what in the world she was going to do with the baby and with Trini...

All of a sudden, that guest room of his sounded very tempting. She hated to admit that even to herself, but it was tempting for that reason alone.

Still, staying here? With him?

"I can't," she said. "If they don't have any power at the shelter, the place will be absolutely crazy. They'll need me, and I can't just..."

She looked up at the sound of footsteps coming closer to her, couldn't help but pull herself up a little straighter, bracing herself for some imagined danger lurking here, within the walls of his apartment.

He stopped two steps away, far enough that she saw no threat from his presence, and she tried to figure out where she'd left off in the explanation she was giving him.

She couldn't remember. It was as if someone had robbed her of all her thought processes.

How did he do that to her? Rob her of the power to think coherently and to speak? He'd cast some spell on her. He'd bewitched her, like some modern-day warlock. Because even though he frightened her, he tempted her, as well. She'd never felt this way, never had her curiosity grow as strong as her inborn instinct to flee—not where a man was concerned.

"They need me," she protested again, as he moved toward her once more.

Whether it was obvious or not, she had to move away. She broke out of her lethargic spell and took one step back for each of his steps forward, until the whole thing became ridiculous and she stopped. He did not, she noted with growing alarm.

"They do need me," she said, chin held high, eyes warily watching him.

He reached out a hand. She tensed even more. His palm settled against her cheek, cupping it, stroking it, almost, setting off alarm bells in her head and making it hard for her to breathe.

His touch was light and gentle, his hand warm on her face, the fingers splayed along her jawbone. She closed her eyes so that she didn't have to look into his dark, dark eyes, so that she wouldn't try to read what was in his expression.

His hand moved along her face, coming down to the point of her chin. She fought—harder than she'd ever fought for anything—against tilting her head a fraction of an inch, bringing it closer to his hand.

She held her breath and opened her eyes, waiting, though for what she didn't know. Nothing happened. His hand fell to his side, and her knees nearly buckled with a strange mixture of relief and regrets. Then his hand was back, stroking the other side of her face this time.

"MacAlister?" She nearly choked on his name.

"What if you don't have anything left to give them right now?"

Her heart was racing, and emotions were welling up inside her. Trini, that tiny baby, the killer storm, this man's ludicrous insinuation that she could once have been a poor little girl named Annie McKay—it was all too much for her.

Her eyes flooded with tears that sat, hot and heavy, against her pupils.

What came next? she wondered. Did the tears just spill over? She couldn't quite remember how the whole process worked, because it had been so long since she'd given in to that particular weakness. But it couldn't be that complicated. People cried every day, bucketfuls of tears. She was afraid that was what would happen to her. That letting go right now would unleash the floodgates inside her, that seven years' worth of tears were just waiting to get out. She couldn't let that happen now. She couldn't fall apart right here, in front of this beautiful, self-assured man.

Her chin still in his hand, he tilted it to one side for a second, and in that instant, all his attention was focused on her.

What did he see? she wondered. What was he looking for inside her?

Just when she thought she couldn't stand it anymore, he backed away. She closed her eyes as his hand dropped away, and breathed in a shaky breath as she felt, more than heard, him take one step backward as well.

A.J. wrapped her arms around her middle, not caring how vulnerable that made her look. MacAlister backed away several more steps.

"Look, don't make this into something it's not," he said evenly, from what she could only consider a nonthreatening distance. "I'm tired. You're tired. There's more than enough room here for both of us."

A.J. hesitated, wondering if she'd imagined what just happened in the apartment. She couldn't have, she told herself. She wasn't so paranoid or so out of touch that she didn't know that something very powerful had just passed between them, that she'd escaped it only because he allowed her to escape.

And now he still wanted her to spend the night? It seemed ludicrous, and it frightened her all over again.

Being in his apartment alone with him, sleeping in the bed across the hall from him . . . she wasn't sure she could do it. But she didn't know how she could get away without telling him things that were none of his business. And she did have some pride, though it had taken a beating in the past twelve hours or so.

Jack MacAlister kept his distance. He considered it an exercise in self-control. He was sure A.J. had no idea how lost she looked, how frightened, how absolutely vulnerable.

Did no one ever touch her? How could that be? She was a grown woman, and this was the nineties.

He didn't remember a time when he'd wanted so much to simply put his hands on a woman, her cheek, her chin, her neck.

How long had it been? He'd been working constantly lately, and at times the job left little time or energy for anything else.

Obviously, it was time to find someone. He'd gone a little crazy tonight and this morning, making A.J. very uncomfortable, and that was the last thing he needed to do.

After all, this was business, he reminded himself. With luck, she would be a material witness in a case he was prosecuting, and there wasn't any room here for personal involvement.

If he found her fascinating in some way, then he'd just have to live with that. He'd have to forget about it, because this whole situation was complicated enough.

There she stood in front of him, obviously wary, but determined not to show it. And she had to be exhausted. God knew he was.

Once again, she reminded him of Miranda. Once again, he remembered the guilt he'd felt over her death.

He'd met Miranda while in college. They'd dated for about six months, and he'd loved her—as much as any twenty-year-old male was capable of loving a woman.

She'd been having some problems at home, with her parents, but he hadn't understood the depths of those problems. And he hadn't pressed her for information on them. He'd been too busy trying to keep his grades up so that he could graduate at the top of his class and get into one of the country's best law schools. He'd been selfish, where she'd been generous and understanding. And he simply hadn't paid as much attention as he should have when things went from bad to worse for her at home.

Then it had been too late. She was dead, and he was left with nothing but guilt.

A.J. was like Miranda, in that they both had a way of taking on other people's problems and making them their own. He couldn't imagine where this urge to help A.J. had come from, unless it all went back to Miranda. Maybe he could make amends in some small way. Maybe he could be the one to help this young woman who carried the weight of the world on her shoulders.

He wanted to know who'd hurt her so badly and left her in this shape. He would have liked to be the one who prosecuted the bastard. Or at least beat the man to a pulp.

She'd lived on the streets; she'd told him that herself, last night. But either he'd conveniently forgotten what it could be like out there or he hadn't looked at it as anything more than a piece of information about this mysterious young woman. Of course, at the time, he hadn't thought of her as anything more than the person who could help him get a conviction in this case that had come to be so important to him.

And now . . . now he had an irresistible urge to help her in some way, to shield her from the ugliness of the world those kids of hers lived in, to spare her the pain he knew it would cost her to remember her past as Annie McKay—if she actually was Annie McKay.

Amazingly, he found himself hoping, for her sake, that she wasn't, even as he fought to keep any of that from showing in his face. If he wanted to keep her here, he had to play this exactly right, and pity was the last thing she wanted from him or from anyone else. He was certain of that.

MacAlister backed up, giving her the space she so obviously needed from him, and tried to be as nonthreatening as possible. He couldn't help but wonder if she saw all men as a threat, or if it was just him. Did he remind her of someone she'd much rather forget? Or had he done something that she found threatening? The thought that he had somehow added to her fear was distasteful to him.

He turned, not wanting to see that particular emotion on her face, and walked down the hallway toward one of the guest rooms. "There's a lock on the door," he told her. "Use it, if it makes you feel any better. There's a phone in both bedrooms, if you want to check in with the shelter and let them know where you are, or if you want to leave the number with the hospital, in case anything happens to Trini or the baby."

He dared to glance back, thought she might have taken a step or two in his direction, couldn't help but remember a frightened doe he'd seen once, on vacation in the woods in Wisconsin. The way she held herself, the way she seemed poised to run at the slightest indication of danger, the way those big, serious eyes watched everything around her so carefully.

"I just want to talk to you, A.J. That's all. And I'd much rather do it while I'm half-awake."

She took one hesitant step over the threshold, then stared off to her right, to the floor-to-ceiling windows that displayed an incredible view of Lake Michigan. When she turned back toward him, he saw that her gaze was steady, and her head was held high.

He had won this round, at least, and he barely suppressed a smile, ignoring altogether how much it meant to him that she hadn't gone running off into the early-morning snow to escape.

Chapter 5

Amazingly, she slept.

Exhaustion took over, drawing her down into a deep, dreamless sleep. She didn't so much as open an eyelid for the next... Could it really have been ten hours? She blinked at the red-orange glow of the digital clock on the nightstand. The room was dark, the sky outside the oversize window the same. The clock read 6:00 p.m. She'd slept the whole day away.

In Jack MacAlister's apartment? Now that she wasn't dead-tired or determined not to let him see that the idea of simply sleeping in his guest room frightened her badly, she knew exactly what she had to do. She had to get out of here. Fast.

Entering the connecting bathroom, A.J. showered in minutes, dried her short hair in seconds and called the man a saint because he'd been thoughtful enough to provide a new toothbrush and some toothpaste for her. With only a mild sense of distaste, she dressed in the clothes she'd worn the day before and gave herself one more minute to brace herself, in case she found him awake and standing between her and the door.

She unlocked the bedroom door, flinching slightly at the sound of the lock clicking back into place, and told herself that he already knew she'd locked the door this morning. He knew she'd been afraid.

Part of the reason she'd stayed was simply the need to prove to herself that she could do it. Part of it was to prove to him that, even if she was scared spitless at the thought of simply sleeping in the same apartment as a grown man, she could do it. And she had.

Now, if only she could get away unscathed.

Walking into the huge living room, she found him in the corner, at his desk. He was on the phone, and giving somebody hell about something. Seemed she wasn't the only one who brought out that attitude in him.

A.J. couldn't help but smile at that. She thought longingly of coffee, and something—anything—to put into her stomach with it, but the idea of rummaging through his kitchen, like someone who belonged here, was too much for her. She headed for the windows, instead, because she didn't have the guts to walk right past him and out the door. Besides, she was sure he'd follow her.

Outside, the lights were coming on in the high-rise apartment buildings that lined the shore. The lake was a big streak of shimmering black that blended so well into the night sky, she couldn't tell where one ended and the other began.

It was like her own memories, she decided. They went back so far, and then, somewhere in the distant past, the memories ceased and the lies began. She didn't know where. The Jenningses had filled her head with the memories of a beautiful little girl named Allison, and A.J. had trouble distinguishing between what had really happened to her with the Jenningses and what was simply the memories of Allison that they had put into her head.

Of herself . . . the real person . . . A.J. simply had nothing. Absolutely nothing.

How hard could that be for Jack MacAlister to understand? She simply could not help him.

"Sorry," he said, hanging up the phone and turning his attention to her. "The office. I had a million things I was supposed to do today."

"So did I," she retorted, determined not to notice that he looked even better today than he had yesterday. He was wearing a suit and a crisp white dress shirt, but his hair was still damp. He wore it short and pushed back from his forehead. His eyes were just as dark in the daylight, his shoulders were just as broad. All in all, he was a very imposing man.

Had he slept the whole day away, as well? Or waited here while she slept in the room down the hall? She didn't like that idea at all.

"I tried to wake you," he said.

She felt a wave of heat climb from her neck to her cheeks before she remembered that she'd locked her bedroom door. He hadn't actually been in that room while she slept. He must have just knocked on the door.

"I guess . . . I guess I needed the sleep," she admitted, then wondered how to get out of the apartment.

A knock sounded on the front door, and MacAlister turned to answer it. "I ordered dinner when I heard you turn on the shower. I'm starved, and I figured you would be, too."

She watched helplessly as he accepted a bag of take-out food from the kid at the door, then walked back toward her, to the elegant dining table in the corner.

She would have protested. She had the words on the tip of her tongue. But the tantalizing aroma of Chinese fried rice hit her right then. Her stomach rumbled in anticipation, and Jack MacAlister gave her a killer smile.

"You are hungry," he said.

She couldn't lie about that; she was once again very neatly trapped into spending even more time with this man.

Would she ever escape him?

"Coffee?" he said.

"Please." She would have begged for that if necessary.

"Have a seat. I'll get the coffee and some plates."

For a moment she considered her determination to leave, but she decided there was no contest between that and her desire for any sort of food available. But fried rice and a cup of fresh coffee? She would have sold her soul for those two things.

She walked over to the gleaming table, which seated six. She doubted Jack MacAlister had Chinese take-out often. A.J. unpacked the brown paper bag, finding carton after carton of food. It smelled wonderful, and there was enough to feed a small army.

He was back in no time with the plates and black coffee—sheer heaven to taste—and offered her a choice of a fork or chopsticks. She took the fork, as did he, and they both dug in.

"I don't remember the last time I was this hungry," she said, trying to do nothing more than make polite conversation with him. But she did remember days like that.

Unbidden came the image of herself, on the streets, never knowing where her next meal was coming from. Food never tasted so good as it did to someone who'd gone without, and this, her first meal in more than twenty-four hours, reminded her of those days.

Looking at the man, seeing the casual elegance that encased him, this huge apartment on the lake that he called home, she knew he had never gone hungry in his life, had never worried about where he would sleep at night or whether he could find someplace safe, for just a few hours, in this crazy world of theirs.

He had no idea how she'd lived, or why she'd lived that way. He would never understand.

They were worlds apart.

Not that it mattered at all. She was nothing to him. As soon as she convinced him that she couldn't help him with his case, he'd be gone for good. She would never see him again. Their paths, so completely opposite from one another, would never cross again.

She found that incredibly reassuring. Maybe it would be enough to get her through the rest of the time she had to spend with him.

They finished their meal in blessed silence, cleared the table together and stacked the dishes in the dishwasher. She noted with wry amusement that he didn't give a thought to saving the leftovers. Instead, he dumped two cartons that they hadn't even opened down the garbage disposal.

No, she told herself, he would never understand where she'd come from or how she'd lived. Not in a million years.

"I'm never here," he explained when he caught her staring. "I usually grab something on the way to work and something on my way home."

A.J. said nothing, but she thought it was such a waste. He had all this space, this magnificent view, and he was never even here to enjoy it.

"I guess you're anxious to get out of here," he said, wiping down the already spotless counter with a dish towel.

Oh, yes. She needed to leave.

"I'm sure there's a lot of work waiting for me," she told him.

He walked back to the desk, closed the file he'd been flipping through when she came into the room, then walked back to the oversize sofa and sat down.

"This won't take long," he said.

She intended to make sure it didn't.

With some trepidation, A.J. walked over to the sofa, then took a seat in the big chair sitting at a ninety-degree angle to it. He moved to the corner of the couch and placed the file on the coffee table in front of them both.

"I told you yesterday," she began, "I don't see how I can help you."

He took his gold watch off his wrist and pushed a series of buttons, then placed it on the table beside the file.

"Fifteen minutes," he said.

The watch was ticking those minutes off like a stopwatch. He was going to demand his time.

"Fine." She surrendered.

"What exactly do you know about these kidnappings?" he asked, before flipping open the file.

"As little as possible." She hadn't let Nick tell her anything about Annie, because she hadn't wanted to know.

"It's been all over the TV and the papers," he said, obviously having a hard time understanding how she could know so little about it.

Well, it hadn't been that hard. She'd been out of town at a conference when the man was arrested, so she'd missed most of the media frenzy over the case. She didn't have a TV in her room at the shelter, and the one in the common areas the kids shared seemed to be stuck on MTV. The one in the staff lounge was most often blaring some soap opera.

Newspapers depressed her—and the politicians featured most prominently in them angered her—so she didn't read a lot of news, either.

She lived in her own little world, and that suited her.

MacAlister stared at her for a moment, but she remained silent. Once he realized she wasn't going to explain anything more on this particular subject to him, he went on. He pulled a color photograph from the file in front of him, one of a darling little dark-haired girl, maybe eight or nine years old, smiling into the camera. A.J. found herself strangely drawn to the picture, the way some people lean over and crane their necks for a better view of a ghastly accident on the highway.

The girl had on a green plaid skirt and a crisp white blouse with embroidered flowers on the collar that matched the flowers stitched into the green sweater. A.J. could just imagine the hands of the girl's mother pushing and pulling the needle through the material to make those little flowers. She couldn't help but wonder if the girl's mother still had that sweater, if she ever took it out and sat in some darkened corner of her house and wept into the soft green material.

A.J. turned away, cursing Jack MacAlister as she did.

"What's the matter?" he asked, and she had a sense of what it would be like to face him in court. "Do you know her?"

She shook her head. She would never forget the child's face now. Not as long as she lived.

"The kidnapper took her." She managed to get that much out.

"And this one." He tried to push another picture in front of her face, but she shoved it back at him, then jumped to her feet.

She was shaking badly, so she didn't go far, just stood beside the chair, with her head turned toward the lake. "What kind of a man are you?"

"I'm the man who's supposed to put away the bastard who snatched these little girls. All five of them. I have photographs of the other three, if you'd like to see them."

A.J. closed her eyes and tried to breathe. In the silence that fell between them, she heard his watch ticking off the seconds and knew that she would be lucky if a full minute had elapsed yet. She wondered whether he would try to stop her if she made it to the door. Remembering the tone of his voice just now, she decided he probably would.

"I can't look at those pictures."

"Fine," he said. "But could you live with yourself if you let that man go free?"

She whirled around and wished she had the nerve to slap his beautiful face. "I am not going to let anyone go free.

None of this is my responsibility, and don't you dare try to make it mine!"

"If you are Annie McKay, you're probably the only chance I have of getting this man convicted. And if I can't, he's going to be walking the streets again. He's going to find another little girl, and another, and another. Until some-one manages to stop him."

"I couldn't help you, even if I wanted to," she said, slowly and carefully. "Don't you understand that? I don't remember anything about my life from the time I was thir-teen years old. So how could I possibly help you?"

"If you're Annie, the memories are there somewhere in-side your head. We'll get them out some way."

"Think about what you're saying." She was almost beg-ging him now. "Think about what that man did to Annie and those other little girls. And ask yourself why anyone in her right mind would want to remember something like that."

That seemed to get to him for a moment. Maybe even shamed him into looking away and backing off. He'd stood up when she thought of bolting from the room, and now he sat again.

"Please," he said, gesturing for her to take her seat, as well.

"No more pictures," she insisted.

He nodded.

"I know this must be frightening for you," he said, his words giving her the strength she needed to look him in the eye. "But you have to understand what I'm fighting for, why I'm pushing so hard. If you were fighting for one of your kids, you'd do the same."

A.J. felt something akin to pity for the defense attorneys who had to match wits with him. He knew just where to hit, just how hard. How could she ever hold out against this man?

"We don't have to fight about this," he said. "No one's seen or heard from Annie McKay in nearly eleven years. I'm certainly not naive. I know the odds against finding her alive and well."

"Then why are you doing this to me?"

"Because if there's the slightest chance that you're Annie, I have to check it out. A.J., it's so simple to verify something like this these days. Annie's mother is there at your shelter. All I need is a blood sample from her and one from you, and we'll know. All of us will know for sure whether you're Annie."

"I can't." Hadn't he heard her?

"Why?"

"You would never understand."

"You don't have to decide right this minute. Just think about it," he urged her. "Odds are, you aren't Annie. And if that's the case, I—"

"You'll what?"

"I won't . . . hound you about this anymore."

She wondered what he'd been about to say before he caught himself.

"Think about the blood test," he said. "Surely it would be worth it to get me off your back."

"All right," she said. "I'll think about it." It wasn't exactly a lie. She wouldn't be able to put it out of her mind anyway, and if he felt better thinking she was considering going through with it, if it gave him the reassurance he needed to let her walk out of this apartment, then it was well worth it.

She stood, feeling as if she were actually going to escape. "Is that all?"

He glanced down at the watch, picked it up, then pushed a button on the side to stop its seemingly incessant noise. He showed her the watch face. Only four minutes had elapsed. Eleven minutes left. "Maybe I'll save them for another day."

She held her tongue, letting him think there'd be another day when she'd be willing to sit down and listen to him.

"I'll get your coat," he said, turning away.

She felt herself go weak in the knees at his words. She'd done it. She'd survived a night and day with him, and now she was free to go.

"Oh, I almost forgot," he said, frightening her all over again. "I called someone from my garage to go and get your van. They checked it over this morning. Do you want the grim details, or the final verdict?"

"Just the verdict."

"It's hopeless."

"We'll see about that," she said, just imagining what his mechanic's opinion was going to cost her. "I know someone who works wonders with beat-up old vans."

"A.J. you can't drive around the city at night in that thing."

She was intrigued by his concern, and tired of butting heads with him, especially over things that were none of his business.

"Why, Jack, I didn't know you cared." She said it just as Trini had said it to countless staff members around the shelter, sugary-sweet, yet at the same time dripping with cynicism.

She expected him to respond in kind, and for that to be the end of it. But it wasn't.

He suddenly turned all serious on her. His eyes took on an intense look as he stared down at her. She felt the tension escalating moment by moment, surrounding them and holding her in place when she wished she could flee.

Suddenly she was aware of every move he made, every flicker of emotion that crossed his face. He took a step closer to her, then another, invading the space she always tried to keep between herself and others.

"I realize this isn't any of my business," he said. "But I have to know."

He held out his hand to her, fingers spread wide, palm flat and open. Moving slowly, obviously trying not to frighten her, yet doing it in spite of the care he took, he reached for her hand, captured it, pried open the fingers and laid her palm flat against his.

He didn't try to hold it there in any way, just let it rest there, her palm against his. She seemed to be caught up in some spell he'd conjured. She couldn't have moved if her life depended on it. And it felt as if her very life did depend on what she did in the next few seconds.

"Is it just me?" he said. "Have I done something? Said something to frighten you? Or do you react this way to any man who touches you?"

A.J. shivered. She glanced around the apartment, taking in the dark green leather sofa that had creaked and crackled when he sat down, the antique rug, the breathtaking view of the lake. She tried very hard not to look at the man, not to think of the way it felt to have her hand lying in his, the heat of him seeping into her whole body.

He would never understand her world, or the things that had made her the way she was today.

Never.

"A.J.?" His other hand came up to stroke the back of hers—down her fingers, one by one, across her knuckles, over the flat, smooth back of her hand. His touch was as gentle and as easy as the brush of a feather, the pads of his fingers smooth and maybe even a little soothing.

She snatched her hand away when, amazingly, that gentle stroking started to feel good. Too good.

"Men don't touch me," she told him. Let him make of that what he would.

MacAlister thought about going after her, but he was too stunned by the way she'd run out of his apartment, too surprised by what she'd told him.

Men don't touch me.

Never?

Thinking of the possible reasons enraged him. He had to sit down, to calm down. Leaning forward in his chair, he put his elbows on the coffee table in front of him, folded his hands and rested his forehead on them.

He wanted to go and find her, to bring her back here and... and what? Tell her that she didn't have to be afraid of him? That she could trust him? That he would never hurt her, the way someone obviously had?

And he wanted her back in his arms again, the way she had been when he carried her in from the car.

How would she react if he explained to her the old-fashioned need he had to shield her and to protect her as best he could? He could just imagine. She'd call him a caveman and tell him she didn't need anyone or want anyone to take care of her.

How wrong about that she was. Everyone needed someone.

MacAlister shook his head. He'd known the woman for twenty-four hours, and he'd decided that he wanted to be the one she leaned on? How could that be? He knew hundreds of women, none of whom feared the mere touch of his hand, none of whom had ever fled his apartment the way she had.

And none of them had brought out this overwhelming protective streak in him. He couldn't remember the last time he'd brought a woman to his apartment to hold hands, couldn't ever remember the simple touch of a woman's hand lingering in his mind this way.

What in the world had happened to him? He couldn't get involved with A.J. With any luck, she could be the key to his case. It would be irresponsible of him. And that was just the beginning of the reasons he had for avoiding her.

Chapter 6

She'd fled from his apartment. There was no other word to describe it, A.J. thought, settling herself in a cab. Thankfully, he hadn't tried to stop her. She'd run out of the elevator, across the lobby and outside, where, by some miracle, a cab had been waiting by the curb.

It was still bitterly cold, the wind coming off the lake making it even worse, but the snow had given way to light flurries.

The driver did a double take when A.J. gave him the address of the shelter, and they spent the next five blocks negotiating over someplace he could drop her where she'd be able to catch a train and he wouldn't feel as if he were taking his life into his own hands by simply being there. Even if he didn't take her the whole way, it was going to cost her a fortune to get from MacAlister's Lake Shore Drive neighborhood to hers.

They were simply worlds apart, yet he'd held her hand in his and stroked it, the way a man might try to soothe some small wounded animal.

Was that how he saw her? Wounded? That was what she was, wasn't it? One of the walking wounded? This city was filled with people just like her—battered and bruised in some way. Doing the work he did, he couldn't be oblivious of that. What could one more wounded woman matter to him? she thought.

Yet, somehow, something inside her knew that it did matter, that she mattered, to him.

It was the most insane idea, yet she knew it to be true.

When she told him, in that split second of blinding honesty, that men didn't touch her, she'd thought she was going to cry again. Because she'd told him the absolute truth—men *didn't* touch her. But there he'd been, running his fingers so gently over the back of her hand. And it had felt . . .

She had to breathe deeply for a moment.

It had felt good.

There—she'd admitted it to herself. It had felt good to have him touch her that way.

Was it just him, he'd asked, or did she react this way to all men? And his question hadn't had anything to do with ego. It had been genuine and earnest, and he'd asked as if the answer meant a great deal to him. Which was crazy.

For how could a man like Jack MacAlister care about her?

She didn't even know him, for God's sake. But a part of her . . . Oh, Lord, a part of her wanted to know him better.

She finally made it to the shelter around eight-thirty. As usual the place was packed. She waded into the mess like a general taking charge, snapping orders at anyone on the staff who wanted to know where she'd been, what had happened to Trini and where the van was.

Carolyn left around nine, but not before coming to find A.J. and asking very softly if she was all right. A.J. assured her she was fine, then heard from Carolyn that her friend Nick was in the shelter looking for her.

She did a quick round of the shelter, finding everything running as smoothly as was possible when they were stretched to the limit like this, then made her way to the administrative offices, where Nick and a few other health professions who volunteered here had an office that they all shared.

Quite deliberately, A.J. let herself remember the instant when she'd realized that only one person could have revealed the kind of information about her that Jack MacAlister had, and that that person was Nick. She'd been furious, and she wanted that feeling back. She wanted Nick to see it, wanted to dump the anger and frustration onto him, where it rightfully belonged.

Dr. Nicholas Garrett was the closest thing she had to a friend here. He'd been working at another shelter farther west of here when she first arrived in Chicago, and for some reason, she'd trusted him. She'd told him more than she'd told anyone else about what she knew of her own past. No one but Nick could have told the authorities about her.

If not for Nick, Jack MacAlister wouldn't know about her. He would never have come looking for her, and she wouldn't have all these mixed-up feelings to deal with right now.

When she arrived at the door to his makeshift office, she didn't bother to knock. He didn't deserve that small courtesy from her. She opened the door and found him sitting at his desk, jotting down some notes on a yellow pad.

"Be right with you," he said without looking up.

She let him take his time, using the moment to assess him as she hadn't in the longest time, as a man. She guessed Nick was in his early thirties, and that Jack MacAlister would be as well. They were both tall, strong, with dark hair and dark eyes. Both deeply committed to their work, driven to succeed, hardworking.

Yet why did she find Jack MacAlister so fascinating, so infuriating, so... different from her friend Nick. Why did she still remember exactly how the touch of his hand had felt to her?

She'd never had feelings like that for Nick, though she worried that he had feelings for her that went beyond friendship.

"A.J." He stood and let the pad of paper fall to the desktop, then started to come around the side of the desk.

"I can't believe you did this to me," she said, the words fueled by remembered anger and the humiliation of being blindsided about her own past by a total stranger, one who'd neatly turned her whole life upside down.

Nick said nothing.

"How could you tell him those things about me? What gave you the right? I could get your license pulled for this, and you know it, Nick, so—"

She nearly lost it then. The anger drained away as quickly as the words flew out of her mouth, deserting her, even though she wasn't nearly done with him. Left in its place was nothing but a tightness in her throat, a heavy feeling in her eyes that left her vision blurring.

Given the state of her knees and her trembling limbs, A.J. decided that sitting was a good idea. Nick sat down again himself, watching her. He had a way of watching everyone intently, as if he could look inside people's hearts and tell whether they were being straight with him. God knew, he'd always managed to do that with her, somehow.

Who was she kidding? He'd always been great with her, and to her. If he hadn't stayed on her the way he had, she might still be living on the streets today, if she was still alive.

She owed him her life. And she'd trusted him more than she'd allowed herself to trust anyone in years.

"How could you do it?" she asked again.

"I'm sorry," he said. She found it totally inadequate, considering what he'd done. "But you can't run from your past forever, A.J. I've always told you that. I think, deep down inside, you know it. All that crap from the past—it's going to catch up to you, and you're going to have to deal with it."

"And you think it's up to you to decide when I do that?"

"I tried to talk to you about the McKays, but you wouldn't listen," he said.

"Which is certainly within my rights," she shot back at him. "I'm mad as hell at you."

"I think you're scared as hell."

"Well, thank you for that analysis, Dr. Garrett. How much do I owe you for this session?"

"Don't, A.J. Don't try to pull this act on me, because it won't work. I know you too well. I know this is important to you. I know you're furious, and I know you're scared. Can we deal with that first, because that's the heart of it?"

"Wait a minute," she said. "I'm not in therapy here."

He swore softly. "I'm the best friend you've got in this town, A.J. Who else are you going to talk to?"

She was at a total loss. He hadn't treated her this way since she was seventeen years old. She couldn't believe he was doing it now. "You have no right to interfere," she told him.

"Sure I do. If I don't, who will?"

"I can't do this," she said, standing abruptly.

"Why not?"

"I just can't."

"What is your gut instinct telling you?" he asked. "Why are you so afraid?"

She didn't sit back down, but she didn't walk away, either. She silently damned him to hell and back instead.

"I think somewhere, deep inside you, you already know. These people are your family, and some part of you recognizes that. The only problem is, you've got a whole lot of lousy memories standing between you and them. And you can't get to those wonderful memories of your family again without plowing right through those lousy memories, as well."

"You've got to be kidding," she said, praying that he was.

He shook his head. "That's why you're so mad at me, and that's why you're so afraid."

"How could you possibly know that?"

"Because I know you."

And then she wanted to cry. Except she never cried. "Nick..."

"Look, I'm sorry about this prosecutor barging in here and throwing all this stuff at you the way he did," he said. "I never meant for that to happen. I certainly never told him anything you and I discussed about your past. And I never thought he'd try to pressure you into testifying like this."

"You talked to someone," she said, not ready to let him off the hook.

"Just Drew. And not for the FBI. For Carolyn. I heard her on TV one night, A.J. I saw her, and I saw the picture of her little sister. Did they show you the picture? Of Annie McKay when she was thirteen years old?"

She shook her head. The girl MacAlister had shown her had been much younger.

"It's you."

She found that impossible to believe. "You put me through all this because you think I bear a resemblance to some eleven-year-old picture of a missing kid?"

"Sit down," he said, his tone daring her. "I'll tell you exactly why I did it, if you can take it."

She could have slapped him for that. There were times when she thought he was the most arrogant man in the world. Then, when she saw him working with some lost little kid, when he was so kind and so gentle, she thought he was the most wonderful man on the entire earth. And she didn't understand how he could possibly be both those men at the same time.

Unbidden came the image of Jack MacAlister, the tenderness in his eyes, the intensity to them, when he'd bent over her hand, stroking it so gently, asking if she was afraid of all men, or just him.

But Nick was here now. He leaned back in his chair, his arms crossed in front of his chest, one of his hands visible on his forearm.

How would it feel to have him touch her? He'd done it before, casually—testing her, she thought. She'd failed each and every test, and he'd retreated again and again.

How would it feel to have him touch her the way Jack MacAlister had?

She trusted Nick, more than she trusted any man. And he cared for her in some way that had nothing to do with the work they shared or the way he'd helped her in the past.

She could trust him now. She could find the answer to Jack MacAlister's question, which had so unsettled her. Was it just him? Or did she react that way to any man who touched her?

Of course, he didn't know the half of it. It had unsettled her, frightened her a little. But there was more. She liked it, too, when Jack MacAlister touched her. She'd felt drawn to it, soothed by it, comforted. And she had no idea what to do about that.

"Well?" Nick said.

She shook her head, uneasy at the turn her thoughts had taken, unable to recall the last thing she'd said to Nick.

"You remember when you let me hypnotize you that one time?" he said.

"Don't," she warned him. She'd come out of the hypnosis abruptly. It had been like awakening in the midst of the worst nightmare, made even more frightening by the knowledge that it was all too real. She'd known that whatever demons had surfaced during that session were real. And they were inside her, buried somewhere, just waiting for the chance to attack her again.

Why in the world would anyone think she'd give those demons another chance at her?

"Someone took you, A.J. Someone snatched you away from your mother and your father and someone else you obviously loved very much. That's where we were that day I hypnotized you. That's why you came out of it so frightened."

"I don't want to hear it," she said.

"Believe me, I hated hearing it myself. I'll never forget it. It's haunted me all these years."

She didn't want to hear Nick's reaction to what had happened that day. He'd seen and heard more than his share of horror stories, and if hers had made such an impression on his mind, it must have been terrible.

"A.J., it's time. You're so much stronger now. You can face it now, I promise you that. And you have a mother waiting for you now."

"You don't know that," she said. "Even Jack Mac-Alister admits that it's a ridiculous long shot."

"We don't have to guess," he said. "It's there, inside you somewhere, and someday it's going to come out. I know you can handle it now, A.J. I'll be with you every step of the way."

"Oh, Nick." She had never felt so bad about seeing him as nothing more than a friend. She was angry at him for what he'd done, but she believed him when he said he would stand by her. He would not let her down. And if she'd finally turned some corner in her life, finally decided that she might be ready for some kind of a relationship with a man, why couldn't it be with a man like him?

She would be safe with him.

"I'm sorry," she said, knowing he would take it as an apology for a totally different thing, but saying it anyway.

"Think about it. But before you go, I have to warn you— about Jack MacAlister."

"What about him?"

"I talked to some people around the courthouse."

Nick was often called upon to provide testimony as an expert witness in cases involving just about every lousy thing that could happen to a child. He also worked with prosecutors in preparing children to testify in court cases.

"And?" she prompted.

"A.J., it's a big case. I doubt you realize just how big. It's the kind of case that can make or break a prosecutor's career, and MacAlister has to know that."

"So?"

"I hear he's catching all kinds of hell from his boss for not having this case ready to go to trial."

"My heart bleeds for the man," she said, with as much sarcasm as she could muster. She wasn't ready to explain to anyone the mishmash of feelings she had for Jack MacAlister. And she certainly didn't want Nick offering to analyze those feelings for her.

"All kinds of hell," Nick repeated, "and it looks like it's going to get worse. That means you have to be very careful. From what I hear, MacAlister's a very ambitious man. You don't know what he might be willing to do to win this case."

What would he do to win it? she wondered. Pretend an interest in someone like her? She felt a little sick at the idea.

"What are you telling me?" she asked.

"Watch out for yourself."

"I always do."

In the next instant, the phone on Nick's desk rang. He answered it with a clipped "Hello," then explained to her, "I've been waiting for this. I need to take it. But will you think about what I've said."

She nodded.

"And think about taking the DNA test, A.J. Prove me wrong," he said, reminding her of Jack MacAlister then. "It would be so easy to do. And if you're so sure I'm wrong..."

Then it shouldn't bother her in the least.

She would love to do it—prove Nick and Jack Mac-Alister wrong at the same time.

There was only one problem. She was scared to death that there was a chance, even a slight chance, that they might be right.

Chapter 7

Later that evening, when A.J. had a minute, she called the hospital and spoke briefly to Trini, who was much better after having slept for about twelve hours. And the baby was holding his own. They couldn't ask for much more than that.

About an hour later, someone from the front desk called to her. "Need you up front, A.J."

"Can't it wait?" she called out from down the hall, where she was rummaging in a closet, trying to find just one more blanket. "Can't you handle it?"

"I think you need to see this for yourself, girlfriend," said Betsy, one of her streetwise teenage volunteers. "Because I'm sure my eyes are playing tricks on me."

A.J. glanced at her watch. Nine-forty. Although she'd slept the entire day away, she was exhausted. And yet she went on. "Coming, *girlfriend.*"

There was a crowd gathered around the shelter opening, and A.J. worked her way through it. At the entrance, she found Betsy, who held a package, obviously wrapped by someone who made a career out of bow-making, in her hand. "That's it?" A.J. said. "That's what you called me down here to see?"

Betsy shook her head and smiled, then pointed to the street in front of the shelter.

A.J. turned back around. Through the crowd of bodies gathered at the entrance, she saw what all the fuss was about. Illegally parked at the curb was a brand-new white van with a Hope House logo on the side.

A.J. looked from the van back to the crowd gathered there, then to Betsy and her package.

"It's for you," she said, holding out the keys and an envelope.

"What is?"

"All of it."

"Someone sent me a van?" she said stupidly, thinking of the limited number of people who knew the shelter's van had given out the night before and been declared officially dead this morning by an uptown mechanic. She thought about the severely limited number of people she knew who could afford to donate new vans to charities, not sure whether Jack MacAlister was among them.

"Guess nobody ever told him about sending something simple, like flowers or candy," Betsy added with a smile.

"Al-li-son," the group of kids behind her started chanting. No doubt they knew all about the mystery man who'd been here the night before, looking for Allison Jennings. She wondered if they were also aware of the fact that she'd been gone all night and all day.

Probably. The kids always seemed to know things before she did.

A.J. looked at the van. It was all shiny and clean, not a dent or a scratch on it. It would run like a dream, and the shelter desperately needed it.

Still, a van? She ripped open the envelope and pulled out the card.

"Be safe," it read. Then she saw a scrawl that must have been his signature, then a couple of phone numbers that she could barely make out.

The man had sent the shelter a brand new van. She was dumbfounded.

"Don't forget this," Betsy said, holding out the package to her.

She wasn't that scared of the package. It was small enough to fit into her hands, after all. How expensive and inappropriate could it be? She fought with the big gold ribbon and finally won, then pulled off the pretty flowered paper. Inside, she found a tiny cellular phone, the kind very important people carried around in little leather bags.

Be safe.

He'd been shocked that she didn't have one in the van so that she could at least check in with the shelter, or call 911 if she needed to. And now she could.

A.J. couldn't help but remember that strange look in his eyes when he'd told her she couldn't go driving around the city at night in that beat-up old van. He'd said it without the arrogance that was evident in so many things he said. He'd said it without making it seem like a command—and that was another annoying habit of his. She'd have sworn it was born of nothing more than simple concern for her safety.

Of course, this went way beyond simple concern.

"So who sent it?" Betsy said.

"I don't think you've been introduced."

"The dude who was here last night?" someone called out from the crowd behind her.

A.J. colored profusely.

"He was one fine-lookin' man," someone else added, in case anyone had missed him.

"Well," Betsy said, "do we get to keep it?"

"I'll have to think about," she said, knowing he'd made it nearly impossible for her to refuse without making an even bigger impact on the whole shelter staff and all the kids here.

He'd boxed her quite neatly into this corner. She'd have to see that it wasn't so easy for him in the next round.

A.J. tossed the keys to Betsy and asked her to find someone to park it in the lot around the side so that it wouldn't get towed away, then took her new phone inside, working her way deeper and deeper inside the shelter, until she found a little privacy. Finally she figured out how to make the phone work, then dialed one of the numbers scrawled on the card. She heard MacAlister's answering machine click on, heard a clipped message from him. His voice was brusque, not at all as warm and appealing as she remembered it. Surely it hadn't been as tempting as she remembered it.

She dialed the other number. Judging from the way he barked his last name into the phone, she decided, he must be at work.

"We got your present," she said, feeling every bit as awkward as she had at his apartment earlier, still remembering that last, shocking confession she'd made to him.

"You don't like it?"

She bit her tongue. "I didn't say that."

"They had one in blue, if you'd prefer that. I thought the old van must have been white at one time, but it was so beat up, I couldn't tell for sure."

"It was white," she told him. "Are you out of your mind?"

"You wouldn't have liked the blue?" He sounded so smug.

"I can't believe you sent us a van."

"And a phone? Did you get the phone?"

"Yes, the phone came, too. I'm using it now. The only problem is, I don't know what to do with it, or the van."

"Sure you do. Your van died. You need another one. And the mobile phone is an absolute necessity, if you're going to be on the streets alone."

"This is none of your business," she said, growing more and more irritated with him.

"It's no big deal, A.J."

"You give away vans and mobile phones all the time?"

He laughed at that. She'd never heard him laugh so freely or so easily. It sounded incredibly appealing. She couldn't help but wonder if there was some other woman who made him laugh.

"I give away all sorts of things all the time to worthy causes. Wouldn't you say Hope House is a worthy cause?"

"The worthiest."

"What was that?" he asked. "I must not have heard you correctly. You're agreeing with me."

"Don't be an ass, Jack."

"Didn't I tell you? Nobody calls me Jack."

"But I'm sure it's not the first time someone's called you an ass."

He roared at that, and it occurred to A.J. that she was having a lovely time sparring with him.

"It's no big deal, A.J. Send me a receipt for my taxes. Believe me, I can use the deduction."

"I didn't know prosecutors were so well paid."

"We're not," he admitted. "I made my money the old-fashioned way. I inherited it."

"Oh." Even better. Not only was he incredibly handsome and entirely too unsettling, he was wealthy, as well. She couldn't have found a more unsuitable man if she'd tried.

"Keep the van, A.J.," he said—as if he had any doubts that she would.

"You knew there was no way I could turn it down."

"There's no reason you *should* turn it down, is there?"

She couldn't think of a one that sounded even remotely reasonable.

"I'll be in touch," he told her.

And before she could tell him not to bother, he hung up. He'd gotten in the last word once again.

The man just wouldn't stay away. He showed up around midnight, when she'd finally finished sorting through the mess the day had brought, when she was once again feeling exhausted and vulnerable and totally inadequate when it came to dealing with him.

Was she doomed to always feel this way around Jack MacAlister? Was she cursed where he was concerned?

He'd told her he would be in touch, and she supposed that should have been fair warning. She should have been prepared, but she wasn't.

A.J. had been making one last check with the person manning the front door, with the intention of turning in for the night. Suddenly, there he was—walking through the slush and ice as he made his way toward the shelter.

There were snowflakes in his dark hair and on his coat, and there was a wary smile on his face. And she was afraid that she was actually glad to see him. Part of it was sheer curiosity. Could he actually be as sinfully attractive as she remembered? Could he set her on edge, somehow bring all her senses alive, just by walking into a room?

She'd been sure that part was simply her imagination. Now she had her doubts.

Damn, she was glad to see him.

"You're not closed for the night, are you?" he asked.

A.J. wished, for the sake of her sanity, that they were. She held the door open as he walked through, then stood back as he brushed off the snow.

"What in the world are you doing here?" she said.

"Would you believe I was in the neighborhood?"

She shook her head.

"How about I was desperate for coffee and thought you might take pity on me?"

"No one's ever pitied you in your whole life, Jack MacAlister."

"One cup?"

"It's almost midnight. How will you sleep tonight?" she said, then instantly regretted it. She didn't want to know how or where or when he would sleep, and especially not with whom he might be sleeping.

"One cup," she said grudgingly. Walking with him into the staff kitchen, she saw that there was none left. She'd have to wait until another pot brewed.

A.J. put her back to him and sorted through the cabinets until she found what she needed to start the coffee.

"How's Trini?" he said.

"She slept most of the day, which isn't surprising. But she sounded better when I talked to her a couple of hours ago."

"And the baby?"

Did he care? She couldn't help but wonder about that. She wanted to know what made him tick, what had brought him all the way across town tonight to find her. "The doctors are cautiously optimistic about the baby's chances."

"So what's going to happen to the two of them now?"

She emptied the coffee into the filter, then poured in the water, which left her nothing to do but face him again. The snow still clung to a few strands of his hair, his eyes were still too dark for her to read anything in them, and he was watching her. Why did he always seem to be watching her this way?

"I don't know what's going to happen to them." She thought about that for a moment, and then her conscience forced her to add. "You saved their lives."

"I was just following orders—yours."

"I don't think I would have found them on my own."

"A.J., I think you can do anything you set your mind to."

She dropped her eyes and felt a rush of blood to her cheeks. That sounded suspiciously like a compliment—something she hadn't expected at all from him, and felt guilty accepting, considering what she was about to do.

"I am grateful for the van," she said, also grudgingly. "We needed it desperately... but then, I guess you knew that."

He nodded. "Do I make you that uncomfortable?"

"Yes."

He seemed to like that, because he came one step closer. She had visions of them playing that awful cat-and-mouse game again, the way they had in his apartment this morning. She couldn't allow that.

She put out her hand to ward him off. "Look, Mac-Alister—"

"I'm not such a bad guy," he said.

Taking a breath, she held it to the count of three to calm herself. If it worked when dealing with small children, surely it would work with a grown man, as well. "I don't know what you're doing here, but—"

"Would you believe I was worried about you?"

"No." At least she didn't want to believe that.

"That I simply wanted to see you again?"

"No." Oh, please, don't let it be that.

He gave a long, low whistle. "I guess I have my work cut out for me."

A.J. swore as the color burned in her cheeks. Why was he doing this?

And then she remembered what Nick told her. Mac-Alister was a very ambitious man. And he wanted something from her, something she didn't intend to give him. And that something had nothing to do with anything he might feel about her personally.

That had to be it. That was so much easier to believe than the idea that he might be attracted to her.

"Someone told me you'd do almost anything to win a case," she said, stopping him cold.

His chin came up. He settled himself back against the cabinets and crossed his arms in front of his chest, then watched her for a long moment. "Someone isn't far from the truth."

She was taken aback for a second. She hadn't expected him to admit it so easily. "And he told me that this is a very big case you're working on, the kind that could easily make or break a prosecutor's career.''

''And naturally you'd believe anything this someone tells you, and nothing that comes out of my mouth?'' He looked angry then. ''Spill it, A.J. If you're going to accuse me of something, go ahead and do it.''

She flinched at the icy calm that had come over him, the rock-solid quality to his voice as he dared her to finish what she'd started. She looked around the room, then into the hallway, aware now, as she hadn't been before, that it was very late, that there was no one from the staff near here at this hour, that she was once again alone with him.

She wasn't afraid of him. Not exactly. Not in the traditional way a woman might fear a man. She was afraid because he tempted her.

And now she'd dared him to bring this whole thing out into the open. But her pride wouldn't let her drop it.

''I'm saying that you're a very ambitious man.''

''I wouldn't argue that with you.''

''That it's a big case,'' she continued.

''An *important* one.''

''And that you'd do anything to win.''

''*Almost* anything,'' he told her. ''And now you want to know if I'd stoop so low as to come on to a woman because I needed something from her, some kind of help on a very important case I'm working on? Is that what you're asking me, A.J.? If this has to do with the damned case that means so much to me?''

''Yes.''

She was sure he'd be furious at her response. Sure he'd come back with some blistering retort. But he didn't. Instead, he seemed a little saddened. He looked off to the side, then up at the ceiling, then shook his head.

And then he was back to looking at her—looking right through her, it seemed. ''Do you think so little of me?''

She could have sworn she'd hurt him with her accusation, but then, before this she would have sworn that nothing could hurt him, that very few things ever touched him in such an elemental way.

"Do you?" he repeated. "Or is the problem something else altogether?"

"I don't know what you mean," she retorted.

"I don't believe you doubt me nearly as much as you doubt yourself, A.J. Do you really think so little of yourself that you can't imagine a man who's honestly interested in you as a woman?"

At first, she was sure she hadn't heard him correctly. Then she could only wish she hadn't. Her back went ramrod-straight, and she had to fight to look him in the eye.

There was nothing she could say. Absolutely nothing. Never in a million years would she believe a man like Jack MacAlister could be attracted to a woman like her. It seemed so obvious to her. Surely it was to him, as well.

Did she think so little of herself?

She simply didn't think of herself at all in those terms. There'd been no reason to do so. Until now. Until he'd come barreling into her life and turned it upside down.

"I think you should go," she said, unable to look him in the eye a second longer.

He hesitated for a moment, just enough to totally unnerve her all over again, then said, "All right. This time, I will."

Chapter 8

Ten days later, Jack MacAlister slammed the phone down in disgust, jerked his tie loose from his throat for the third time, then started to tie it once again, in hopes of finally getting it right. Then the doorbell rang.

"Coming," he called out impatiently, still fooling with the tie and wondering who could have gotten past the doorman without him hearing about it first.

For a moment, he thought about the person he'd most like to see on the other side of that door. The woman whose face he saw morning, noon and night, the one who thought he was a perfect ass and made him feel like ten different kinds of a fool.

How long had it been since he'd felt so foolish with any woman?

Jack MacAlister didn't have trouble with women. He knew all sorts of women, and he enjoyed them. He flirted with them, dated them, took them to bed. Beautiful women, ambitious women, sophisticated women.

He'd fallen in love once in his life, and so far that had been more than enough. He didn't lead women on.

And he'd always been able to find a woman interested in the same things he wanted in a relationship: a little companionship, a few laughs, good sex. Until now, that had always been enough.

But those other women weren't nearly as fascinating, as complex, as tough—or, at the same time, as fragile—as A.J.

He didn't see their faces first thing in the morning before he even opened his eyes, didn't think about them late at night before he fell asleep.

He didn't spend precious time he couldn't afford to waste dreaming up excuses to see them again. He didn't feel something close to a murderous rage at the idea of another man hurting them so much that they couldn't stand to have his hands on them.

As he saw it, he was in trouble. And he was greatly disappointed when he opened the door to his apartment and saw that the woman on the other side was not A.J.

"Hi, Jack." Kitty gave him a quick kiss on the cheek, then headed for his bedroom. "Sorry I'm running late. It took longer than I expected to get everything ready for the party tonight, and the catering staff is giving me fits. You don't mind if I shower and change here, do you? That would save some time, and I can't be late."

"Help yourself, Kitty," he said to her back as she walked into his place as if she owned it.

He found himself mildly annoyed. It wouldn't be the first time she'd showered and dressed here, yet he felt uneasy about her doing so now.

"Someone's sending over my dress and my makeup. The doorman's bringing it up as soon as it arrives," she called from inside the bedroom.

He came to stand in the doorway, then saw that she was already inside the bathroom. She hadn't bothered to close the door, and he could see her reflection in the mirror over the vanity. She was shedding her clothes quite rapidly. He looked away.

"I haven't seen you in forever, Jack."

He looked back, relieved to see that she'd wrapped a big towel around her and was doing something to her long blond hair. His gaze caught hers in the mirror, and he noted the mild censure there.

"I've been busy at work," he said, even though he didn't owe her any explanations. They didn't have the kind of relationship that required explanations or excuses.

She walked out of the bathroom, her hair piled high on her head, the towel looking none too secure in the way it was wrapped around her body.

He knew her body well. He'd known her for years, though they were more friends than anything else. Friends and sometime lovers.

How long had it been since they'd been sometime lovers? He found he couldn't remember, realized he hadn't missed that particular aspect of their relationship at all.

She stood in front of him now, and took the ends of his tie in her hands and started to fix it.

"You never could get these things right," she said with a smile, standing too close for comfort. "I don't know how you've managed without me."

He looked down at her, his gaze settling on the generous curve of her breasts, which were barely covered by the towel. It was going to fall to the floor any minute.

"Kitty," he said, disentangling himself from her, "we need to talk."

"Do we?" she said, dropping the towel. "I thought you might get in the shower with me."

She had an incredible body; he couldn't deny that. In the next minute, she had her hands all over him, and he was pushing her away.

He simply didn't feel anything for her. He had no desire to take her into his bed. And he was in serious trouble. If he hadn't realized it before, he did now. All he could think about was A.J.

A.J. paused at the entrance to the main ballroom of one of Chicago's most elegant hotels, trying not to feel so out of place in the richly appointed room. It was useless, but she tried. She hated these things, though she suspected it was better to be here, surrounded by people, then in her room at the shelter, brooding.

She had tried to keep her mind off Jack MacAlister, and everything else except her work, but the rest of the world was not cooperating with her.

Carolyn McKay was at the shelter every day, as was Carolyn's mother, so A.J. tried to stay out of the administrative offices and the kitchen.

Her friend Nick was still pushing for her to at least take the DNA test that could tell them whether she was Grace McKay's long-lost child, but so far she had refused.

Trini was almost ready to be released from the hospital, and the baby would come soon after her. A.J. kept thinking that if it hadn't been for MacAlister, the girl and her baby never would have made it.

Now that she'd heard a little about the case Jack MacAlister was trying to prosecute, she seemed to see news of it everywhere—on TV, in the newspapers, even on the radio. She couldn't keep herself from looking for stories about the string of child kidnappings that had been attributed to Ray Williams, the man MacAlister was trying to prosecute. And it all left her feeling very uneasy, even a little sick to her stomach.

She couldn't be part of this case. How could they ask that of her? And yet they did, continuously. MacAlister kept calling her on the mobile phone he'd given her. He'd let a few days go by; she'd finally start to feel comfortable answering the thing again, and then she'd do so and find him on the line.

He wanted her to think about the case, think about the kids and the blood test. She'd done little else but try *not* to think about it. He wanted to show her the rest of the pictures of the missing girls, but there was no way she was going to look at those.

So, they were at a standoff, and she was stuck coming to this party. It was early February, time for the Valentine's Day Have-a-Heart fund-raiser, an annual event that raised money for a number of children's charities, including Hope House. In a weak moment, A.J. had agreed to attend on behalf of the foundation that ran the shelter.

She hated things like this, and always felt out of place with all the society types in their glittery ball gowns, their spike heels and their elaborate jewels. Nick was supposed to come and suffer through it with her, but was called away on an emergency at the last minute. So, here she was by herself in the crowd, hating the whole ordeal.

A.J. followed a group of people to a corner next to the bar and ordered a ginger ale for herself, because it would give her something to do with her hands. And when she backed away from the bar, she found herself face-to-face with the last person in the world she wanted to see tonight.

Jack MacAlister, in a black tux, a black tie and a killer grin. Damn.

"A.J.," he said softly, the grin even more devastating now.

She didn't want to think about what the sound of her name on his lips did to her, but she had an idea why he was so happy. She'd have bet her last dollar that he'd known she was going to be here tonight, that it would give him another chance to pressure her into doing what he wanted. With any luck, they could at least avoid all talk of anything personal.

"Jack," she said, as sweetly as she could manage, because he'd told her no one called him Jack. "What in the world are you doing here?"

"It's a worthy cause, wouldn't you say?"

Oh, he was the very image of the devil himself. "Yes, I think it's a very worthy cause. Hope House is one of the beneficiaries of the fund-raiser."

"Oh."

"As if you didn't know already." She wasn't about to let him off the hook.

"Me?"

"Give it up, Jack. You don't have an innocent bone in your body."

"I've been meaning to call you."

"I'll just bet you have."

"I hear Trini's getting out of the hospital."

That surprised her—that he'd obviously been checking up on Trini, that he still cared. "She'll be out of the hospital in a couple of days."

"And the baby?"

"Holding his own. Trini was very lucky. He doesn't have any major health problems."

"So, what's going to happen to her and the baby when they're released from the hospital?"

"The most amazing thing happened the other day. She agreed to call home and tell her mother about the baby."

"She's going home?"

"Not exactly. Her mother's involved in an abusive relationship. That's why Trini left, and she could never take the baby back into a situation like that. But her mother's sister, after hearing about the baby, offered to let Trini and the baby come live with her. And I think it's going to work out."

"That's wonderful."

She nodded.

"You could go back home, too, A.J."

"Don't push it, MacAlister. I was just starting to think you were a nice guy."

"I am a nice guy."

"As long as you get your way," she said.

"Okay, so I never learned to lose gracefully. It's not exactly considered a virtue in a prosecutor."

"But it is in a man." A.J. wondered what he'd make of that. Would he think she was interested? In him? As a man? Surely not. Still, she was thinking of some way to back herself out of that corner when an incredibly beautiful woman walked over to the two of them.

"Darling, there you are," the leggy blonde, who was wearing a glittery, flame red dress, said to MacAlister as she slid her arm into the crook of his elbow and plastered herself to his side. "I've been looking all over for you."

The woman pouted prettily and tilted her head toward him, dismissing A.J. with one glance. A spray of diamonds in her ears, at her neck and on her fingers glittered and danced in the light with every move she made.

A.J. wished the floor would open up and swallow her whole. She'd actually been worried that MacAlister might think she was interested in him, when he had someone like this hanging on his arm?

"I came to say hello to a friend of mine," MacAlister said to the pouting blonde. "Kitty, this is A.J. She's the director of the runaway shelter at Hope House. A.J., this is Kitty Whittaker. She helped organize the fund-raiser."

A.J. had no option but to shake the woman's hand, once Kitty managed to force herself to let go of Jack MacAlister long enough to offer it.

"So nice to meet you," the woman said, reminding A.J. of a cat about to pounce.

"The party's lovely," A.J. offered, then remembered she was here representing Hope House. She had to be nice. Turning back to the cat she smiled. "I can't tell you how much all of us at the shelter appreciate all the hard work that goes into this, or the money that comes out of it. We need it desperately."

The woman purred. "And you actually work there, with those . . . poor, unfortunate children?"

"Yes," A.J. said, wondering if the woman would faint if she knew A.J. had once been one of those poor unfortunates.

"How...interesting."

"Yes, it is. Now, if you two will excuse me, I...see someone I need to speak with."

And then she escaped, pretending not to hear MacAlister calling her name.

She hid behind a huge potted fern and sipped her ginger ale while she tried to tell herself that there was no reason to be upset. He was a man, a gorgeous one, a rich one. Naturally women would be crawling all over him at any opportunity. That should come as no surprise to her.

And the cat with the big red claws and the killer dress— Kitty—obviously had some claim to the man. She had her hands all over him, tucking her hand in the crook of his arm, leaning into his side, pressing the side of her breasts against his biceps. A.J. got the she-cat's message loud and clear—hands off. She was surprised the woman saw fit to even post the warning, surprised that Kitty would see her as any threat at all.

A.J. was fine with that. After all, she certainly had no claim on Jack MacAlister. A night in the snow and at the hospital with him, a day spent in the bed in his guest room, an evening meal at his apartment, a new van for the shelter and a phone for her, lots of accusations, a few confessions and a mountain of doubts—that was not the stuff of which relationships were made. Even A.J., who knew nothing of relationships with men, understood that.

Still, she continued to hover behind the potted plant as the party swirled on around her. And she couldn't take her eyes off Jack and the catwoman. The music started. Kitty plastered herself against him, and they slowly circled the dance floor.

Sick with fascination and what she could only describe as envy, A.J. watched every move they made. They were a stunning couple, looking as if they belonged together. And surely they did.

A.J. tried to remind herself that she wanted nothing to do with the man, and that more than likely he wanted only one thing from her: help with his case. And if he'd decided to play some sort of mind game with her—namely flirting like the devil and then, when that didn't work, trying to make her think she was incredibly insecure in believing he wasn't actually interested in her—it only showed that he'd do anything to win this case.

Yet she continued to watch them circle the dance floor. She remembered what it felt like to be caught against MacAlister's big, powerful body. What would it feel like to have his arms around her that way? To have her body brushing against his as they slowly moved in time to the music? To have his cheek come down and nuzzle against hers? To have his mouth settle over hers?

A.J. turned away in disgust at the path her thoughts had taken. She was going crazy. He was making her crazy. And she simply couldn't get thoughts of him out of her head.

It took MacAlister a good fifteen minutes to escape from Kitty and find A.J. again.

He had been meaning to call her, but he'd wanted to see her again, as well. And his reasons had nothing to do with business.

He followed her through the ballroom, admiring her trim figure, encased in a pair of silky black trousers and a shiny red vest that left her arms bare and a hint of the curves of her breasts exposed. It was a very simple outfit, one that had no doubt cost a fraction of what most of the elaborate gowns worn by the rest of the women in the room had. Leave it to her to find something totally different, and to look fantastic in it. The outfit suited her perfectly. And he thought it was sexy as hell.

"Wait a minute." He finally caught up with her as she slipped into an alcove just outside the main ballroom. He wished he could just reach out and grab her by the arm, but he remembered her reaction the last time he'd done so. And he'd never forget what she'd told him right before she ran out of his apartment.

Men don't touch me.

"A.J.," he called out, worried she'd slip away from him. Finally, she turned around and stopped.

"Don't run away from me again," he said, counting on her pride alone being enough to keep her here. He thought she might try to deny the fact that she'd been avoiding him, but she didn't.

"Did you lose something, Jack?"

"What?"

"That woman hanging on to your arm. How did you ever manage to escape?"

He smiled. She actually sounded jealous. "Kitty had some business to take care of."

"Oh. She's . . . lovely."

"She works very hard at it. Puts in amazingly long hours to achieve that look."

That won a smile from her, and a catty "I'm sure she does."

"In case you're wondering, I've known her since she was six. Her parents are good friend with my parents."

"How nice for you."

"She asked me to come to this thing with her," he added. "I didn't invite her."

"In case I was wondering?" She seemed outraged by the thought. "Believe it or not, I have better things to do with my time than wonder about which woman you're dating at the moment."

"Since when did dating become a crime?"

"It hasn't."

"I try to date a wide variety of socially prominent women," he said. "It gives my mother hope, and it keeps her off my back."

"You expect me to believe that you see *that* woman just to keep your mother happy?"

"I love my mother very much," he declared. "But when Kitty asked me to the dance, I only agreed to come because I thought you might be here."

That did it. He'd scored a hit with that one, managing to throw her off-balance and make her blush at the same time. He didn't know women still did that.

"You wanted to talk to me about something?" she said, taking a step backward.

He wasn't about to let her get away with changing the subject now that he had her on the run. "I wanted to talk about you. And me."

She opened her mouth, but closed it again. He watched the delicate muscles in her throat and her neck as she swallowed hard and tilted her head to the side, couldn't help but look down into that enticing bit of curves and shadows at the V neck of her glittery vest.

She caught him doing it, too, and he wasn't sure that was such a bad thing. She turned nearly as red as her vest. Clearly, he'd succeeded in throwing her off-balance. Of course, that hadn't been his main objective. He'd simply wanted to let her know that her confession that night in his apartment hadn't made a difference in the way he felt about her. He was still interested, definitely interested, and she might as well get used to it.

She could try to put him off with this smoke screen about him coming after her for no other reason than to get the information he needed for the trial, but it simply wasn't true. He wasn't *that* ambitious. She'd just have to figure that out on her own, in time.

But he didn't see a reason to be anything but up-front with her about the fact that he was interested, if he could do so without scaring her off.

"I don't know what you mean," she finally said.

"I mean that I haven't been able to get you out of my mind."

She looked even more uncomfortable at those words, and took another step backward.

He wasn't that close to her, he told himself. Not enough to send her scrambling to get away. But then, she wasn't any woman. She was A.J., and he couldn't be sure how deeply the scars of her past still haunted her today.

"I told you," she said. "I mean . . . I thought you understood." She took another step, putting her back against the wall. Her chin came up a notch.

Again he watched her throat as the muscles moved with every breath she took. He didn't think he'd ever been so fascinated by a woman who obviously hadn't dressed to call attention to herself. He was certain she had no idea how sexy she was in that outfit, certain she never would have dressed to create such a look.

"I heard what you said at my apartment, and I think I do understand. But surely you're not going to live your whole life alone, A.J. Surely there'll come a day when you meet someone you want to get to know better. . . ."

"And you've decided you're that man?"

"I think I'd like to be."

He watched as she looked away and smiled incredulously.

"You think a lot of yourself, don't you?" she asked.

"No. I told you, I've been thinking a lot about you." He was absolutely serious. "A.J., I mean it. This isn't a line I throw at women. It isn't a game, because I don't play games with women. And it doesn't have anything to do with the trial."

"Oh." It was a small, breathless sound, and it told him that he'd broken through the teasing and the flirting. He meant what he'd said, and he thought she finally believed him.

Unfortunately, she was also afraid. And he hated the idea of her being afraid of him. He decided it was definitely time to back off.

"I'm sorry," he said lightly. "We don't have to settle this tonight. I can be patient."

"Oh, really?" She was bouncing back.

"I am capable of being patient. I don't like it, but I can do it."

"At least you're honest about that."

"I'll be honest with you about everything."

"And I thought you just wanted to talk about the case." She sighed heavily.

He watched as some of the fight seemed to drain out of her and she relaxed just a little.

"Damn," he said softly.

"What?"

"I do have some things I need to tell you about the case."

"I knew it," she said.

"I told you I'd be honest with you. Well, I am. This case is an issue between us. It's just not the only one."

"So, tell me."

He couldn't help but feel he'd just confirmed her worst fears about him, couldn't remember the last time he'd felt so clumsy and so foolish around a woman.

"We don't have to do this tonight," he said, offering her an out.

"You're here. I'm here. We might as well get it over with."

He'd bet she thought she'd never have to see him again. He'd have to show her how wrong she was about that.

"You should know," she said, "I haven't changed my mind about the blood tests, or anything else."

He put his hands in his pockets, thinking it might ease her mind a bit if she didn't have to worry about him touching her. His attraction to her was complicated enough because she was a potential witness, but this obvious and real fear of hers . . . that should have been more than enough to tell him to back off. Trouble was, he didn't know if he could.

"I found out some things this week and I thought you should know." He forced his mind back to the business at hand, where it should have been all along. "I dug through some old records. Want to know what I found out?"

"I'm sure you want to tell me."

"No, A.J., I don't want to tell you. I don't want to frighten you, or make you any more uncomfortable than you already are. But I have a job to do, a very important job. I think you can understand that, and I wish you'd try not to dislike me so much because of it. I'd hoped it wouldn't cause a lot of problems for us, but I guess I was wrong."

"MacAlister, there is no *us*."

She didn't give an inch, and that made him mad. He thought about calling her a liar right then and there, because something was definitely going on between them.

"There was something you wanted to tell me?" she said. "About the case?"

"Fine," he said, struggling to control his temper, wondering how this conversation had ever gotten so out of hand. "We'll talk about the case. First, those pictures I showed you?"

"Yes."

"There was nothing disturbing about them. Nothing that should have caused you to become so uncomfortable. Why did they make you uncomfortable, A.J.?"

She shrugged, her shoulders coming up a little and the vest shifting and settling again around her body. He tried his best not to notice.

"Those were photos of the girls," she said. "The ones who are still missing, right?"

"Right."

"You wanted me to look at them and remember their faces and feel guilty because I wasn't doing what you wanted me to do. Well, that was a rotten thing to do."

"I didn't show you their pictures for that reason," he said. At least not for that reason alone, he added to himself. "Could you have seen any of those photos before? Did you recognize any of the girls?"

She shook her head. "Where would I have seen them before?"

"Think about it. It's important. Why did the pictures upset you so much?"

"I just . . . I don't like photographs."

"Why?"

"I never have."

"Never?"

"For as long as I can remember."

"A.J., did anyone ever take pictures of you that made you uncomfortable?" He hated what her answer might mean, hated even asking her to consider it.

"I don't understand."

"Yes, you do," he said softly.

"I've just never liked having my picture taken. I don't know what else I can tell you."

"The man I have sitting in jail is a photographer."

"I know."

"If he's the man who took those five girls, and I'm convinced that he is, then I'm willing to bet he photographed those girls while he had them."

Suddenly her eyes took on a frightened look. Then her gaze turned almost pleading, and he thought that any minute she might turn and run.

He felt like a complete bastard. At the moment, he hated this impossible job of his, and he hated the idea of hurting her even more than she'd already been hurt.

MacAlister held out his hand to her, hoping the action wouldn't frighten her more. "Hold on to me," he said, thinking to steady her.

He held his hand out in the space between them. Magically, miraculously, she took it. With a touch as light as a feather, she laid her palm across his. His fingers curled around the back of her hand, squeezing it once, and suddenly he felt about ten feet tall. She did trust him, at least a little bit.

"That's not all I found, A.J."

"Of course not," she said, resigned to his revelation.

"I told you he was a photographer. That's how he found the girls. He came into their schools and photographed them all." MacAlister squeezed her hand again. "Eleven years ago, he photographed Allison Jennings."

Her face turned paper-white, and her hand clenched his in a death grip. If he'd thought she would allow it, he'd have hauled her into his arms right then and there.

"Steady," he offered instead.

"Are you sure of your information."

He nodded.

"The real Allison Jennings?"

"Yes, the one who drowned."

"You have done your homework, counselor."

Of course he had. He was a careful, conscientious, thorough investigator. But he wished at the moment that he hadn't been quite so thorough. "Are you all right?"

"I'm still standing," she said, and he couldn't help but admire the woman.

"There's more." He squeezed her hand again.

"With you, there's always more."

"The Jenningses lived in Indiana their entire lives. But one summer, in August, they packed up everything they owned and left. Why did they do that?"

"I don't know."

"Do you have any memory of being in Indiana?"

"No, just Wisconsin."

"They never talked to you about why they left?"

"No."

"The first records," he went on cautiously, gauging her reaction as best he could, "at least the first I can find, showing the Jenningses in Wisconsin, were from October, nearly eleven years ago. They showed up there about two months after Annie McKay disappeared."

He watched as A.J. took the information in.

"It doesn't mean anything," she insisted.

He doubted she believed it herself, even as she said it. "Don't be so quick to dismiss this, A.J. You said there wasn't any connection between the Jenningses and this kidnapper. Well, I just found one."

She struggled with that. He felt the fine trembling in the hand he still held, saw the way the light caught her eyes and reflected the tears held stubbornly in check there.

"Just think about taking the tests," he said. "That's all I'm asking you to do right now."

She nodded.

"I'd help you, A.J., if you'd let me. I'd be with you every step of the way, and I'd do anything I could to make this situation less painful for you."

She looked at the floor, at the ceiling, at the party going on in the next room, anywhere but at him.

"I don't want to hurt you," he added.

"Then don't ask me to do this." She was almost pleading with him.

"I'm sorry." What else could he say?

"Damn you. You can't make me do this."

"No, I can't." He gave it one last try. "I'm asking you to do it for the children, for the ones this guy's going to grab next year and the next and the one after that, if we can't convict him. I'm asking you to do it for Sara Parker, because there's no way she'll hold up on the stand as a witness. But that's wrong of me, too. Maybe you should be doing this for yourself." And with that last remark, he released her hand and walked away.

A.J. watched him go, and tried to figure out whether she was relieved by his departure or not. She had wanted to force him to stop revealing these things, to stop making demands on her that she couldn't satisfy. But she hadn't wanted him to let go of her.

Imagine that. Her welcoming the touch of a man's hands. Would Jack MacAlister never cease to amaze her? And he'd found a link between the Jenningses and the man who'd taken those little girls.

Up until this point, she'd been certain that the possibility of her being Annie was just wishful thinking on the part of Carolyn and Grace McKay. And she could understand their hopefulness. She knew people became desperate when their children were lost. They would grab at every little piece of hope, and hang on to it for dear life.

But this...this was something more. At some point in her life, the real Allison Jennings had crossed paths with the kidnapper.

Could that be nothing more than a coincidence, as well?

The Jenningses had arrived in Wisconsin, with A.J., two months after Annie disappeared. That was truly unsettling. There was only so much she could blame on coincidence.

She was going to have to stop running from the secrets of her past. She'd have to face the real truth one day; Jack MacAlister was going to make sure of that.

What else would he push her into? she wondered. He'd said he'd missed her, said he hadn't been able to get her out of his mind. What did a woman say to a man who'd confessed such a thing? A.J. had no idea. This was totally out of her range of experience with men.

What could MacAlister possibly want from her? A date? A kiss? To go to bed with her? What? She couldn't imagine. It was all so ridiculous, anyway. A man like him would never be interested in a woman like her.

He had Kitty with her fancy gowns, her socially prominent parents and her charity balls. And A.J. had no business spending her time thinking about him.

Now that he was gone, she looked down at her hand, once so safely enclosed by his. Could she have gotten used to the touch of his hand so quickly that she already missed it? Because, for reasons she couldn't begin to explain, now that he was gone, now that he wasn't here beside her, she felt absurdly alone.

It was absolutely amazing. She'd spent the past seven years of her life almost totally alone. She'd gotten used to it, and she'd come to feel safer that way, with no one to depend upon except herself.

Could MacAlister have taken that away from her already? And what else would he take from her before this case was over.

Chapter 9

He wanted lunch.

A.J. was certain that there was much more to his request than that, but for now, Jack MacAlister claimed he simply wanted to share a meal with her. And he'd practically dared her to turn him down.

So she'd agreed to lunch. How much could that involve? They would share a meal, downtown, near his office, with hundreds of other people around them sharing meals. How dangerous could it be?

A.J. had no idea. She hadn't gone on a date since high school, back in her other life, when she'd believed herself to be Allison Jennings. Football games, dinner at the pizza place, a trip to the movies, with a *boy*. That was what she knew of dates.

But Jack MacAlister was no boy, and they weren't going to a football game.

A.J. had agonized over what to wear. She'd fussed with her hair, though it was too short for her to do anything really different with it. Though she'd chosen to put on some lipstick, she'd chewed it off on her way downtown to meet him.

He'd picked a new Chinese restaurant that he'd recently discovered, and she found him just inside the door, wearing his lawyer attire and looking a little stern and very intimidating. Then he smiled, making her even more uncomfortable than before.

"I wasn't sure you'd come," he said.

"Neither was I."

"I'm glad you did."

The hostess interrupted then, saving A.J. from having to reply. With a very deferential attitude and several inquiries as to Mr. MacAlister's preferences, the woman led them to a booth in the back.

A.J. took her time getting settled, finding a spot for her purse, arranging her napkin, looking around the room, only to find her attention drawn back to the man across from her. He was watching her. What was it about the way he looked at her that made her feel as if someone had turned the heat in the room up a notch too high?

"Comfortable?" he asked.

"Yes."

"Hungry?"

"Yes."

She picked up her menu. Luckily, it was tall, and totally blocked out his face, making her feel better for a moment. Was this how men treated women they dated? she wondered. Was this how they affected them? She didn't remember this part from high school. And she was no good at this.

Putting down her menu, she blurted out, "Why are we here, MacAlister?"

"I thought you liked Chinese food. That night at my apartment, you couldn't wait to dig into the fried rice."

"I was starving," she said.

"You don't like Chinese? Because we can go somewhere else."

"No." Was the man deliberately misunderstanding her? "I mean us, together. Why are we here together? Why did you ask me to come here today? And what do you want from me?"

"Do I have to answer all that on an empty stomach?"

She glared at him. He could be so obtuse at times.

"Come on, A.J. You're here. I'm here. I'm hungry. We might as well eat. And we can work out the rest of it over lunch, all right?"

The waitress arrived before she could come up with a rebuttal. A.J. thought about the time—shortly after noon. Her alarm had gone off at 5:30. She'd eaten something on the run earlier, and she was very hungry, despite her nervousness. She ordered Moo Shu pork and fried rice, then, regretfully, gave her menu to the waitress and looked for something else to hide behind. But there was nothing left.

He was directly in her line of vision, so she had no choice but to look at him. The room was definitely too warm. She chewed on her lip for a moment, but that only made her realize again that her lipstick was long gone.

"Do I make you that uncomfortable, A.J.?"

It was a loaded question if she'd ever heard one. She decided to go for honesty. He'd probably recognize anything less than that, and challenge her on it.

"Yes," she admitted.

"I *was* surprised that you came."

"I was surprised that you asked. And I'm still wondering why you did."

"I wanted to see you again." His words sounded sincere.

"Try again, Jack."

"I'm giving it my best shot," he said.

Oh, no. He really did want to see her. He'd made that more than clear at the party the other night, but she'd thought she'd made it equally clear that she didn't want to start any kind of relationship with any man.

Obviously, he wasn't going to let that stop him. What in the world was she going to do about that? Already she felt color flooding her cheeks, felt little butterflies fluttering around in her stomach. And all they were doing was sitting across the table from one another.

She decided to start with "I don't know if this is such a good idea."

"Tell me why," he shot back.

Who was asking, the prosecutor or the man? She had no idea. "Why?"

"Why you're so afraid of me. Or any man. What happened to you, A.J.? All I heard was a bizarre story about how the Jenningses raised you and convinced you that you were their daughter, and that you didn't find out otherwise until the couple had died."

She swallowed hard, then reached for her water glass. She hadn't told anyone that story except Nick. She wondered if she could repeat it to this man, wondered if it would hurt as much as ever, even after all this time. She wondered if that would be enough for him, if he would leave her alone then.

Could she tell him? Could she do it without falling apart? Could she prove to herself that it didn't hurt that much anymore?

"There's not that much to tell," she said.

"Tell me anyway. What's the first thing you remember about being with the Jenningses?"

That was hard. She'd heard so many stories about Allison Jennings. The little girl's memories had been planted in her head, and it was difficult to figure out where A.J.'s real memories ended and Allison Jennings's began.

"I remember the new house, the one in Wisconsin, the day we moved in. I remember being in the pickup truck before that. And I remember Mrs. Jennings holding me and crying over me. I remember crying with her, but I'm not sure why I was crying."

"And before that?"

"I remember being frightened." More frightened than she'd ever been in her life. "And that's it. There's nothing before that."

MacAlister shifted in his seat to lean across the table toward her. "So this couple—they lost their daughter in an accident, then somehow got a hold of you and tried to convince you that you were their daughter."

"They did convince me. I believed every word they said." That realization had left the most lingering pain. She'd believed them with every fiber of her being, and they'd lied to her, every day she'd spent with them.

"How did you find out the truth?" he asked.

"After the Jenningses died, I went to see their attorney, and he wanted to have me thrown in jail. He thought I was someone who decided to try to grab what was left of their money and run with it. He didn't believe a word I said to him, because he already knew the truth. Allison Jennings was dead. She had been for years by then."

"He told you, just like that?"

She shrugged helplessly, the pain just as deep as it had been that day so long ago.

"Of course I didn't believe him," she said. "Who would have believed him?"

"What did you do?"

"I decided to prove him wrong, except I couldn't. I went to the town courthouse, and found the death certificate. Allison Jennings drowned when she was thirteen. I went to the library and looked up the story in the newspaper. The Jenningses were at the lake, and Allison had an accident. She hit her head on the side of the dock and fell in. The water was deep there, and it had been raining the day before. The sediment in the water made it murky. No one found her until it was too late.

"That's what the Jenningses told me, that she—that I—fell and hit my head on the dock and nearly drowned. Nearly. And when I woke up, I didn't remember anything."

The waitress returned at that moment, pulling A.J. back to the present. MacAlister waved the woman away, and A.J. tried to pull herself together.

"What did you do then?" he said, his voice low and steady, almost mesmerizing. She wondered if he used that tone in court, wondered if people told him anything and everything when he talked to them that way.

He was a very dangerous man.

"I still didn't believe it," A.J. continued. "Who would have? But I went to the junior high school and looked up her yearbook picture from the year before she died. And once I saw her picture, I knew. I'd seen her picture before."

"Where?"

"In the family photo album—the Jennings's photo album. They had tons of pictures of her when she was little, and then there was a gap of several years when there weren't any. Later, there were more, except the pictures were of me." A.J. shrugged, trying to ease away some of the tension building in the muscles of her shoulders. "I guess I should have known there was something strange about that, but I didn't see it while I lived with them. Allison and I had the same coloring—our hair, our eyes. I guess it wasn't that hard to pass her baby pictures off as mine. But as she grew older, it would have been more obvious. So they must have hidden those pictures away."

"It's a bizarre story," he said.

She nodded.

"What did you do then?"

"I found her grave. And then I couldn't lie to myself anymore. I wasn't the Jennings's daughter. I had absolutely no idea *who* I was. That's when I ran away."

"Did the Jenningses ever hurt you? Physically, I mean?"

"No. They were very kind, very loving. I couldn't— It sounds so silly to say, but I couldn't have asked for better parents. The only problem was that they weren't my parents."

"Do you think they could have been mentally ill? That the trauma of losing their daughter was just too much for them?"

"I don't know." She looked down at her hands, clasped together in her lap, the thumb of one hand busy worrying the thumb of the other, and willed her fingers to be still. "I've thought about it a lot over the years, and I felt like Mrs. Jennings believed what she was telling me. She wasn't being treated for depression, and she wasn't on any medication that I knew of, but she was always very emotional, maybe even manic-depressive. I don't know. I try not to think about it anymore."

"You've buried it all, you mean."

A.J. wanted to growl at him, but she stopped herself in time. It would only let him know that he'd gotten to her again. She fell back on what was almost a reflex for her— sarcasm. "Thank you for that expert opinion, Dr. Mac-Alister. I think we're making great progress with my therapy, don't you?"

He swore softly. "You really think I'm an ass, don't you?"

A.J. held her tongue, with difficulty. Much as she'd have loved to say yes, she didn't see how that would be fair, because she honestly didn't know what she thought of Jack MacAlister.

"If one of your kids was in trouble," he continued, "you'd fight just as hard as I am to save them. Don't even try to tell me you wouldn't. Yet you're ready to condemn me for doing the same. Darlin', I don't think you're being fair."

"Life isn't fair, MacAlister. Didn't anybody tell you that?"

He swore again.

"Why *did* you ask me to come here today?"

"Two reasons," he said. "I did want to see you again."

She tensed at that, believing him. "And the second?"

"You know, I wasn't sure if I could do this. I didn't think I could be as hard or as unfeeling as you've decided I am. I'm sorry, A.J."

"About what?"

"The little girl in that booth over there."

A.J. looked toward the front of the restaurant. She saw a little girl of six or seven, dressed in her Sunday best, a red bow in her hair and shiny black Mary Janes on her feet. She was sitting very close to a woman A.J. suspected was her mother, and looking a little uneasy.

"See her?"

"The one with the red bow?" A.J. said.

"Yes. That's Sara Parker."

A.J. recognized the name. She'd heard it before, though she wasn't sure where. Then it came to her. "She's—"

"The girl Ray Williams grabbed off the sidewalk near her house and kept for four days. She and her parents are meeting me at the jail later. We're going to see if Sara's willing to pick him out of a lineup. She fell apart the day we asked her to I.D. his photograph. This will be even harder for her. Then I'm going to decide whether I can stomach the idea of putting her on the stand to try to get him convicted, or whether I might as well spare her the experience. Because even with her testimony, I don't think there's any way I can win the case."

"That's why you brought me here today," she said, hating him in that instant. "You wanted me to see her and feel guilty about what she's gone through, that she's going to have to testify. That's the only reason we're here today, because you knew she was going to be here."

"Believe that, if it makes you feel any better. Or if it makes you feel safer. But you and I both know it's not the only reason we're here today."

And then he stood up and left. A.J. watched him stop at the little girl's table briefly, watched Sara Parker huddle closer to her mother and look up at him with a sad expression.

MacAlister said something to the girl's parents, handed some money to the passing waitress, then left the restaurant.

A.J. propped her elbows on the table, laid her head in her hands. She wanted to believe him, wanted to believe that he did want to see her again, that their being together was about more than his job. Still, she cursed him with every step he took.

A.J. wasn't sure whether she was in the hands of a master manipulator, a down-and-dirty street fighter or a truly dedicated man wrestling with his conscience. But she still found herself at the county jail that afternoon.

MacAlister's name opened all sorts of doors for her. She just kept telling everyone that she was meeting him this afternoon to pick someone out of a line-up, and they took her deeper and deeper inside the facility, until she was standing in a corridor outside the observation room.

She wondered if he would gloat over his success in getting her here, or worry that he'd pushed her too far. She didn't know. She seemed totally incapable of reading the man.

But she hadn't come for him, anyway. She'd come for the little girl.

Her friend Nick did a lot of work preparing young children to testify in court, so she knew what Sara faced. More than likely she'd be put through the agony of testifying, only to have the judge or the jury decide she wasn't a credible witness. Either she would be considered too young to be trusted, or someone would decide she might not understand the difference between the truth and a lie.

So A.J. was here, mostly for Sara Parker, but partly because she wanted to be done with Jack MacAlister.

If she could simply look Ray Williams in the face and show MacAlister once and for all that she didn't recognize the man, that she had no recollection of ever having seen him, the whole mess would be over. MacAlister would have to understand then that she could not help him with his case. Maybe then he'd give up and leave her alone. He claimed he didn't have the evidence needed to take Williams to trial and have a prayer of winning. And he seemed to think she was his last hope. Well, if this was what it took to take that last hope away, A.J. could do it.

All too soon, the door opened. She heard low-pitched but urgent voices. MacAlister's was clear, and easy to distinguish from the others. A.J. thought she might recognize one other voice, but she couldn't place it right away.

Sara Parker's father came through the door first, carrying his daughter. The little girl was wrapped around him, her arms around his neck, her legs clutched tight around his waist, her head buried in his shoulder. A.J. was glad she couldn't see the girl's face. Mrs. Parker followed close behind. And then A.J. watched in surprise as Nick walked out of the room.

A.J. wondered if she'd been set up again.

"We'll talk tomorrow." MacAlister finally came through the door after Nick. They were talking in the corner when the little girl's mother interrupted.

"I don't think she can do this," Mrs. Parker said, wiping tears from her eyes. "I don't see how her dad and I could put her through it."

"It would be difficult, at best," MacAlister said. "But you have to consider one thing, Mrs. Parker. How are you going to feel if the man is walking the streets again?"

He cut right to the heart, A.J. thought, like an arrow piercing a target. Nick gave him a murderous look and A.J. saw what it cost Sara's mother to hear the words. Yet she couldn't blame Jack MacAlister. What he'd said was absolutely true. He had a rotten job to do, and he knew that even if a parent was reluctant to have a child testify in a case such as this, that same parent would be ready to crucify him for letting a man like Ray Williams back on the streets.

Sara Parker's parents needed to think about their decision, because if the situation was as desperate as MacAlister made it out to be, Ray Williams might actually walk.

A.J. understood all that. So she gave him the benefit of the doubt with the Parkers. But could she be as generous with him where she was concerned?

"Think about it tonight," MacAlister said to Mrs. Parker. "We can talk tomorrow."

The poor woman wore a dazed look as she turned to Nick for help, but Nick was staring at A.J. She watched as her friend pulled himself back to the woman at his side. "Take Sara to the interview room we used before, and I'll follow in a minute. We'll talk this thing out."

A.J. watched the Parker family leave. She waited for Sara's head to pop up off her father's shoulder, waited to give the girl a little smile, some small sign of reassurance, but she never had the chance. The three of them disappeared around the corner without Sara ever lifting her head.

"A.J.?" Nick said. "What are you doing here?"

She looked from Nick to Jack MacAlister. The first man looked honestly surprised, the second guilty as hell. She decided Nick wasn't in on this one.

"Why don't you ask him?" she said to her friend.

Nick glared at the man at his side. "You son of a—"

"Wait a minute, Nick." She grabbed his arm and did her best to turn him back toward her. It wasn't like him to fly off the handle. She wondered again if she hadn't totally misread the depth of his feelings for her. "I can handle this by myself, okay?"

"Do you know who's in that room?" He pointed to the one they'd just left.

"Ray Williams, among others."

"Why didn't you tell me you were going to do this?" he said to her, before turning back to MacAlister. "Why the hell didn't you tell me you were going to bring her here?"

"I didn't see the point," MacAlister said, looking from one of them to the other.

"You saw the point perfectly. You knew that I'd never let her do this," Nick said.

"Hold it." A.J. was sick of them acting as if she were ten years old and they were going to decide what was best for her. "I don't need a keeper, and I will decide what I do and what I don't do today. Understand?"

MacAlister looked happy, Nick exasperated.

"You wanted me to try to remember," she reminded her friend.

"This isn't the way to do it," he said. "You should have come to me, A.J. Come with me now, and I'll help you. But don't do this. Not without any kind of preparation."

Though some part of her was afraid, she still didn't believe she was Annie McKay. And if that was the case, then Ray Williams didn't have any power over her. Confronting him wouldn't hurt her at all. As she saw it, it would only help. It would get Jack MacAlister off her back—and out of her life.

"Come on, A.J.," Nick said. "I have to go talk to Sara and her parents. Come with me. We'll go over this when I'm done with them."

She looked from one man to the other. She trusted Nick, but, in a funny way, she trusted Jack MacAlister as well. Most of all, she trusted herself. And she wanted this whole thing to be over.

"I want to be done with this, Nick. Surely you can understand that."

He swore and, before walking away, turned to MacAlister. "I hope you know what the hell you're doing."

Chapter 10

A.J. took a deep breath. She'd made her choice. But that didn't mean she wasn't still angry at the way she'd been pushed into making it. "Isn't this what you wanted?" she asked MacAlister bitterly.

He weighed her question in his mind for a second. "It's what I need."

"Then let's do it."

He turned and stepped inside the room for a moment, said something to one of the officers, then turned back to her. "Come this way."

A.J. felt every bit of courage she had desert her, and that was quite odd. She honestly believed that there wasn't anyone or anything he could show her that could trigger the memories locked inside her. She'd buried them so deeply for nearly eleven years now, and she had no desire to remember. And still there was this certainty that she wasn't Annie McKay.

So what if Annie's disappearance and A.J.'s appearance with the Jenningses had come within two months of each other? It was sheer coincidence. What if this man, this Ray Williams, had once photographed the real Allison Jennings; it didn't have to mean a thing.

But that didn't explain why she'd gone weak in the knees all of a sudden.

"A.J.?"

She sensed more than heard the question and, looking up, found Jack MacAlister watching her with what she would have sworn was concern.

"Come inside."

Still, she hesitated. Her heart rate kicked into high gear, and her breathing became shallow and agitated.

"The room's empty," MacAlister told her. "I sent an officer to have someone bring the men back, but it's going to take a few minutes."

Reassured by the thought of having time to prepare herself, A.J. stepped through the doorway. MacAlister closed it behind her, and they were alone in a small rectangular room with what looked like a long, narrow window along the front of it. A.J. stepped up to the glass and put one hand against it. It was smooth and cool to the touch, to all appearances an ordinary window.

What would it be like to look through something like this into her past? To have the mere sight of a man dredge up all those memories she was so determined to leave buried forever?

She heard MacAlister moving around behind her, felt his presence at her right side, braced herself for a touch that never came.

"Are you sure about this?"

He was close enough that his warm breath stirred the hairs on her neck, something she found oddly unsettling and reassuring at the same time. She didn't trust her voice to speak, so she just nodded.

"There'll be five of them. They'll walk in from the door on the right, stand under the numbered squares and face you. Take your time looking them over. This is special glass. They won't be able to see you at all, they won't be able to get to you. There's no reason to be afraid."

A.J. searched for something, anything, to take her mind off what was going to happen. Sara Parker, she thought. Little Sara must have been afraid at the thought of doing this. Surely A.J. could do this—for Sara Parker.

The door in the other room opened, and A.J. had the sudden urge to scream. But all she saw was a police officer coming into the room. He closed the door behind him. She made one desperate grab for air.

"They're ready, A.J."

"Go ahead." Her voice sounded pathetically weak, even to her own ears. Like a coward, she closed her eyes the second the door started to open again. The sound of her own heartbeat pounded in her ears, blocking out nearly everything else.

She was afraid—desperately, blindingly afraid. But of what?

She felt MacAlister's hand against her back and willed herself to stop shaking, but she couldn't have made herself pull away if her very life depended on it. She wanted to move even closer to him.

If only she could get out of this room. It was much too small and narrow. She looked at the wall to her side, then behind her, and finally hung her head in desperation. MacAlister came one step closer and placed his arm around her waist, his tall, solid body against her side.

"They're in front of you, A.J." He said it softly, with his lips nearly against her ear.

Just look at them, she told herself. Just look. They couldn't see her, couldn't touch her, couldn't hurt her. There was nothing on the other side of the glass capable of hurting her.

She took a deep breath and looked. Like a magnet homing in on metal, her gaze was drawn to the man under the

number *4,* although at first glance there was nothing at all
remarkable about him. He was short, balding, rounded in
the stomach, a totally unmemorable man.

Yet the other men in the room were remarkably similar to
the man she'd been drawn to. Why him? she wondered.
What was it about him that affected her so?

A.J. forced herself to look into his eyes, and felt as if the
temperature in the room had suddenly dropped ten de-
grees.

MacAlister pulled her against his side, no doubt to keep
her from falling. She didn't even think about objecting.

"Talk to me, A.J.," he said.

She broke her gaze away from the evil eyes and found
herself breathing as if she'd just run a marathon. Realizing
she was practically in Jack MacAlister's arms, A.J. stepped
away shakily and held on to the windowsill to steady herself. She concentrated on the crevices in the textured wall
covering, staring at it until she could no longer see the man's
evil eyes.

Evil. She could have sworn that she'd felt it, like a tangi-
ble thing. She was inhaling it with every breath, smelling it,
tasting it. She gagged, then covered her mouth with her
hand.

"Get 'em out of there," MacAlister said harshly into the
speaker that sounded in the other room, then came to stand
in front of her. He took each of her hands in one of his own.
"Hang on to me."

She did. If she'd thought she had the power to move on
her own, she would have flung herself into his arms. Let him
make whatever he wanted to out of that; at the moment, she
didn't care.

She had no idea what had just happened. She just hung
on to Jack MacAlister until the world steadied around her,
the temperature in the room returned to normal and she
didn't feel as if she were going to choke on the next breath
she took.

Once she convinced herself to let go of him, he pulled a chair over and helped her sit down. She was grateful she hadn't fallen on her face. She hadn't actually hyperventilated, hadn't actually cried or screamed—proof that she was still able to exercise some self-control.

Jack MacAlister was sitting beside her, looking shaken. Her reaction must have been pretty bad, to affect him like that. A.J. tried to remember whether she'd actually said anything to him. For a moment, everything had simply faded to black.

MacAlister handed her a cup of something hot—coffee, she realized. Maybe it would kill the metallic taste in her mouth.

She took the cup and sipped, burned her tongue, then heedlessly took another sip. She needed it. And when she sat the cup down in her lap, her hands wrapped around it, she noticed the ends of a man's jacket around her.

"You were shivering," MacAlister said as he put his chair directly opposite hers and sat down again.

A.J. remembered shivering, but not having him put his jacket around her. She looked around the room—still that same claustrophobic rectangle of a room. At least she knew they hadn't moved.

"Can you tell me what happened?" MacAlister asked.

She cleared her throat, then took another gulp of coffee. "I don't know any of them."

MacAlister swore with the gusto of a Chicago street punk.

"I don't," she insisted.

"Then why are you so afraid?"

"I don't know." She felt ridiculously close to tears then, and reminded herself that she never cried. "I swear to you, I just don't know."

A.J. wrapped her arms around her waist and tried to hold herself together. It sounded crazy. She knew that. But it was true. She had no recollection of ever having seen that man before in her life. And yet he'd scared her to death.

"Did you ever have a really bad dream," she began, "when you were so scared you couldn't move? You could barely breathe, you couldn't even scream? You knew something awful was going to happen to you, but you couldn't break out of the paralyzing fear soon enough to stop it?"

"Yes."

"And you can't really see who or what is after you, but you know it's coming and you're not going to get away? It comes closer and closer, and you just lie there, terrified?"

She doubted he truly did understand.

"Go on, A.J."

She tried. She fought against the fear that she could still taste. "It's always the same. The minute the monster grabs you, you wake up. You jump up out of bed and can finally scream. You know it was a dream, but that doesn't help at all—you're still terrified. And the worst part is, you don't even know why you're so afraid.

"That's what it was like, Jack. I was scared, and I didn't know why. But I swear I saw something evil in his eyes."

A.J. risked looking up at him then. She doubted he'd accept her account, but it was the truth. She couldn't explain it any better.

"*One* of those men scared you," he said.

She nodded. She should have known he'd pick up on that. "Which one?"

A.J. held up four trembling fingers, then looked away. She didn't need to hear his reaction to know she had just picked Ray Williams out of the lineup.

The room started spinning, the lights blinding her, the dark beckoning. She felt MacAlister take her hands in his.

"Hold on," he said. "Hold on to me."

She did. She shivered in the cold, in the midst of the fear and the revulsion.

She knew that man. Oh, God, she knew Ray Williams.

"Look at me," MacAlister said, in the tone of a man used to giving orders and to having them obeyed.

She looked at him, found him hunched forward in his chair, found his face inches from her own, found herself unable to look away.

"Steady," he said.

She nodded. She would try. Concentrating on nothing but his dark eyes and his commanding voice, she steadied herself.

"Can I hold you, A.J.? Would it help?"

"I . . . I don't know."

"Would it hurt?"

"I . . ."

"Why don't we find out?"

He came forward slowly, giving her time to back away if she wanted to. But she didn't. She watched, fascinated, as he inched closer.

He put one hand beneath her knees and the other around her back. "Hang on," he said, then lifted her into his arms and settled her on his lap.

She leaned into him, as if it were the most natural thing in the world. Her head fell to his shoulder, and she heard his heart pounding beneath her ear. His arms were like bands of steel around her; surely she would be safe within this embrace. And surely that wasn't such an awful thing to want—to feel safe for just a minute because a man had his arms around her, a man who wouldn't hurt her.

"I'm sorry," he said.

And she knew he was sincere, knew the situation wasn't one of his own making, knew it was hopelessly complicated and terribly unfair.

But that was the world. It wasn't him.

So she lay trembling within his arms, trying to make sense of the whole mess.

She'd recognized Ray Williams, a child kidnapper, maybe even a murderer. No wonder she was so afraid.

* * *

Jack MacAlister cursed himself over and over again for having left A.J. alone in the viewing room. He'd known she'd been terrified of Ray Williams, and he felt like the scum of the earth for putting her through that lineup.

But, honestly, he'd just been trying to help when he left her there for a few moments. He'd been sure her friend Dr. Garrett was still in the building with the Parkers, and he'd thought the doctor might be able to help. God knew MacAlister didn't know what to do, except hang on to her for a while until she stopped shaking.

Dr. Garrett had cursed him all the way from the interview room to the place where he'd left A.J., and he knew he'd deserved it. Once she'd finally stopped shaking, A.J. had taken on a dazed expression. She'd frightened him, and he knew she needed help, knew he'd pushed her too far and that she was suffering the consequences.

And now she was gone.

When he and Dr, Garrett returned to where he'd left her, A.J. hadn't been there. That had been twelve hours ago. It was now nearly two in the morning. No one had seen her since.

MacAlister didn't think he'd ever been this scared. Bone-deep and mind-numbing scared—over a woman.

He'd only known her for a few weeks, yet he'd come to care about her so much in such a short time.

And he had never hated his profession more than he did right now. God knew he'd hurt people before in the name of his job, and still been able to sleep at night. Because he hadn't taken any of these cases personally. He hadn't seen the people involved in them as anything more than witnesses, victims or criminals.

A.J. was different. A.J. had gotten to him on a deeper level, and he didn't want to lose her. He couldn't lose her.

They had started something, something very fragile and very special. They needed time to figure out what it was, time to nurture it and watch it grow. And MacAlister was going to find that time for them, as soon as they could put this trial behind them.

He didn't want to think about what the trial would do to her, or about what price she was going to pay if those memories came back to her. He'd felt sick inside when he saw her reaction to Ray Williams.

He simply hadn't known what to do to help her. It was like being with Miranda all over again. Then, he'd missed the signals, hadn't understood how upset she was or what she might be planning to do. And one night Miranda had swallowed a bottle of pills.

But A.J. wouldn't do anything like that, he told himself, though that had been his first, irrational fear. A.J. was much stronger, braver, more determined. She would come through this. And he was going to stand by her. He was going to help her, if she let him.

She could be anywhere in the city. Anything could have happened to her by now.

He'd been at Hope House earlier, and he'd caught all kinds of hell from everyone there. He wondered if she realized how many people were worrying about her tonight, if she had any idea how sorry he was for what had happened.

She wouldn't run away again, he told himself. She had done so before, but she'd been a teenager then. She wouldn't run now.

So where the hell was she?

MacAlister drove the streets of that godforsaken part of town she called home for the longest time, hoping to catch a glimpse of her. And then he gave up, because it was almost morning and he knew what he had to do.

He still hadn't had time to totally examine the myriad of feelings he had for her, but three things were uppermost in his mind. He was scared to death that something terrible might happen to her, he was angry at himself for ever leaving her alone this afternoon, and he felt something close to a murderous rage for Ray Williams.

MacAlister could scream when he thought about A.J. at thirteen, about Ray Williams finding her, grabbing her, taking her away from anyone and everything she'd ever known, and then . . . then . . .

He closed his eyes and tried not to imagine the rest. He tried not to remember the almost frantic way she'd avoided the touch of his hands at one time, the pride—mingled with something else he hadn't been able to identify—in her voice when she'd told him that men didn't touch her.

He could kill Ray Williams, coldly, ruthlessly, without any regrets, either through the legal system or with his own two hands. He could do that. In fact, that had been his first thought.

And then he'd considered the price A.J. would pay.

He found himself unable to think about the whole situation from anything but her point of view, because she had become his first priority.

What did she need right now? What could he do to help her?

He had a meeting scheduled for early tomorrow regarding the Ray Williams case. And now MacAlister knew he was going to walk into that meeting and tell everyone that he was dropping the charges against Ray Williams, thereby leaving the man free to walk the streets again.

And he was doing it because, at this point in his life, a woman had become more important to him than the case on which he was working.

He was doing this for A.J.

And he hoped to God that one day he'd be able to explain that to her and make her believe him.

Chapter 11

MacAlister was crucified by the local media the next day. A.J. watched in horror as the cameras rolled, the headlines screamed and the people of Chicago registered their outrage on talk radio.

The governor was furious, as was the mayor. People were scared to have their kids walk the streets in broad daylight, which was nothing unusual in some parts of the city. But this had the people in the 'burbs worried, too, and they weren't taking it well at all.

Ray Williams was going to walk, and the people of Chicago wanted someone to pay for that. A.J. knew exactly who would pay, and couldn't help but feel a little guilty.

She was scared, too. She didn't want Ray Williams loose on the streets. The possibility that any minute she would come face-to-face with him on the sidewalk filled her with fear.

She'd spent the night walking the streets, talking to some kids, thinking about the terrible urge she had to run away from everything. But she'd come to terms with that at some point during the night. She was too old to run, and it wouldn't solve anything anyway.

A.J. had slipped into the shelter around 5:00 a.m., with no one seeing her, and then she'd hidden out in her room sleeping away most of the day. She'd simply been too exhausted to deal with anyone that morning.

When she woke up, it seemed the whole shelter was in an uproar over where she'd been, Carolyn and Grace included. She hadn't been sure how to handle that, not being used to having to explain her actions to anyone, and definitely not being accustomed to having people worry over her. It felt strange, a little uncomfortable, but not altogether bad.

After she'd done her best to calm down everyone at the shelter, she'd found out the whole city was up in arms over what Jack MacAlister had done.

Funny, he'd threatened to do that very thing—let Ray Williams go—but she hadn't actually believed he'd do it. She'd heard enough about him from Drew, from Nick and from some of the friendlier cops she knew to feel certain that MacAlister wouldn't give up. If there was any way to keep that man in jail, MacAlister would have found it. Obviously, when he told her he was desperate for her help, he'd meant it.

Now that she'd seen Sara Parker in person, she understood *how* desperate.

A.J. couldn't help but feel she'd let Sara down, that she'd let MacAlister down as well. And she felt guilty, especially listening to some of those crazy people on the radio who were ready to lynch him. She'd never thought she'd feel protective of Jack MacAlister, but she didn't know what else to call it. She wanted to make sure he was okay, maybe even tell him she was sorry.

And because she hadn't come to realize that until nearly ten o'clock at night, and because she didn't want to wait until morning, what else could she do but go to his apartment? It wasn't as if she hadn't been there before. He couldn't read anything into her visit. Still, she was as nervous as a sixteen-year-old about to embark on her first date.

In a way, Jack MacAlister *was* her first date. She'd bet he'd get a kick out of that idea, and she was smiling when she heard that low, rumbling voice of his answer the intercom, telling the doorman to send her right up. She was still smiling when the elevator opened and, to her surprise, he was waiting for her there, instead of inside his apartment.

A.J. thought for a moment that he might sweep her into his arms and forget all she'd ever told him about her reluctance to be touched. His eyes looked even darker than usual. She thought she could drown in them. And there was something so... sexy about the way he looked at the end of the day, when he started to come unbuttoned, untied, untucked. Lord, she was in trouble.

He took one step toward her before he caught himself, then put out a hand to hold the elevator doors open until she stepped into the hallway.

His shirttails were hanging out, the top buttons of his shirt were undone, and the sleeves were rolled up to his elbows. He looked tired and rumpled and very... sexy.

"I've been worried about you, darlin'." He extended a hand, and she placed her palm in his. He slid his fingers through hers, then held on tight.

And his touch, the feel and sight of him, broke through every defense she'd struggled to build in the past thirty hours or so.

"I've been worried about you, MacAlister."

"Me?" He tugged on her hand and led her down the hallway to the open door of his apartment. They went inside, and then A.J. led the way to the windows. He came with her, still holding her hand.

She looked down at the lights and the darkness, and it all seemed so far away. It seemed as if nothing could touch her from up here, as if nothing and no one could hurt her. Or maybe that was because she was with him now.

"Why were you worried about me?" he asked.

"Last I heard, someone on the radio was advocating shooting you on sight and asking questions later. Most of the other callers were agreeing with the guy."

He shrugged. "It's not the first time. I'll lie low for a while. Believe me, it'll blow over."

"Your boss was on the radio, too, tonight. He sounded like he was as outraged by what you'd done as the man with the gun. He sounded like he'd have your job for it."

"Makes him look like a reasonable, responsible man to the public, and he's very conscious of his public image."

"Jack, he's your boss."

"And he's just telling people what they want to hear. He knows as well as I do that it would have been a waste of our time and the taxpayers' money to take Ray Williams to trial right now. There's no way in hell we'd win."

"I knew you said that . . . but I guess I didn't think about what that would mean to you."

He stepped directly into her line of vision. "You really are worried about me."

"I guess no one ever worries about a big strong man like you?"

He shrugged. "I really hadn't thought about it."

She couldn't tell if she'd offended him, or simply surprised him—or if he was thinking that she didn't have any worrying rights where he was concerned.

"I'll be fine, A.J," he said.

He seemed to mean that, and she wondered if she was overreacting to this situation. Was it possible that the job simply didn't mean that much to him? But that couldn't be right. She knew his job meant a great deal to him. Maybe he simply didn't think he was in any danger of losing it.

"And Sara Parker?" she asked. "What about her?"

"Her parents didn't want to put her through the trial. I couldn't, in good conscience, encourage them to do that. She's barely seven years old, and her testimony's shaky. How could I make her take the stand, when I believed the man was going to get off anyway?"

"She's bound to be so scared right now."

"She and her parents are going away for a while. And if they come back, the police will be watching them. Ray Williams won't get to her."

"I don't know what I'd do if he did." She shivered at the thought.

"It's not going to happen."

She closed her eyes and tried to hold on to that thought. "I wish I could believe that. I wish I could have done something more ... anything ... to help."

"Darlin', you were right all along. It wasn't your responsibility to see that Ray Williams was convicted. It was mine, and I couldn't do it. It was the job of the FBI and the state and local police to get me enough evidence to convict him, and they couldn't do that, either. None of that is your fault."

"I recognized him, on some level I don't even understand." There, she'd admitted it to herself and to him, and the world hadn't caved in around her yet.

"I know you did."

"Maybe ... maybe if I worked with Nick ... maybe we could figure out why."

"Do you think you're ready for that?"

"I don't know if I'll ever be ready, but maybe it's time."

"Don't do it for my sake," he said. "And don't do it for this damned trial."

"You wanted me to remember. You and Carolyn and Grace McKay, even Grace's son, Billy. I didn't tell you, did I? He walked up to me the other day and asked me if I was his sister."

"He's a cute kid."

''He's Carolyn and Drew's son. Drew ambushed me in the hall one day at the shelter and told me the whole story.''

MacAlister paused, then gave a long, low whistle. ''Damn, how about that?''

''Billy doesn't even know.''

''They're engaged now, right? So what happened to them?''

A.J. shrugged helplessly. ''Drew said everything turned a little crazy after Annie disappeared, that everything just fell apart. I didn't even think of that—how Annie's disappearance would have touched so many lives. All I thought about was myself, and what I believed was best for me.''

''That's what you have to think about, because no one in this world is going to do it for you.''

She shook her head helplessly. ''But there are all these other people's lives involved. I can't just ignore that.''

''Look.'' He turned her toward him. ''If you want to dig back into your past and figure out who you are, I'll do everything I can to help you. But you can't do it for Billy or Carolyn or Drew or Grace. You can't do it for Sara Parker. Do it for yourself, A.J.''

Did she want it for herself? Or for him? She felt something for Jack MacAlister, something totally foreign to her, something that was exhilarating and frightening all at the same time. She wanted a relationship with him, a man-to-woman relationship, with all that it entailed.

This was the first time she'd ever wanted that with a man. She wondered if he wanted the same. How did one go about asking a man such a question?

''A.J.?'' he said, catching her attention again. ''Is this what you really want? Do you want to remember?''

She sidestepped as best she could. ''Nick says I can't run away from it forever. He says someday it's going to come out, whether I want it to or not, whether I'm ready or not.''

''Are you in love with him?'' he blurted out.

''What?''

"Are you in love with the good doctor?"

"Why in the world would you ask me something like that?"

"Because I thought he was going to deck me at the jail yesterday, when he found out how upset you were and that you'd taken off."

"He's a little protective where I'm concerned."

She thought he muttered something to the effect of "So am I," but she couldn't be certain. This conversation was becoming more interesting with every passing minute.

"He's protective as hell where you're concerned," MacAlister said.

"Okay." She could accept that.

"But are you in love with him, A.J.?"

"Why?"

"Because I want to know. Isn't that a good enough reason?"

As she saw it, he was being downright unreasonable, but she was prepared to humor him.

"I care for Nick. I always have. He's the best friend I have, and he was the only one I had for the longest time. He helped convince me to get off the streets, found me a place to stay temporarily, then pulled a lot of strings to get me into Northwestern. I don't know what I would have done if I hadn't been accepted there, or if I hadn't received a partial scholarship."

MacAlister shook his head in frustration. "But are you in love with him?"

As she saw it, she could have easily fallen in love with Nicholas Garrett. And she would have been safe with him, secure—coddled, even. But that wasn't what she wanted. He would always have had more power over her than she ever would have over him. He'd been her teacher, her mentor...her savior, even. And she'd fought with everything she had against falling in love and making herself even more dependent on him than she already was.

It frightened her to think that she could have just as one-sided a relationship with Jack MacAlister, that he would always have more control and more power over her than she would have over him. That she would always have more at stake than he did.

Of course, she wasn't going to explain any of that to him right now. But as he shot her an absolutely murderous look, she decided to put him out of his misery.

"No, Jack, I'm not in love with him."

"Good."

"Is that good?" She was teasing him, but she was a little afraid, as well.

"Yes, A.J., as far as I'm concerned, that's very good. Did you ever consider the possibility that he might be in love with you?"

A.J. had been certain that she was reading this all wrong—that this wasn't a case of a man making his intentions known to a woman, that this wasn't a man making sure no other man stood in his way.

"Right now," she said, "I'm considering the strong possibility that this is absolutely none of your business."

"And you'd be wrong about that."

She opened her mouth to tell him just how arrogant she thought he was, but he silenced her quite effectively by touching a finger to her lips. She felt a shiver work its way down her spine.

Oh, damn. She was in trouble. He was definitely interested. What in the world was she going to do about that?

"Tell the man how you feel about him, A.J. Make sure there aren't any misunderstandings between the two of you regarding your feelings for one another."

"Why?" she said, her lips still tingling.

"Because if you don't, he's going to punch me one day soon. Either that or I'm going to punch him. I don't think you want it to come to that, do you?"

"Jack MacAlister, are you jealous of Nick?"

"Do I have a reason to be jealous?"

"No."

"Good. Tell the man how you feel."

She couldn't believe how happy that made her. Ridiculously happy. Giddy happy, silly happy, like a schoolgirl whose best friend has just told her that the cutest boy in school is going to ask her to the dance.

"Well," he demanded, "you will tell him, won't you?"

"Should I salute, or would a simple 'Yes, sir' suffice?"

He was fuming. Served him right, as far as she was concerned. He really was the most arrogant man. Dictatorial, too. They would have to work on that.

"Are you going to him for help in trying to get your memories back?" MacAlister said.

"What if I do?"

The man seemed insanely jealous. Because of her friendship with Nick? She wanted to laugh, wanted to tell him again that it was none of his business, even though she liked the idea of him insisting that it was. And suddenly all things seemed possible.

"Go to him, if you want," he said.

She fought the urge to tell him she didn't need his permission. "I may do that, Jack."

"Is it what you want? To remember, I mean?"

She supposed they'd danced around that topic long enough. "I'm not sure."

"You need to be sure, A.J."

She sighed. "For the longest time, I didn't think any of that could hurt me if I had no conscious memory of it. But now I'm not so sure."

"Don't do it unless you're sure it's what you want for yourself."

A.J. could hardly believe what she was hearing. "You sound like you're trying to talk me out of doing this."

"I don't want to see you hurt."

"It *is* going to hurt," she said. "I won't even try to kid myself about that."

"I don't ever want to see you as afraid as you were yesterday."

He sounded dead serious; he sounded like a man who cared very much about her and how she felt.

"Have you forgotten your job—if you still have one?"

"I promise you, I still have a job. And don't try to change the subject on me, because it's not going to work. This is too important for that. Do you want to remember?"

She supposed he was right. "If I do, and if I'm Annie, you could win this case and put Ray Williams back in jail by putting me on the stand to testify."

"It may not come to that," he said. "I'd fight with everything I have in me to keep it from coming to that. I promise you."

And she had no doubt that he was telling her the truth. Jack MacAlister would fight for her as best he could.

She closed her eyes tightly and squeezed his hand. She felt as if she'd just been given an incredible and totally unexpected gift. He was going to protect her, to look out for her—and she was going to trust him to do so. The idea that he would be there for her, that she could count on him, felt incredible. No longer was she absolutely alone.

A.J. laughed softly, then felt her eyes flood with tears. Someday she was going to figure out this crying business. But she was a little afraid that, once she started, she'd never stop.

"A.J.?"

She put her hand up to her cheeks. No tears there, although her eyes burned with them. "I don't know what to say."

"You believe me?"

"Yes."

"Do you think I could kiss you?"

Her lashes flew up, and her gaze locked with his. Her heart did a few somersaults in her chest. Her back was against the wall of windows, and the panes of glass were cool against her much-too-warm body.

MacAlister guided one of her hands to his waist and slid his hand down her forearm, to her elbow. A.J. brought her chin up a notch, even though she was dying to look away. She could easily feel the heat coming off him through his unbuttoned shirt, and she was finding it increasingly difficult to breathe.

"All right?" he asked as he placed her other hand at his other side.

She nodded. It was all she could manage to do.

He smiled. "Do you trust me, A.J.?"

"Yes."

"Good." He took one step closer to her. "Just say the word, and I'll stop. I promise."

She was drowning in his dark eyes. She could see stubble on his cheek that told her it was very, very late.

How would it feel to touch his face? His hair? His lips? At the thought, heat flooded her cheeks.

"What are you thinking?" He was teasing her now.

She liked that. She liked his soft, sexy voice, his positively wicked grin, the twinkle in his eye. She liked the way his skin felt beneath her hands, and the way he was careful not to frighten her by pushing too hard, too fast.

"I was thinking about you," she said, avoiding any reference to anything more specific.

"Good, because I've been losing sleep over you."

Instantly, she thought of him in bed, and that reminded her that they were in his apartment, alone, late at night. She was suddenly very nervous. "Jack..."

"Yes."

"There's something I have to tell you."

When she didn't say anything for the longest time, he added, "I'm listening."

"I don't know anything at all about men." She'd blurted out the first thing that came into her head, the guts of her whole problem.

"Nothing?"

She shook her head miserably.

"Nothing at all?"

"No."

He froze for a moment. A flicker of something she recognized as pain crossed his face. "I know you ran away when you were a teenager, A.J. I know you were on the streets for a while. I realize what goes on out there—how young girls survive."

"Not *that*." She was quick to correct him. "I never did *that*."

He considered for a moment. "Someone raped you?"

"A couple of guys tried one night, not long after I came to Chicago. But they didn't get very far. They just grabbed me and tried to pull me into an alley. A couple of friends of mine stopped them fairly quickly."

"So you've been cautious around men ever since. That's to be expected, A.J."

"Cautious?" What a delicate word. "Not exactly. I just . . . I haven't had anything to do with . . . anyone."

"You must have dated in high school."

"Dated. Football games, the pizza place, the movies—that kind of dated."

"Oh." He was obviously considering his words carefully. "And after you got off the streets, when you were in college?"

She shook her head.

"After you graduated?"

She shook her head again.

"No one?" he said incredulously.

"No one."

"Why?"

She shrugged helplessly, wishing she'd never started this conversation. "I told you . . . I'm uncomfortable being touched."

"Do you want to tell me why?"

"It's something . . . inside me, something that must have come from that time before I lived with the Jenningses. Even with them, I wasn't that comfortable being close to anyone. I don't know why. I can't remember anything about the time before I was with them, and it didn't really matter, anyway, until . . ." She closed her eyes, which helped, a little. "Until . . ."

Lord, why didn't she just bare her entire soul to this man? Was there no end to what she would tell him?

"Until now?" he prompted.

Until Jack MacAlister had come into her life and brought out all these feeling she'd never known before. She nodded. "Until now."

Then he gave her a beautiful, blinding smile, and she knew she'd done the right thing in trusting him and telling him all of this. Taking her hands in his, he brought them to his lips.

With a touch as soft as a butterfly's, his mouth pressed against her hands, the backs, the sides, the fingers, across one hand and then the other. He bowed his head over her fingers, nuzzled them with his nose and his warm breath.

"And now it matters," he said, opening her right hand and placing one soul-searing kiss against her palm.

She gasped as a tingling mass of energy shot into her body from the spot he'd kissed so tenderly. So this was it, she thought. The magic, the power, that intangible thing between two people that had proved to be absolutely elusive to her before. She hadn't even dreamed about it, because she hadn't seen the point in dreaming about something she would never have.

"Yes," she told him with a laugh, admitting it to him without one regret. "All of a sudden, it matters a great deal."

Still holding her hands, he kissed his way down to each of her fingertips, making her whole body a tingling, quivering mass of nerves.

"I'll tell you a secret," he said, and smiled. "I've kissed a few hands in my day."

"I'll just bet you have."

"It doesn't usually feel like this, A.J."

She didn't know whether to laugh or to cry.

"This—" he kissed her hands one more time "—feels absolutely incredible."

She smiled again, feeling as if all things were possible.

"Now," he said, "what else do I get to kiss?"

He looked so serious, and she decided he was talking about a serious kiss. She looked down at her hands, which were still encased in his.

Did he know what he'd done to her? With nothing but the touch of his lips against her palm?

"Come over here and kiss me, darlin'," he said, tugging on her hands.

He pressed them against his chest—his *bare* chest. His skin was warm; she'd known it would be. She spread her fingers wide and pushed them through the dark curls covering his chest. The texture, the feel of him, was so different. She felt muscle beneath the warm flesh, felt his heart thudding inside his chest; that gave her confidence to go on.

He seemed so much taller, so much broader, so much more imposing than ever before. All he wanted was a kiss, she reminded herself. Just one.

His mouth seemed like it was a million miles away. She had to stand on tiptoe, bracing one hand against his chest; then she took her other hand and pulled his head down to hers.

She kept her eyes open, watching his face. His eyes had turned smoky and mysterious, his jaw rigid, his lips ... She ran a trembling finger across the bottom one. They opened slightly at her soft caress.

And then she closed her eyes and pressed her lips against his. Again, she felt the touch right down to her toes. His hands came up to her arms, holding her in place, close, but without anything except their lips touching. His grip was strong and tight, and she couldn't tell whether he was trying to keep her from coming any closer or keep her from running away.

But she had no desire to run away.

His lips were soft and smooth, his cheek was rough against hers. His mouth opened, his tongue working magic on her lower lip.

"Don't stop," he said, his commanding tone gone, and something different, but just as compelling, in its place.

She had no intention of stopping.

With her hands on his wonderful shoulder muscles, her body imagining what it would be like to have every inch of her pressed against every inch of him, she opened her mouth completely to his.

He stroked the inside of her mouth. His tongue thrust inside her mouth in a wickedly sexy rhythm that had her imagining the two of them in bed together, his body rocking smoothly and deeply inside hers.

She could see it. She could see the two of them, could imagine how it would feel.

A.J. ran her fingers through his thick, dark hair, then pressed her palm against the roughness of his cheek. She thought he was going to devour her right then and there, the way his mouth was plundering hers.

Her pulse was hammering, and she could barely breathe. Suddenly, the situation seemed to have gotten out of hand.

He was holding her so tightly. She tried to back away, just a fraction, and she couldn't.

"Jack?" she said against his lips, unable to keep the sound of fear out of her voice.

He backed off instantly. His lips spread into a smile, and his forehead came down against hers.

"Scared you?"

"A little."

"Sorry."

She tried to shrug, but he still had hold of her arms. His hands kneaded the muscles there for a moment. She noted with great satisfaction that she wasn't the only one breathing hard at the moment.

"I guess I got a little carried away," he said.

"It's all right. I . . . I know this is silly of me. I'm a grown woman after all, and it was just a kiss . . ."

"A.J., you don't ever have to apologize to me for the way you feel, all right?"

Relieved, she nodded.

"But don't you dare try to tell me that was just a kiss."

"I wouldn't know," she said mischievously.

"I would."

And then he smiled at her, and she knew everything was going to be okay, for now at least. He had the most beautiful smile. Wicked and wild, something to make a woman sure he was up to no good.

She couldn't believe how good he was being to her, how understanding, how patient.

She'd never expected something like patience from a man like him.

"So," she said. "It was a good kiss?"

"Oh, darlin' . . ." He caught her hand and held it against the pulse point on the underside of his neck. "You think just any woman can do this to me? With a kiss?"

"I told you, I wouldn't know about that."

"Then you'll just have to trust me on this. And, A.J.—?"

"Hmmm?"

"Don't get any ideas about going out and practicing on some other man. It just wouldn't be the same."

He didn't need to know that the thought hadn't even crossed her mind. "You're sure?"

"Positive."

"But..."

"Are you trying to make me mad?"

"Jack, I would never do that."

"Like hell you wouldn't."

And she couldn't tell then whether he was actually worried that she might go find some other man to kiss or was just trying to lighten the mood because he knew she'd been frightened for a second.

What in the world was she going to do with him? She didn't want it ever to end, but she didn't think magic ever lasted for long.

And this was pure magic.

Chapter 12

Two weeks later, A.J. and MacAlister were on their way back to Hope House after an incredibly boring reception for a prosecutor who'd just been named to a judgeship.

MacAlister had apologized in advance for dragging her to such a dull event. In truth, it hadn't been that bad. She'd gotten into a wonderful argument with an ultraconservative politician who, if he had his way, would take away every bit of public funding Hope House had, then lock up all the kids on the streets. A.J. had shown admirable restraint in telling the man what she thought of him.

"I'm sorry it was so dreadful," he said.

A.J. smiled and held her tongue.

She and Jack MacAlister were...dating, she supposed one could call it, for lack of a better term.

"Well, I guess if you have to go to such boring parties, I'd rather go with you than have you take someone else."

It was a risk on her part to say it, but this was the best chance she'd had to find out whether he was seeing anyone else. She kept picturing him out with the catwoman; it had her losing sleep at night.

A.J. felt him watching her as they pulled to a stop at the curb near the entrance to Hope House. He put the car in gear, but left it running because it was still near freezing outside.

He unbuckled his seat belt and turned so that he was facing her. "In case you have any doubts, I'm not seeing anyone else but you."

She closed her eyes and tried to hide her smile.

"I'm sorry, darlin', I didn't know I had to say that. I thought it was clear."

She shrugged helplessly, looking for a way to make light of his confession. "I thought...for your mother's sake...to give her some hope..."

He roared. "I guess I need to take you home to meet my mother."

"No, you don't." A.J. could just imagine what his mother was like—the catwoman thirty years from now, all grace and no claws.

She could just imagine the woman turning up her nose at A.J. and asking Jack what in the world he thought he was doing with a woman like her.

"I suppose we could wait a little longer," he said.

A.J. couldn't tell whether he was serious.

"Of course," he said, "it's a risk. If we wait too long, and she hears about you, she might come looking for you."

"Looking for me?"

He nodded, quite seriously. "She wants grandchildren and, unfortunately, I'm an only child, her only hope."

"Oh...and you don't...like children?"

He leaned closer. "I'm still looking for the right woman."

"Oh."

It was dark in the car, so his features were more in shadow than in light. She had an impression of dark, dark eyes, a wide, generous mouth, a cheek she longed to touch.

He was going to kiss her again. Her breath caught in her throat in anticipation. She could sit here all night kissing Jack MacAlister.

She put her hand on the hard line of his jaw, felt him smile in response. She ran her palms over the slightly roughened skin of a cheek in need of a shave, knowing exactly how it would feel against her skin. She wanted to feel it again, right now.

"Go ahead," he said. "Kiss me."

Her lashes fluttered downward, the breath left in her body deserting her. Kissing him scared her just a little, because the feelings were so powerful, so immediate and so intense. She woke up dreaming about kissing him, went to bed with the thought playing in her head. The day before, he'd driven all the way across town at midnight because he said he didn't want to let another day go by without the touch of her lips on his.

It was heady stuff for a woman who hadn't been kissed in years.

She touched her lips to his now, and they opened without any urging. He was impatient tonight, nipping and sucking and licking at her lips, drawing them into his mouth, trying to devour her.

She couldn't get close enough to him, because they were still in the car, and it made her impatient, and more than a little frustrated. During the past two weeks, he'd done nothing besides kiss her. And, as steamy as those kisses got, he'd always held himself tightly under control. At least that was what A.J. thought. But if he felt the same things for her that she felt for him, he must have incredible self-control.

Either that, or he didn't want their relationship to go any further. That was what she contemplated late at night, when he was gone, when she was alone with all her insecurities.

She fought those thoughts off throughout the day, only to have them return full force again every night.

He kissed her one last time, then pulled away.

"You're going to hear about this tomorrow," he said.

"What?"

He nodded over her shoulder. "I think two of your regulars just walked by, and we hadn't been at this long enough to steam up the windows yet."

"Oh," she said, the power of speech once again deserting her.

He just sat and looked at her in his special way that made her feel feverish. A.J. had a million questions she wanted to ask him, a million doubts she needed to admit. But she couldn't find it in herself to voice even one more of them tonight.

"I guess I should get inside. It's late, and I'm sure you have a long day," she finally said.

He nodded. "Meet me downtown for lunch?"

"I might be able to get away."

"I'll come looking for you, if you don't."

He pulled the car forward until it was right in front of the main entrance to the shelter. "Kiss me good night, A.J."

Their good-night kisses were slow and sweet, without all the heat, but still enough to set her to trembling.

"Good night, Jack."

A.J. knew all about having her feet knocked out from under her. She knew all about the way life ran along smoothly for a time, lulling people into a false sense of security, then jerked the rug right out from under them.

Her life had been going along remarkably well. She'd agreed to take the blood tests that would likely prove beyond a reasonable doubt whether she was Grace McKay's child. And she'd resumed her old arm's-length friendship with Grace and Carolyn McKay. They'd even managed to keep the secret that she might be Carolyn's long-lost sister Annie.

She wasn't quite ready to go public with that bit of news, and in truth, she was trying to put the whole thing out of her mind. There was no sense in worrying over something that might not be true. If it was true, she'd deal with it. If it wasn't, she'd be sorry for Grace and Carolyn, because they wanted Annie back so much.

Whatever the outcome of the blood tests, she would go on with her life, and she would work to find out whatever she could about her past. She'd gone back to Nick and started therapy again, although they hadn't dug very far into anything yet. He wanted to take it slow, and they had plenty of time. At least she thought they had time.

And she and Jack were still seeing each other. Quite often, they met for lunch downtown, because he always worked late and her most hectic time at the shelter was in the evenings. And the schedule suited them. It saved her what she was sure would have been those awkward moments alone in his apartment at the end of the night, when she'd be unsure what he expected or needed from her or when she'd be ready to give it to him.

They had plenty of time, he told her, and he was more than willing to wait for her.

It all seemed much to good to be true—and, of course, it was.

One night, about two weeks later, A.J. walked by the staff lounge and noticed many of the staff members huddled around the television, watching the evening news.

A little girl's picture flashed across the screen, and A.J. was riveted by it. The girl was eight years old, the newscaster said, from Abbington, Illinois, and she'd been missing since early this morning, when she hadn't shown up for school.

Two blocks, her sobbing mother told the cameras. It was only two blocks from her house, and it had been a beautiful, unusually warm spring day. She'd let her little girl walk to school, and she'd been able to see her nearly all the way. But something had happened to her. Someone had taken her off the sidewalk, not two blocks from her own home.

A.J. felt as if someone had smacked her in the face. She stood frozen to the spot, horrified, waiting for the last piece of information.

That man.

Ray Williams.

She'd recognized him that day in the lineup. There was no other explanation for her reaction. She'd recognized him, and she hadn't been able to face up to that. At the time, she hadn't pushed herself to remember and given MacAlister the information he needed to keep that man in custody.

And now look what he'd done.

Ray Williams's face flashed across the television screen. A.J. stood there, paralyzed, for a moment, as the anchor team chatted among themselves about the FBI having had the man in custody, only to have the U.S. Attorney's office let him go last month.

A.J. ran for the door.

MacAlister wasn't at his office. She used the fancy phone he'd given her to try to call him there, and when he didn't answer, she called his apartment and still got no response. Figuring that, since he didn't do anything besides work and sleep, he had to be on his way home, A.J. raced toward his apartment in the new van he'd given the shelter.

It seemed like forever before she got across town, past MacAlister's doorman, up the elevator and to his apartment. MacAlister opened his door, took one look at her and steered her toward the sofa.

"I'm so sorry," she said, sitting down. She didn't want to think about how much she'd needed to see him, to be with him right now.

"About what?"

"The little girl." She could barely get the words out. "I couldn't believe it when I heard, and . . . I just had to come and tell you how sorry I am."

"About what, A.J.? What's happened?" he asked, sitting beside her.

"That little girl from Abbington who's missing." She couldn't believe he hadn't heard.

"What about the little girl?"

"Ray Williams—" She choked on the name. "He took her."

"No, he didn't."

He seemed so sure of himself, and she wanted to believe him. But her heart was going ninety miles a minute, and she couldn't erase the memory of that little girl's face.

"I saw her," she insisted. "On TV. I saw Ray Williams's picture, too."

"And someone said he took her?"

She almost jumped right in and said yes, but the fact was, she'd been so upset at that point that she wasn't listening carefully. Could it really not be true?

"They showed his picture on TV, right after the girl's, and they said he'd been in custody but that you'd let him go. I just... I was sure that he took her."

"Oh, darlin'..."

He grabbed her hand, then pulled her closer, so that her head was resting on his shoulder. She didn't even think of resisting. "I was certain that he took her."

"No. I knew he couldn't have done that, but as soon as I heard about that little girl, I checked with the FBI. Williams is under constant surveillance. He didn't go anywhere this morning, and there was no way he could have taken that little girl."

A.J. leaned into him, her face buried in the side of his neck, his big, strong arms around her. She'd gotten used to him touching her like this. She'd come to welcome it, to crave it.

How had he come to mean so much to her in so short a time? What would she ever do without him?

"It's all right," he said.

"No, it's not. He could have been the one who took her."

"Not the way we're watching him."

"Come on, Jack." She felt strong enough now to sit up straight and look him in the eye. "The FBI's lost a few criminals in its day. Ray Williams could get away tomorrow and grab some other child, and you know it."

"They know what kind of man he is, and they're not going to lose him."

"What if they did?" she insisted. "What if he grabbed another little kid? I don't think I could handle that kind of guilt."

"Guilt? Over what?"

"Letting him get out."

"We've been over this," he told her, in his most intimidating prosecutor's voice. "If Ray Williams grabs another kid, then Ray Williams is the guilty party here. Not you."

"I'm the only one who can stop him." She felt a crushing weight settle on her chest as she admitted it, to him and to herself. "I have to do it. I have to remember... everything, so that man will never have the chance to hurt anyone again."

"You're trying to remember. You're working with Nick."

"But it's not enough. And it's taking so long. We haven't gotten anywhere yet, and it's been two weeks."

"So," he said, "it's been nearly eleven years since you lost all those memories. You can't expect them to come back in two weeks, darlin'. Don't push yourself so hard on this, and don't you dare blame yourself for anything Ray Williams does."

"I would," she said. "I wouldn't be able to stop myself. If he ever hurt another child like that, I'd never forgive myself."

He paused for a second, looking worried. "A.J., I need to tell you something. It's about someone I used to know, a woman. I probably should have told you about her a long time ago, but I was sure you'd read something into it that simply isn't true."

She forced her chin up a fraction of an inch, though all she really wanted to do was hang her head. "Go on."

"Her name was Miranda. I met her in college, and we dated for a while."

Dated? She was sure this wasn't about someone he'd just dated.

"Were you in love with her?"

He shrugged off the question. "It was ten or twelve years ago."

"And you were in love with her." She was certain of it.

"Yes," he admitted. "I suppose I *was* in love with her."

And did he still love her? Still miss her? A.J. felt as if she'd been blindsided.

She'd gotten so close to this man, so fast. She felt as if he'd opened up a whole new world to her. And she couldn't imagine trusting another man the way she'd let herself trust Jack. Couldn't imagine baring her soul to another man, explaining her insecurities and idiosyncrasies to him. She didn't think anyone else could possibly be as understanding and as patient as he'd been with her. And she didn't want to find out. She wanted Jack, and no one else.

So this Miranda, this woman from his past, had her scared to death.

"What happened to her?" she managed to ask.

"She died."

"How?"

"She killed herself."

"And exactly why are you telling me this, Jack?"

"Because you remind me of her."

"Oh." The sound was more a long, low sigh than anything else. She couldn't help it. She felt as if someone had laid a ton of bricks on her chest, and she could barely breathe, let alone think. She reminded him of this woman he'd loved and lost? A.J. supposed that explained quite a number of things.

She'd wondered why a man like Jack would be interested in a woman like her. Now she knew.

"Wait a minute, A.J. Let me explain this to you."

She nodded. It was all she could manage to do.

"She had this way of taking the whole world's problems onto her shoulders, especially her family's problems. And her family had serious problems. Her stepfather was abusing her little sister. I think he abused Miranda, as well, but I'm not sure. She never told me, not about any of this. It only came out later, after she died.

"She felt responsible for what happened to her little sister, because apparently her stepfather didn't come after her sister until Miranda went away to college. She made it out to be her fault, instead of her stepfather's.

"A.J.?" He took her hand in his. "You can't take the whole world's problems and make them your own. You can't be responsible for anyone's problems but your own. And you can't blame yourself for the bad things that other people do. If Ray Williams gets off on this kidnapping charge, it won't be your fault."

"I know I shouldn't, but...if I had done everything I could to make sure he stayed in jail..."

"It's not your responsibility," he insisted. "I tried to make it yours in the beginning, and I was wrong. I'm sorry I pushed you like that. I get a blind spot sometimes, when I'm heavily involved in a case, and I just can't see anything else but what it will take to win. But, as I said, I was wrong."

"I understand why you did it," she said. "I can be the same way when I'm fighting for something for the shelter. I'd do just about anything for the kids down there."

"I know, but, darlin', you have to be careful there, too. You can't solve all their problems. You can't save all those kids, and you can't tear yourself up about the ones you lose."

"I care about them, Jack."

"Too much."

"Someone has to care about them. They don't have anybody else." She didn't seem to be getting through to him at all. "Jack, I'm not going to kill myself because of something that happens to a kid who shows up at the shelter."

"I didn't say you were. I said you remind me of Miranda, because you care so much for other people and because you want to hold yourself responsible for things that are totally out of your control."

And she couldn't very well argue with that, because most of it was true.

"You must have loved her very much," she said, changing the subject.

"Mostly I felt guilty as hell because she died."

"Because you didn't see it coming? Because you couldn't stop it?"

"Because I must have been the most selfish man in the world, so caught up in my own life, my own problems, that I didn't have a clue as to what was going on inside her head."

"And now you're going to make up for that in some way by watching over me?" It all made sense now. And it hurt like hell.

"No, dammit," he said. "I knew you were going to make this connection. That's why I didn't tell you sooner."

"It has to be connected, Jack."

"I considered it at first," he admitted. "A.J., I told you I wouldn't lie to you about anything, and I won't. I've turned this over and over in my mind, and I'm certain of it. This thing between you and me isn't about Miranda."

"I can't believe that."

"Then I'll just have to make you believe it."

"Jack..."

"Worry, sure. I worry that you're going to get your memories back, and that you'll need me and I won't know what to do to help you. I worry that you're so damned independent that you won't let me help you. But that's it, A.J. That's where the similarities end. I swear."

He waited. She said nothing, and he made one final plea. "Please try to believe that."

"I will." She could promise to try, even if she didn't see how she could ever manage it.

"And don't shut me out."

"I'll try not to. But I still have to try to remember. I have to do what I can to stop Ray Williams."

"If that's what you have to do. Will you let me help you?"

"Yes."

Chapter 13

MacAlister took her back to Hope, Illinois, the little town where Annie was born and raised, the place where she was last seen alive. Nick had argued vehemently against it, and he'd refused to try to take her back to that time through hypnosis. He didn't think she was ready, and he wouldn't do it, despite her threats that she'd find another therapist who would. And then, because she couldn't imagine going to someone new and having to tell that person everything Nick already knew about her, she backed down and settled for a trip to Hope instead.

MacAlister didn't think she was ready to go back to that little town, but A.J. had stood firm on that point. She didn't know what else to do to try to jog her memories.

And she had to remember. She felt a new urgency about the situation that frightened her. Something bad was going to happen, something very bad, and she had to stop it.

She and MacAlister had driven alone in his car—she hadn't allowed anyone else to accompany them. Nick had wanted to be here. Carolyn and Grace had both wanted to come, as well, but she'd known it would be difficult for them, and she thought they'd make it more difficult for her.

A.J. tensed a little when they passed the first sign for the town limits, and she couldn't help but think of the irony of a place that had been the home of so much grief for the McKays having a name like Hope.

The place had a small-town flavor that made it very different from Chicago. She took in a car dealership and a big chain grocery store, both of which looked too new for Annie to remember. The downtown area had obviously been refurbished recently, with freshly painted storefronts, fancy tiled sidewalks and ornate black lampposts reminiscent of days gone by. But none of it looked familiar to her.

"Do you want to go by the house or the park first?" MacAlister said.

Fortunately for them, the McKays had lived in the same house for thirty-five years, until a few months ago, when Grace and Billy had moved to Chicago. Their old house was still for sale, so A.J. could see it much the same way it would have been when Annie was growing up there.

A.J. knew the park was a few blocks away, and that Annie had been walking from the park to her house that day in August when she disappeared.

No doubt the park would hold the scariest memories for Annie, and A.J. was getting more and more nervous with every passing mile. She wanted this over with as quickly as possible.

"The park," she said.

MacAlister turned right, and A.J. glanced out the side window at row after row of old houses, lovingly cared for, with wide front porches, window boxes that she imagined full of color, big shade trees hanging over the road.

Was one of them Annie's house? She couldn't bring herself to ask.

MacAlister knew where he was going. He'd been here months ago, interviewing people about Annie's disappearance and trying to find anyone who'd seen or heard of a man named Ray Williams.

He found the park with no trouble, and pulled into a parking space. A.J. waited until he got out and came around to her side of the car to open her door. She gave him her hand, holding on to his tightly, and managed to get out of the car.

It was the middle of March, still cool, the wind making it bitingly cold, the sky a gloomy gray. The park was deserted. There was a small playground with swings and slides, a few benches, a wide-open field, and a walking path surrounding the whole park. Then she saw the line of trees. A.J. looked around at the bare branches of the trees, ghostlike on this gloomy, wintry day, and at the occasional evergreens, the only touch of color. There were fallen leaves that no one had bothered to rake from the previous autumn, now trampled down to a washed-out brownish color, and a beaten path leading from the open field into the woods.

"Annie went through there?" she said, hating the thought of going there now.

"Yes. They were having some sort of town picnic that day, here in this open field. Annie's mother forgot something, and she asked Carolyn to walk back to the house and get it. Carolyn ran into Drew, and Annie ended up going back to the house instead."

A.J. had never asked for the specifics; it seemed so sad now, sad for everyone involved. "How old was she? Carolyn, I mean."

"Seventeen. I think her mother didn't quite approve of her seeing Drew, so they'd snuck off somewhere while Annie went back to the house."

"She must have felt so guilty," A.J. said. "I hadn't even thought of that. It would have been torture for her. And Billy's almost ten years old, so she must have either been pregnant then or gotten pregnant shortly afterward. Drew said he never even knew about Billy, so he must have left town shortly after Annie disappeared. What an awful mess.''

They stood there in silence, and A.J. felt ashamed of herself for having made those poor people wait so long to find out whether she was Annie. This whole thing was so much more complicated than she'd ever imagined, and it had touched so many lives.

Could it ever be made right again? If she was Annie, she had no memory of that. Would it all come back in a rush? And if it did, could she just step into this ready-made family? Because she was willing to bet that was what they would want her to do. And they were expecting the old Annie back, the innocent little thirteen-year-old. A.J. couldn't be that girl for them. Too much had happened to her. Too much time had passed. She wondered how they would all manage to deal with that.

''Annie?'' someone called in their direction.

A.J. turned and found a woman, about her age, maybe older, stepping off the walking path and moving toward them. Her eyes were wide, and her expression was one of disbelief. She looked as if she'd seen a ghost. Or as if she *believed* she'd seen a ghost.

''Oh, my God!'' the woman said. She looked around, found no one in the park but the three of them, then cautiously stepped a little closer.

A.J. didn't know what to say. MacAlister came to stand beside her and put a hand around her waist. She leaned into him, in an action that had become so automatic, it should have frightened her.

''Is it really you?'' the woman asked.

MacAlister stepped in and saved her from answering. He extended his hand toward the woman and said, ''I'm Jack MacAlister.''

The woman took his hand, but didn't take her eyes off A.J. ''I'm April,'' she said. ''April Thomas...but that's my married name, so you wouldn't remember it. I used to be April Jacobs.''

The name meant nothing to A.J. ''I'm sorry,'' she said. ''I don't remember you.''

''I was a good friend of Carolyn's, and you look so much like her sister, Annie.''

''I'm sorry,'' A.J. said helplessly. She hadn't anticipated anything like this, though she supposed she should have. After all, Nick had picked up on the resemblance right away, and he'd never known Annie as a child.

''I've been hearing the most outlandish things around town, ever since Grace McKay and her little boy left town. But I didn't see how they could be true,'' the woman said, refusing to let go of the subject.

''We really need to be going,'' MacAlister said.

''It is you, isn't it?'' the woman said. ''You disappeared from this park— What was it? Ten years ago last summer. I'll never forget that day. I was here for the picnic. The whole town was. And all the mothers were too scared to let their kids out of their sight that whole summer.''

MacAlister took A.J. by the arm and turned her toward the woods. ''You're going to have to excuse us,'' he said, as he and A.J. began to walk away.

''But—'' the woman sputtered. ''Wait a minute! It is you, Annie, isn't it?''

A.J. never turned around. MacAlister kept walking, and the way he was half holding her up, she had no choice but to keep walking, as well.

They made it to the edge of the woods before they stopped. A.J. finally allowed herself to turn around and look behind her. The woman was still there, still watching them but, thankfully, not following them.

''You okay?'' MacAlister said.

A.J. could only nod.

''Damn busybody,'' he said.

''Let's get out of here,'' she told him.

He looked back, then forward. "We could cut through the woods."

"Is that what Annie did that day?"

"Maybe," he said. "She either cut through them on her own or someone dragged her into the woods. They found her mother's house keys and a man's footprint there."

"That's it?" A.J. said. "Nothing else?"

"Not a thing. Until you."

She looked up at him, unsure how to take his comment, and still shaken by what the woman had said. "I don't know what to think anymore."

"Do you want to be Annie?" he asked her.

"I don't know."

"I realize you're frightened of what happened to her when that man took her, and I understand your apprehension. But look at what else you'd have, if you were Annie. You'd have a real family, A.J. The McKays are good people. Wouldn't you like to be a part of a family like that?"

She shrugged helplessly. "I'd like to be Annie, for their sakes, because I know how much it would mean to them. They want her back so much. But how would they handle it if, after getting their hopes up like this, I'm not Annie?"

"What about you?" MacAlister said. "I know Annie's family wants her back. I know you'd like to give Annie back to them. But what about you? What do you want for yourself?"

"I want my memories, my past." And she wanted him. She wanted to come to him knowing every deep dark secret held within her. She wanted to be whole again, to be free of the ghosts of her past, for him.

And she wanted to start over, for the fourth time in her life.

Now there would be a new beginning, her life come full circle, all the pieces fitting together, all the possibilities spread out before her. She wanted it for Jack. She wanted to be with him, in every way possible, wanted to spend the rest of her life with him. Of course, that was still just a dream. She couldn't confide that in him now, when neither of them knew what this trip might reveal.

Part of what she was doing was for Sara Parker, and for that little girl taken a couple of days ago. But she couldn't lie to herself. Part of what she was doing was also for herself—and for Jack. She wanted that new beginning for them. And she was prepared to go through hell to get it.

They walked hand in hand along that path through the woods where Annie had disappeared. They came to a small white cross stuck in the ground beneath an old oak tree. The inscription on the cross read Annie McKay—Gone but Not Forgotten.

A.J. closed her eyes and listened to the sound of the wind blowing through the trees and thought about what it must have been like for Annie.

She remembered Ray Williams when she'd seen him in the lineup that day. She remembered the feeling of evil that had pervaded the room.

Was it here, as well? Would she feel it just as strongly as she had when Ray Williams was in the next room?

But she didn't feel it now. She felt sad for Annie, but she didn't recognize this place, she wasn't frightened of it. Nick had told her not to expect miracles, that memories buried so long and so deep didn't just come flooding back at once. They would probably come slowly, in bits and pieces, like small clips of a movie flashing through her head. He'd said she would never know when one would start running or when it would end.

Nick had told her to take her time, to look carefully at every little detail, to see if anything smelled familiar or sounded familiar, to see if she knew things that only someone who'd been in this town before would know.

So far, she'd found nothing.

"I don't... There's nothing here, nothing that I remember."

MacAlister pulled her to his side and held on to her for a long moment. He wasn't sure whether he was relieved or saddened by the fact that, so far, nothing was coming back to her.

He didn't want her hurt any more. He wanted to stand between her and everything in this world that had the power to hurt her. He wondered if she'd even have thanked him for that. She was, after all, a fiercely independent woman.

He was scared about what they were going to find in this town, about how she would handle it and how he would handle it. He didn't care what anyone had done to her in the past—it wasn't going to make a difference in the way he felt about her. Mostly he worried that it would make a difference in how she viewed herself. He knew that some victims irrationally blamed themselves for things that had happened through no fault of their own.

If he could take her pain upon himself, he would. That was how far over his head he was for the woman. Yet these feelings between them that had grown so strong were still so new. The whole relationship was so fragile.

Reluctantly he loosened his hold on her and stepped back. "You all right?"

She nodded.

"Say the word, and we'll be on the road back to Chicago, okay? This town isn't going anywhere. It will still be here when you're ready to do this."

"It's never going to be easy, Jack."

"I know, but you don't have to do this right now, either."

She pulled completely out of his arms, though he wished she'd stay right there. She straightened her shoulders, stuck that cute little nose of hers up in the air and tried to erect that invincible air of hers—damned stubborn, independent woman that she was.

"A.J., give it a week or so. A few days, at least."

She shook her head. "The house isn't far from here, is it?"

"A few blocks."

"We can walk? Through the woods? The way Annie would have that day?"

"Sure." At least they wouldn't risk running into that woman from the park again.

"Let's go."

The walk didn't take long. A.J. timed it by the watch on her wrist. Five minutes. Imagine that—losing a child in the space of five minutes.

People waited that long for elevators. Waited that long in lines at the grocery store. Did a million mundane things in that time span.

MacAlister walked briskly down the sidewalk, past old but well-maintained houses and lawns. He paused at the wrought iron gate to a two-story home with a For Sale sign in the front yard.

A.J. looked up at the place. It had a wide front porch. She wondered if there'd ever been a porch swing there, if Annie had ever sat in it. What would it have looked like with a tricycle on the front lawn and toys scattered on the porch and in the grass? She couldn't imagine, although the Mc-Kays had lived here for thirty-five years.

"Well?" MacAlister said.

"Nothing. Can we get in? Do you have a key?"

"Carolyn gave me one."

They walked through the gate, down the path and up the steps to the porch.

"Are you ready for this?" he said, the key in the door.

A.J. waited, hoping the house would somehow speak to her, that she would feel some sense of homecoming. But she didn't, not yet.

"Let's go inside," she said.

He turned the key, then took her hand. She absolutely loved the feel of her hand in his, thought she could get through anything if he was at her side. And she wondered if she'd ever find the courage to tell him that, if she'd ever feel clean and whole and capable of giving to him as much as she knew he would give to her—if they ever managed to have the kind of relationship she wanted from him.

She wouldn't settle for less. If she never answered these questions about her past, never knew what terrible things had happened to her when she was little, she didn't see how she could trust herself to enter into any kind of relationship. It simply wouldn't be fair.

They walked across the threshold and were surprised to see some personal items still in the house. A comfortable-looking old sofa, two chairs beside it, some photographs still on the walls. She glanced into the kitchen; it was small, old-fashioned. It looked like the kind of place where someone would still make homemade bread, something Grace McKay did very well. She could see the woman working here, could imagine Billy playing in the backyard in the tree house she glimpsed from the kitchen window.

"Why would they leave all this behind?" she said.

"Their home? It's about fifteen miles from Ray Williams's house, for one thing."

"Oh . . . I didn't know that. I was talking about all their furniture."

"I think they've bought a duplex in Chicago, but the sale hasn't gone through yet. I supposed they left some things here, rather than put them in storage while they were in their smaller apartment," MacAlister said. "Plus, when they moved out, they already knew about you. I think they wanted Annie to be able to come home one last time."

A.J. put her hand over her mouth. "How incredibly sad."

"You need to be prepared for something else."

"What?"

"Annie's room. It hasn't been touched. It still looks the way it did the day Annie disappeared."

A.J. took in that bit of unsettling news. "Well . . . I guess that's where we need to go." She headed down the hallway to the right, then turned back to MacAlister. "I don't have any idea where it is."

"That's all right. I do." He turned and headed up the stairs.

A.J. held the railing in a death grip. She couldn't say why. It was just a room, after all. A lost little girl's room. And if the memories were there, well . . . that was what she wanted. In the end, that was what needed to happen. She had to push through the bad ones to get to the good. And obviously there had been a lot of good times in Annie's life. There were still good memories to be made—memories of a loving mother, a sister, a little boy raised to think of himself as Annie's brother.

She knew, from working with the kids at the shelter, that a loving family was a very precious thing, and not something to be taken for granted. How would it feel to have a family again? A real one?

"Here it is." He paused in the doorway. "Sure you're ready?"

She nodded and he opened the door. Pink was everywhere—pink ribbons and pink flowers on the old-fashioned bedspread, stuffed animals sitting on the bed and against the wall. The furniture was off-white wood with burnished gold trim. There were hair ribbons draped over the side of the mirror, and pictures of other kids stuck into the sides of the mirror.

It was such a sweet room, a little girl's dream room. And A.J. didn't remember a thing about it.

In a daze, she walked over to the bed and sat down. She grabbed a white stuffed bear, because it was closest to her, and held it in her lap.

Her throat felt funny, and her vision had become blurred. MacAlister dropped down on one knee in front of her so that he could look her in the eye.

"What is it?" he said gently.

"Nothing—" She choked on the word. She'd been so sure this would do it, and so sure she was Annie. The McKays were so certain, she'd almost come to believe them. That was why it was so hard to admit, both to herself and to him, "I don't feel a thing."

"Wait. Just sit there. Give it a minute. Remember what Nick told you. Look at the details. Smell the smells. Touch the little things. Feel them in your hands. Listen to the sounds around you."

She shook her head. "There's nothing."

"A.J., it's been more than ten years. You didn't expect that you'd walk into this room and everything would come rushing back, did you?"

"I thought ... if I could make myself do this ... come here ... that it would. It sounds so silly now. But I thought it would just come back to me."

A.J. ran her hands over the bedspread of pink flowers threaded through with pink ribbons, then walked over to the closet and looked at a few of the dresses. The shoes were there, too, worn-out sneakers, scuffed-up party shoes. It looked as if Annie had been a tomboy.

She pulled one of the hair ribbons through her fingers. Annie had had a ponytail, as well.

And then she picked up a small silver chest with the daintiest legs. It was heavy. She wondered what kind of treasure a thirteen-year-old would keep inside. She wondered what else—

MacAlister's beeper went off, reminding her that he was still in the room.

"Sorry," he said, turning it off and checking the number. "I need to get to the car and use the phone. Will you be all right while I'm gone?"

"I'll just come with you," she said.

"Are you sure? This will only take a few minutes. Or it can wait. The world's not going to fall apart if I don't return a phone call within two minutes."

"What?" She said. "I must not have heard you right. You ignoring a phone call? And thinking that your office can do without you for that long?"

He smiled—she suspected because he knew she needed to smile as well.

"You work just as hard as I do. And you're the one who thinks the shelter's going to collapse if you're not there for one night."

"I do need to call them," she said, determined to ignore the things left unsaid about the house and her nonexistent memories. "Why don't we just go check into the hotel?"

"You're sure?"

She shrugged. "We'll be here tomorrow. If I need to come back, I can do it then."

She'd been so sure there would be something here that she would remember. Some little thing that would trigger a memory that would let her know, in her own heart, that she was Annie.

But there was nothing.

The message on his beeper indicated that Drew had called, but MacAlister couldn't get through to him, because the phone lines were busy. So they drove to the bed-and-breakfast where they had planned to spend the night.

It was a beautiful house, huge, whitewashed, with porches and balconies and lots of windows. A.J. didn't remember it at all.

They checked into separate but adjoining rooms on the top floor of the house, then went out to dinner. A.J. didn't eat a thing. And she couldn't help but feel as if half the people in the restaurant were staring at her. She heard the whispers behind her back, saw the heads turn toward her, then quickly turn away when they were caught staring.

Finally, a waiter they hadn't seen before came to their table to offer them an after-dinner drink, then knocked over a glass and broke it when he got a good look at A.J.

"Let's go," she said. "Now, please."

"Of course," MacAlister said, reaching into his pocket, finding his keys and handing them to her. "Go out to the car. I'll be there in a minute, as soon as I pay the check."

Grateful for the chance to get away, she took the keys and left. She thought every eye in the room was on her as she made her way through the restaurant and to the car.

She climbed into the vehicle, turned on the ignition so that she could start the heater, then sat there in the darkness and tried to calm herself. All those people seemed to be staring at her, whispering about her—she hadn't even thought of encountering anything like that. Did she look that much like Annie? Was it that obvious for anyone to see?

So why didn't she feel like Annie? Why hadn't the house or that spot in the park triggered any memories for her?

The car phone rang, and she gave a start. MacAlister hadn't come out of the restaurant, and she knew he still hadn't gotten in touch with Drew.

She picked up the phone. "Hello."

"A.J.?"

"Yes."

"It's Drew. I need to talk to Jack. I've been trying to get him for hours. Is he there?"

"He's on his way. He should be here in a minute. Do you want me to have him call you?"

"I beeped him, about three hours ago, and I've been waiting to hear from him." He hesitated. "It's important, A.J."

"Something's happened, hasn't it?"

Again he hesitated. "I need to talk to him."

"About me?"

"About a case we're working on."

"Ray Williams's case?"

He took a deep breath, then let it out. "Yes."

A.J. felt a nasty shiver work its way up her spine. The car door opened, and she jumped again, then realized it was Jack.

"What is it?" he said.

She got out and stood on shaky legs, then handed him the phone. "Drew, for you."

A.J. leaned against the car and crossed her arms in front of her, then hung on for dear life.

She knew what was coming. She'd felt it that day she saw Ray Williams. She'd known that something bad was going to happen, that she had to hurry and remember everything, because she was the only one who might be able to stop it.

And now it didn't matter anymore. It was too late.

Jack leaned against the open doorway. She heard him swear, once, then again. "How the hell did that happen?"

She closed her eyes tight.

"When?" Jack said into the phone. "And no one's seen him since?"

No one's seen him since.

It wasn't what she'd feared—that he'd snatched another child. But it was still bad. And it was something she hadn't even considered.

A.J. looked around her, into the night, and the town seemed unusually dark and quiet to her. The shadows had turned menacing, the peaceful quiet now utterly eerie.

Ray Williams was loose out here somewhere.

Chapter 14

She couldn't sleep that night. She tried soaking in the bathtub, reading, counting sheep. Nothing worked.

Finally, sometime after midnight, not caring how cowardly it was of her, not even caring if she looked like a clinging, helpless female, she knocked on the connecting door between her room and Jack's.

He opened it quickly enough that she knew he'd been awake, too. "Couldn't sleep?"

She shook her head.

"We *could* not sleep together," he suggested with a sly grin.

"That's the best invitation I've had all night." She took the hand he offered and walked into the room. Only once inside did she start to feel a little uncomfortable. A huge antique four-poster bed dominated the room. MacAlister was only half dressed. His shirt was completely unbuttoned. She took one quick glance at his powerful chest, then blushed and looked away.

She hadn't seen him this way since the night she'd confessed exactly how little she knew about men. And she couldn't say that she'd learned a lot since, except that kissing him was better than chocolate. And A.J. had a serious thing for chocolate.

She made her way to the window that overlooked the now deserted street and asked, "Have you heard anything?"

"No."

Looking into the moonless night sky, she asked, "You said he doesn't live far from here?"

"About twenty minutes."

Her breath came out in a long, unsteady rush.

"A.J., I know where he's going. We all know where he's going. He has a cabin somewhere in the woods of southern Illinois or Indiana, and I bet there's enough physical evidence there alone to convict him. If he's smart—and I think he is—he's gone there to destroy that evidence."

"Which means he'll go free." That thought made her sick inside.

"No," he said. "We're fairly certain we know the approximate area where the cabin is, but there are tons of them down there. And I can't get a search warrant to go through them all. But we have cops all over those woods. We're going to find him, hopefully right after he leads us to his cabin. And then we've got him."

"I don't know," she said, laying her forehead against the coolness of the glass. "I've had such a bad feeling about this...ever since I saw him that day. I knew something awful was going to happen. I thought for the longest time that it was what he'd done to Annie so long ago or to me, that I was going to remember it, and it would be just awful. But now I'm not so sure. Do you believe in premonitions?"

"No."

That was just like him—practical, logical man that he was.

"I do," she said. "I think something terrible is going to happen."

He came to stand behind her. Slowly he settled himself against her back, putting his arms around her. A.J. rested her head against his shoulder, feeling better than she had all night, now that she was safe and in his arms.

How had she ever made it without him for so long? And what would she do if she ever lost him?

"Nothing bad is going to happen here," he said.

She wished she could believe that. "He's out there, somewhere. He could be right across the street, and we'd never know."

"Think about it, A.J. Why would he come here?"

"Because I'm here." That possibility hadn't hit her until the past hour.

"Williams doesn't even know about you," Jack said.

"You're sure?"

"We've been very careful to keep this quiet. If the TV people had any idea that one of his victims might have gotten away from him years ago and been located again, that person wouldn't have had a minute's peace. *You* wouldn't have had a minute's peace. So believe me, we've been very careful with this information. Ray Williams has no idea who you are or where you are."

"The people in this town know. I bet that woman we ran into at the park went home and called everyone she knows and told them Annie was in town today. And you saw how all those people were staring at me at the restaurant tonight."

"Do you want to leave tonight?" he said.

"No...I just...I want you to hold on to me tonight, and not let go."

It was the closest she'd ever come to telling him how much she needed him. She held her breath, waiting for his response.

He only held her tighter. She soaked in the warmth of him, the strength, the solidness. It was heavenly, in the face of all her irrational fears.

"I know it's silly," she said, "but I'm just so scared."

Jack kissed her cheek, then put his lips against her ear. "You need to understand something. He'd have to kill me to get to you."

And he meant it. She knew he did. She'd never thought she'd take comfort in the fact that one man might take the life of another to protect her, but she did. Right then, she took great comfort in that.

"Oh, Jack . . ." How had it ever come to this? A madman on the loose, her in a town only minutes away from him and in love with a man she didn't think she could ever have.

She *was* in love with Jack, she realized. She loved him for his strength, his determination, the way he had of making her laugh when there was nothing funny about anything. She could even overlook his incredible arrogance and his tendency toward bossiness.

Because she loved him. She needed him desperately. She wanted him in her life, today and every day. Forever.

His arms pulled her even closer. He kissed her cheek once again, and his voice was slightly unsteady as he told her, "I'm not going to lose you now."

A.J. caught her breath. She wanted to know exactly how he felt, but was afraid to ask. She didn't think she was up to hearing the answer. When they were like this, when he talked to her like this, the possibilities seemed endless. But when she was alone at night, thinking about the kind of life he led and about how different his past was from hers, she didn't see how anything could come of this relationship.

Could she even call it a relationship? He hadn't done anything more than kiss her and hold her like this. And she found herself wanting more. At times, when she felt particularly brave, she wanted much, much more.

But as she saw it, men like him had either sexual relationships or pure friendships. This thing between them didn't fit into either category. And if he wanted it to be more than it was, he'd never told her or shown her.

So she could only assume that he didn't want anything more from her, and she still had enough insecurities about her past to think she knew why.

She couldn't say for sure, of course. Only he could, and in order to find out what he thought, she'd have to ask. She didn't think she had the courage. And she'd thought they would have all this time to sort these things out. But now that man was out there somewhere.

What if they didn't have any time but now?

What if these feelings she had—these premonitions of evil, of danger—came true? What if they came true tomorrow, and this night was all she had with him?

She'd want to spend it with him. It was as simple, as exhilarating and as frightening as that. She wanted to be with him, tonight.

How would a woman with experience go about that? Would she show him somehow? A.J. shied away from that. She could just tell him. They could be perfectly rational about this. Surely it didn't have to be that complicated.

"Jack?"

"Hmm?" She still had her head against his shoulder. He still had his lips next to her ear, and she shivered with pleasure as his warm breath settled against the sensitive skin of her neck.

"Do you think...we might..." She took a deep breath and forced herself to go on. "I mean...I was wondering..."

"What, darlin'?"

"If you might want to make love to me. Tonight?"

It sounded ridiculous to her own ears, and she closed her eyes and wished she could take back the words and just stay here in his arms all night.

She felt him go still behind her, felt what she thought was a smile creep across his lips.

"Is this a trick question?"

"Don't you tease me now, Jack MacAlister."

"Okay," he said, then had the nerve to laugh. "I must not have heard you correctly."

"You're a rat, Jack."

"And you want to know if I *might* want to make love to you."

"Tonight," she added. That part seemed vitally important.

"Darlin', I don't see how you could possibly have any doubts about that. You want to explain that part to me?"

Not really. A.J. swallowed hard and wondered how much courage she had left. "So you do? Want to, I mean?"

Again, he laughed, then turned quiet enough to really worry her. One of his hands moved downward, coming to rest flat against her abdomen. The muscles quivered and clenched beneath his palm.

"Be still," he said.

His voice had taken on a low, husky tone that she didn't think she'd ever heard from him before. It did funny things to her. Her cheeks flooded with heat, her knees went weak, her breath caught in her throat.

She felt him settling himself carefully behind her, bracing himself with his legs wide apart, then pushing her back against him with his hand still over her abdomen.

He pushed her back until her hips were flush against him, and then she felt it. She felt him, big and hard against her.

A streak of pure, unadulterated sexual attraction shot through her, from that point where their bodies pressed so intimately together. It spread through every inch of her being.

Her skin felt different, ultrasensitive. The hair on the back of her neck was standing on end, and she wasn't sure she could have stayed on her feet if he hadn't been holding her so tightly.

"Don't be afraid," he whispered against her neck.

"I'm not," she insisted.

"You are, but there's no reason to be."

"But you're..."

"Aroused?" He seemed to take delight in the fact that she wouldn't say it herself. "But we don't have to do anything about that."

"What if... I *wanted* us to do something about *that?*"

"Wait a minute." He backed away from her, then turned her around to face him, still holding her by the arms. "Let's get something absolutely clear between us. I swore to myself I wasn't going to pressure you in any way to do anything you're not ready for."

"I know."

"And you took that to mean that I didn't want you? Is that what you're telling me, darlin'?"

He looked incredulous, and she wondered if she hadn't actually misread the whole situation. She'd told him she didn't know anything about men. Maybe she knew even less than she thought, she decided miserably.

"And here I thought I was being such a gentleman," he said.

"Oh, Jack. I'm sorry. I don't—"

"How could you think I didn't want you? Why, A.J.? I think that's the real question here. Why would you think I didn't want you?"

She was even more miserable than before. "I think I need to sit down."

"Okay."

She sank into the chair by the window. He sat on the wide edge of the windowsill and faced her.

"Could we turn out the lights?"

"If you want."

She nodded. Not having to look him in the eye right now sounded pretty good. She felt more vulnerable than she ever had in her life.

He clicked off the overhead light and came back to sit on the windowsill. "Why would you believe I didn't want to make love to you?"

"You think I'm Annie," she said, hoping that would be enough.

"Go on."

"You know what happened to her. Surely we can both make a pretty accurate guess. Surely I don't have to spell it all out for you."

"I think you do."

"I feel so dirty," she said, nearly choking.

"*No.*" Jack said it like a curse, feeling as if he'd been blindsided.

I feel so dirty.

That heartfelt confession made him feel like a heel.

She was ashamed about something over which she had no control, something that had happened to her when she was just a child, something that in no way was her fault. Yet she was still ashamed.

Jack wanted to break something. He wanted to smash something into a million pieces, wanted to hear it shatter.

He wanted to break Ray Williams apart. If he could find the man, he would do it. But this wasn't what A.J. needed right now. She didn't need to hear about how angry the situation had made him.

"I could understand," she said, "if you didn't want to be with me, because of what that man did to me."

"No, darlin', no." He put his hands against her lips. Then he fell to his knees in front of her and took her face between his hands, leaving her no choice but to look at him. "I never thought that. I never felt anything remotely like that."

And then Jack knew that she had no idea what he felt for her. He wondered if she'd let him tell her tonight, wondered if she was ready to hear it.

He turned away for a moment, trying to get hold of himself. He didn't have a lot of experience with love. He'd certainly never gone looking for it. Not too long ago, he hadn't even been sure he believed in it. He understood honesty, commitment and trust—surely they were the basis of most of the relationships he'd seen, the ones that had lasted, at least.

But what else was there? What was this elusive thing called love? He'd thought he loved Miranda, but that had been so long ago. He hadn't been nearly as cynical back then, or as jaded.

Now there was A.J., and in the space of a couple of minutes she'd told him that she would understand if he didn't want to make love to her, and that she felt dirty because of something she couldn't even remember.

There was a burning sensation in his throat and his eyes, a pressure that had settled into them.

"Oh, darlin', what am I going to do with you?" He caught her chin in his hand and gave her a quick kiss on the lips.

And then he didn't know what to do.

He wanted to keep her, forever. He wanted to love her and take care of her and pamper her, lock her away somewhere so that no one could ever hurt her again.

He wanted her to be his and to belong to no one but him. He would gladly give himself to her in exchange.

His throat was even tighter than before, and his vision had gone blurry. He wasn't sure what was happening at first, and then he felt the wetness of tears on his cheek for the first time in years, probably since he was a kid.

"A.J.—" He choked on her name. "I had no idea you felt that way. I swear it. And if I ever did anything to make you feel like that—"

"No," she said. "It's not you. It's me."

"I'm so sorry, darlin'."

A.J. watched the tears form in his beautiful, dark eyes, as they had in hers. And then she watched those tears spill over onto his cheeks.

She was amazed as she watched him, this big, powerful man with tears on his cheeks because of her.

She was struck by that. It seemed a terribly intimate and powerful thing, to see them and to know that they were for her, that they somehow indicated how strongly he felt about her.

Something shifted inside her, some deep-seated and monumental thing. He'd always had a way of loosening the grip she maintained on her emotions, and he'd done it again now.

A.J. put her hands on his face and followed the path of his tears with her fingertips.

"I don't want to hurt you," he told her. "Not ever, not for anything in this world."

"I know that," she said.

"We need to get some things straight," he said, then stood and pulled her up beside him. "Are you cold?"

"A little."

He moved to the bed and threw back the covers. Then he situated himself in the middle of the enormous bed, his back against the polished mahogany headboard. "Come and sit with me."

She eyed the bed warily.

"Do you trust me?" he asked.

"Yes," she replied, climbing onto the bed.

He pulled her close, her head against his bare chest, her side pressed to his, his arms around her, the covers pulled up for added warmth. He ran his fingers through her hair for a moment, then kissed the top of her head. She shivered yet again, not knowing at all what to expect from this.

"A.J., there's nothing you could possibly find out about that man, about anything he might have done to you, that's going to change who you are or what you are. Surely you know that."

Maybe she knew that. Maybe she could reason it out that way in her head. Her feelings were another matter altogether, and they had nothing to do with logic or reason.

"He can't hurt you anymore, darlin'."

And then, miraculously, she started to cry.

She brought a trembling hand up to her cheeks, amazed by what she felt there. She wiped the moisture away, only to have the tears fall faster than she could catch them. They spilled down her cheeks, onto his chest, catching in the fascinating curls there.

She tried to wipe them off his skin, then realized that she'd been looking for some excuse to touch him.

"I didn't think you ever cried," he said.

He caught her hand flat against his heart. It was pounding, she noted with great satisfaction.

"I haven't cried in years," she said. "I didn't think I could anymore."

"Darlin', you can do anything. I promise you that."

She smiled through her tears. "How is it that you seem to know exactly what to say to me? Exactly what I need to hear?"

"I'm telling you what I believe in my heart. No matter what happened in your past, it doesn't have any power over you except what you give it. Don't let it hurt you any more."

"I...I'm trying not to, but it's hard. Nick told me the same thing, and—"

"Wait a minute," he said. "Could we leave good old Nick out of our bed, please?"

A.J. laughed. Jack always knew when she needed to laugh. "If I didn't know better, I'd say you were jealous, Jack."

"You know damned well I'm jealous."

She supposed she'd hoped he was, though it had seemed like a lot to hope for.

"You really don't have any idea how I feel about you, do you?" he said.

"I know that you care about me."

"That's putting it mildly, A.J."

And that scared her so much, she decided there was nothing left to do but change the subject. "But I know you're uneasy about my past. What man wouldn't be?"

"I think you're changing the subject, darlin'."

"We can't ignore it."

"We can't ignore how I feel about you, either," he insisted, pulling away so that he could see her better in the near darkness of the room. "But if you don't want to know..."

She was afraid to know, and some of that must have shown on her face, because he was watching her even more intently now. His hand came up to her face, to tilt it up toward his.

"A.J., would it be so terrible for me to fall in love with you?"

She thought her whole heart was lodged in her throat. It seemed to have lurched inside her, then started pounding. And she couldn't say anything. She could barely breathe.

"A.J.?"

He could be so gentle at times, could lose all that cockiness, that teasing tone of his. He touched her so gently, so softly, held her so tightly, made her feel so safe and so at home with him. She'd never thought she'd find that with any man. And if she did find it, by some miracle, she didn't see how it could possibly last.

"Don't say any more," she begged him. "Please, don't."

He looked as if he were about to argue with her, but in the end, he didn't. "All right. What is it you do want to talk about? Tell me why this can't work."

She cleared her throat with some difficulty. "My past. I know you're . . . uneasy about my past."

"*Darlin', you* are the one who's uneasy about *your* past."

"You can't tell me that it doesn't mean anything to you, Jack. Don't lie to me about that."

"I'll never lie to you. Never."

"I'm sorry. I do know that."

"We're back to sex, right?"

She nodded.

"You think I don't want to be with you, because of whatever that man might have done to you. Is that it?"

"You can't tell me you don't have some reservations about it."

"Okay, yes, I have some reservations. But I don't think we're talking about the same things, A.J. Tell me about yours, and then I'll tell you about mine."

She closed her eyes and searched her heart for the worst of her fears. "I'm afraid it's going to bring back bad memories for me, that I won't be able to separate in my mind what he did to me and what you and I will do, even though I know they're totally separate things."

He pulled her back toward him, pushed her head down to his chest and held her tightly. "So maybe it's going to take some time to work it out. We have time, A.J., all the time in the world. We'll stay in this bed until we get it right, until it feels as incredible to you as I know it's going to feel to me."

She smiled, in spite of herself. "We'll stay here until we get it right?"

"Believe me, I'm more than willing."

"I love you, Jack MacAlister." She hadn't meant to say that. It had just come out, but it felt so right. And then she looked up and pressed her fingers against his lips. "Don't say anything, please."

"A.J. . . . ."

"Please. You said you'd give me time."

"But I wasn't talking about time to tell you how I feel."

"You promised," she said. "And you said if I told you about my reservations, you'd tell me about yours."

"Okay," he said finally. "First, I don't want to frighten you. I don't want to push you into anything you're not ready to do. I don't want to bring back any bad memories for you. And I'm worried that I won't know how to help you, if this does upset you."

"That's it?" she asked tentatively.

"I want to make this good for you. I want you to enjoy it as much as I will. What else did you expect me to say, A.J.?"

"That man . . . We don't even know what he did. . . ."

"We don't have to know what *he* did. We know what you did, A.J. And you haven't done anything wrong. You don't have any reason to be ashamed about anything."

But shame wasn't something logical, she decided. And she couldn't seem to believe it was all so cut-and-dried to Jack either.

"It has to have some bearing on your feelings for me," she said.

"It does. I just told you about them. I told you everything except this. Whatever that man did to you, it doesn't make me want you any less."

"You're sure?"

"Positive."

"Oh, Jack." She wanted to believe him. She wanted that so bad. "I don't know what to say."

"I do. I want you in my bed, whenever you're ready, and we can do whatever you think you're ready to do. I can wait for that, A.J. I'll wait as long as it takes."

He was too good to be true. Patient, kind, generous . . . What more could she want in a man?

She wanted him. She'd wanted to be with him for a long time, but she hadn't known how to tell him that, hadn't been sure she had the courage to go through with this.

But she trusted him. She'd trust him with her life, and with her deepest, darkest secrets—once she figured out what those were. And he said it didn't matter to him, anyway. Maybe she could get to the point where it didn't matter to her, either.

"I guess you didn't notice," she said, "I'm in your bed right now."

"Believe me, I noticed."

"I think I'd like to stay."

Chapter 15

A.J. felt Jack tense. She couldn't help but be conscious of the fact that they were safely locked away from the rest of the world, in this room, in his bed, together.

She was scared, but impatient. She wanted to do this, wanted to get past this first time, which she thought was certain to be awkward at best. She wanted to get past all that, to the laughter, the joy, the love, that she thought was waiting on the other side of this void in her memories.

"A.J.?" Jack said, his hand on her head, stroking through her hair, then working through some of the tension in her shoulders.

"Hmm?"

His hands were big, warm and strong. She couldn't help but shiver at the thought of the pleasure those hands could give her, by doing nothing but stroking slowly along her body the way they were doing now to her back.

"If you change your mind, at any time, tell me to stop, and I will."

"I know."

"You don't have to be afraid."

He slid down the bed, lying now instead of sitting, and eased her on top of him. She was surprised by just how much bigger and stronger he was than she, how easy it would be for someone of his size to overpower her. But she wasn't afraid of him.

"So . . . are you going to tell me what to do?"

He laughed huskily. "There are lots of things we could do. Why don't you tell me what you'd like to do?"

"Uh . . . I'm not sure. I really hadn't thought about it."

"Then I must be doing something wrong."

"Okay," she said. "Maybe I've thought of a few things."

"Name one."

"You could kiss me."

"Where?"

She pointed to her cheek. His lips touched her, softly, slightly. She shivered, and he pulled the covers up higher around her shoulders.

"I'm not cold," she told him.

"Neither am I, darlin'. What else can I kiss?"

She worked up her nerve and set her lips against his, felt his harshly drawn-in breath, felt his hands shift to her arms and pull her a little closer, his tongue slip inside her mouth, his taste as sweet and as intoxicating as the finest wine.

Her breasts felt strange—full and heavy, her nipples puckering into little points that pressed against his chest. She wondered what it would feel like to lie against him this way, with absolutely nothing between them. And the thought excited her.

He kissed her again and again, deeper, stronger, faster, as if he couldn't get enough of her. His hands were in her hair, then on her face. His breathing was suddenly as unsteady as hers, and he shifted his legs, opened them, and once again she felt his arousal. Pressed this way against her, she couldn't help but wonder how he would ever fit inside her.

"What's wrong?" he asked, picking up on her tension.

She felt utterly ridiculous for asking. "Are you sure it will fit?"

He smiled against her lips. "You're going to have to trust me on this one, darlin'."

And she did.

"Kiss me again," he said.

And she did that, too. He kissed her back, kissed her cheeks, her eyes, her ears, her neck. She couldn't help but moan aloud when he came to the spot where her neck met her shoulder.

"That's good?" he said.

"That's very good."

He did it again, and pleasure shot through her body. He rolled onto his side, taking her with him. His hands moved down her back until they cupped her hips, and he fit her to him, then rocked gently against her.

A.J. felt a strange tension building inside him, felt a heat, a heaviness, an insistent throbbing at the juncture of her thighs, felt an answering response in his body.

She struggled to get even closer to him. His lips were moving downward now, along her collarbone, along the upper curve of her breasts. She buried her hands in his hair, urging him closer, urging his mouth lower.

He took her nipple into his mouth, through her shirt, and the tension was more than she could stand. Her body jerked in a bewildering spasm over which she had no control, and she cried out in surprise, in pleasure, and held on to him.

She felt for a second as if the whole world had fallen away—every problem she had, every fear, every insecurity—leaving nothing but pleasure so intense she'd never known it existed. There was nothing but the pleasure and Jack.

She opened her eyes, noted that he'd gone still beside her, and that he was smiling like the devil himself.

"Was that—?"

He nodded, still smiling.

"Just like that?"

He laughed.

"I mean, I knew that happened, sometimes, to some women..."

"Darlin', let me tell you something. This isn't going to be as difficult for you as we thought it would be."

"Oh." And then she smiled, too. Then she laughed. She'd never thought she'd find herself in bed with Jack Mac-Alister and laughing. It felt wonderful. "I'm so happy."

"So am I, darlin'. So am I. And, A.J.—?"

"Hmm?"

"It gets better."

It did get better, much better. He stripped her naked, and the look in his eyes when he saw her that way for the first time was enough to set her whole body trembling again. His breathing wasn't as steady as it had been, and it became even more ragged when she undressed him and started exploring.

A.J. felt a heady thrill of sheer feminine power when she realized that this was affecting him as much as it was her. Somehow she'd assumed that he would be the one with all the power here. She was relieved to find out she'd been wrong about that.

She ran her hand along his shoulders, through the dark cloud of hair on his chest, then lower. The muscles of his stomach clenched, and she heard him moan.

Curiosity driving her on, she moved her hand still lower, stroking him lightly with her fingertips. She felt his whole body stiffen in response.

"Are you sure this is all right?"

"*All right* doesn't begin to cover it," he said.

She smiled, loving the feel of him in her hand. She used her fingertips, then the palm of her hand, then let him show her what he liked. To her surprise, she found it as arousing touching him as having him touch her. She was starting to understand exactly what it meant to make love with a man.

And she wanted more. She wanted everything. Her body was starting to demand it, and Jack must have sensed her need. His hands were all over her again, stroking, teasing, finding the warm, wet, aching spot between her legs. She forgot all about what she was doing to him, couldn't think about anything but his hands down there, between her legs, stroking her that way. She felt the tension building within her again, knew this time what that meant, and soon she went spinning out of control all over again. The feeling was stronger this time, sweeter, even more intoxicating, than before, when she hadn't known what to expect.

She came back down slowly, a smile spread across her lips, which he kissed again and again.

"You are an amazing woman," he said, rolling on top of her.

Her thighs parted automatically as she welcomed him. He nuzzled her neck and shoulders for a minute, giving her time to come back down before they started again.

How many times could they do this? she wondered. How much pleasure could one woman take in a single night?

"Still want more?" he said.

"Yes."

"In the top drawer, in the nightstand, there's something I think we're going to need."

"Oh," she said, all flustered, when she found a small foil packet. "I forgot all about that."

She fought the urge to ask him when he'd bought them— or, worse, for whom he'd bought them.

"A man has to have hope, A.J.," he said, showing again that uncanny ability to read her mind.

He took the packet from her hand, and she waited while he put it on.

"You're sure?" he asked again.

"Yes."

She felt the weight of his body settle heavily over hers, felt him draw in a long, unsteady breath. Obviously she wasn't the only one eager for this to happen.

His mouth came down on hers, hard and insistent. She writhed against him, trying in vain to get close enough to him. And she clung to him, praying that the day would never come when she had to let him go.

She felt him nudge her legs apart, felt the blunt tip of his arousal poised against that aching emptiness of hers.

"Don't be afraid," he said.

She put her hands on his hips and urged him closer. She felt the pressure, slight at first, then stronger. It did frighten her a little. She tensed. He backed away.

"What's wrong?" she said.

"Nothing." He kissed her mouth. His fingers were inside her by then, stroking and opening. She forgot to be scared, because it felt so good.

Just when she thought she was going to come apart again in his arms, he stopped. She cried out in frustration until she felt him position himself above her again. This time, it was going to work. She was determined that it would. And she wanted him inside her, all of him.

Still, A.J. felt the resistance in her body return. He started to pull away again, but there was no way she was going to let him.

"Don't you dare stop now," she said, putting her hands on his hips and pulling him to her.

The pressure continued, enough to make her uncomfortable, but not enough to make her back away.

"Wait a minute," he said.

"No. Don't leave me, Jack."

"I won't. I . . ."

And then the resistance was gone. He surged forward, burying himself completely inside her. And it felt . . . it felt so good.

He didn't move at first, and she thought she'd done something wrong. Her body started to move beneath his. She rocked back and forth, tentatively at first, then with greater confidence. He let her know just how much he liked that.

She'd thought she understood the power, the urgency, the depth, of the desire, that a man had for a woman. But what she'd felt before was nothing to compare to this. He was on top of her, his arms around her, his mouth on hers, his body joined together with hers in the most intimate way possible, and still she wanted more. She needed more.

She felt him tense again above her, saw his jaw clench, his eyes close, then realized how greedy she'd become.

"Don't," she said. "Don't stop."

"A.J." He groaned her name, then ground his hips against hers in long, deep strokes, faster and faster, until she thought she couldn't stand it anymore.

She sank her fingernails into his back, fighting him for something she didn't even understand. Then she felt a deep, heavy throbbing inside her; it was him, his body reacting in just the way hers had before, the way hers did again. She felt him shatter in her arms, and then she followed him down into a well of pleasure unlike anything she'd ever known.

In spite of his gruffness, his tendency toward bossiness, the self-assurance that bordered on arrogance, Jack MacAlister had a definite tender side, one he was showing her in abundance.

Cradling her in his arms as if she were made of the thinnest, most fragile glass, he stroked her, crooned to her, kissed her tenderly, all while she cried her eyes out.

It took her forever to convince him, through uncontrollable tears, that nothing was wrong, that nothing had gone wrong, that what he was seeing was nothing more than relief.

Making love to him had been unlike anything she'd ever imagined, and it hadn't brought back any dire memories for her. Not a one. She felt cleansed by the whole experience, freed by it. She felt whole again, strong again, in control again.

She felt incredible, and so relieved that she simply could not stop crying.

"God, you nearly scared me to death," he said, once she'd finally explained it all to him.

"I'm sorry."

He kissed her briefly. "It's all right. I'm not worried about me. I'm concerned about you."

"I'm fabulous."

"Yes, Miss Jennings, I'd have to say that you are."

She found she could still blush quite easily, where he was concerned.

"I can't believe how easy it was and how wonderful it felt. I was sure that if anything made me remember, it would be this."

"No bad moments?"

"No."

"A.J., did I hurt you?"

"No, why?"

"You were so... tight."

"I was nervous." She couldn't understand what he was getting at.

"Darlin', it wasn't a case of nerves. You were ready for me. I made sure of that."

"Then... I don't understand." Had she done something wrong? "You liked it."

"I loved it."

"But there was a problem?"

He took her face in his hands and smiled down into her eyes. She felt marginally better.

"No, darlin', not a problem."

"Then what?"

His face wore a silly grin. "I'm no expert on this... but...darlin', I don't think you've ever done this before."

"I told you I hadn't."

He turned his head to the right and laughed a little. "We're talking pure as the new-fallen snow, A.J."

"Pure?"

"Innocent. As in...virgin."

She didn't move for a second, didn't even blink an eyelash. "Me?"

He nodded.

A.J. thought her heart had just stopped beating. She'd never considered that. Never. She'd been so sure that...that she was Annie McKay...and that man had taken Annie, and he'd...surely he'd done that.

"I don't understand," she said. "How could that be?"

"I don't know, darlin'."

"Oh." And then she just sat there with her mouth hanging open, not knowing what to say. A few minutes later, she had even more tears running down her cheeks.

"Hey," he said, wiping them away. "I thought you'd be happy about this."

"I am." She struggled helplessly. "I'm... I can't believe it."

"Believe it, A.J. Whatever that man did to you, he didn't rape you."

"I was so sure. And this...this takes some getting used to."

"I know. Did I mention that you happened to be incredible in bed?"

She shook her head.

"You don't have anything to worry about on that score. And the rest of it, whatever it is, we'll handle it, A.J. I promise."

She believed that she had come to him as pure as the new-fallen snow, as he'd put it. And she would have loved to believe that she was fabulous in bed, and that they could handle absolutely anything that happened from this point on.

She prayed, as she hadn't prayed for anything in years, that Jack MacAlister loved her with the kind of love that endured forever, because she couldn't imagine going through this without him. It frightened her how very much she'd come to lean on him, to trust him, to need him.

How many men could possibly have been so understanding about her past? So kind, so caring, so absolutely sure that she could handle this? She needed that from him, needed it desperately.

And she was scared of losing it.

When she woke up the next morning in his arms, after they'd made love again sometime shortly before dawn, she couldn't have been happier.

He showered, dressed, then went downstairs in search of coffee and something for them to eat. She soaked in the tub and dressed, all the while dreaming of staying with him in this room, locked away from the rest of the world, forever. Surely their life would be perfect.

And then he came back upstairs and showed her the latest edition of the local newspaper.

Annie's picture was on the front page, next to a photo taken of an unaware A.J. sometime yesterday afternoon.

The headline read: Annie McKay—Home At Last?

She didn't bother to read the story but Jack told her the highlights of it. From the innkeeper he'd learned that the woman who'd spotted them in the park yesterday afternoon was the daughter of the man who owned the newspaper. Someone from the paper had been calling the inn all last night, but Mrs. Adams had refused to put the call through to A.J.'s room. Of course, A.J. hadn't been there anyway.

"It gets worse," Jack warned.

"How?"

"I gave Drew a call this morning while I was downstairs. He said apparently someone from the paper here started calling the papers in Chicago to get information on the status of the Williams case, and once they explained why they needed it, the Chicago papers got interested in the story, too. You made the Chicago front page, too."

"Oh. So leaving town isn't going to help." She walked to the window, spotted a satellite truck with a television-station logo and half a dozen people milling around outside, two of them with cameras.

"I'm sorry," he said. "When we came here, I didn't even think about people recognizing you."

"It's not your fault," she said. "I didn't think of it, either."

"It's going to be even crazier in Chicago."

"I know." She looked longingly around the room, taking in the big, old bed that had held such magic, the lock on the door that she had thought could hold the world at bay. Couldn't they have had one more day? One more night? "Do we have to go back?"

"Not today. But we can't stay here."

"I could have stayed here forever," she said.

"Believe me, darlin', I had plans for us in that bed. But they're going to have to wait."

"It's…it's so unfair," she said. They had just made love for the first time last night, had just figured out that her worst fears about her past simply were not true.

No man had ever touched her the way he had. There were no demons waiting in her past to ruin what the two of them had found together in this room.

And she wasn't ready to leave. She wasn't ready to let reality intrude upon this precious time she had with him.

It was too new, she warned herself. Too fragile. She still hadn't worked up the nerve to ask him exactly what all this meant to him, wasn't ready to hear him say that he was falling in love with her, when she would still have so much trouble believing his words.

And things were so crazy that she simply hadn't had time to sort out her own feelings. She was still getting used to the idea that she'd come to him as innocent as the day she was born.

"I don't want to go," she said.

"I know. Neither do I. But we can come back someday. Or we'll find another inn just like this one, where no one knows us. We'll turn off the car phone and refuse to tell anyone where we're headed."

She thought for a moment that she was going to cry again. The tears came so easily now, she couldn't seem to stop them. And she hated the idea of turning into a helpless, weeping, clinging woman.

"Hey," Jack said, cupping her chin in his hand and turning her face to his. "We have the rest of our lives to lock ourselves away. Besides, you still have a lot to learn."

"Oh, I do?"

He grinned. "And I can't wait to teach you."

She smiled back at him, but couldn't help wondering if this was some novelty that would wear off in time. How long could innocence be that seductive? How long could she hold on to him?

She still saw them as worlds apart. She'd seen the kind of women who inhabited his world. Beautiful, sexy, full of self-confidence, raised in the mansions along Chicago's Gold Coast, their mothers friends of his mother, their fathers with social and political connections.

What if Jack had some political ambitions of his own? She could see one of those women by his side, but she couldn't see herself there.

She imagined that one day she'd go back to her world—the South Side and her kids, and he'd go back to his, the penthouse on the lake.

"A.J.? You're a million miles away."

She shrugged with as much nonchalance as she could manage.

"And I don't think I'm going to like hearing what's going through your head right now."

"It's nothing," she said, wondering if he had any idea how much she needed him, and how she hated needing anyone this much.

"I guess we have to get out of here," she said.

"Not this instant," he replied, reminding her that he made his living prying information out of people.

She decided to try telling him a half-truth, hoping he wouldn't see it as such. "I don't want to leave this room, all right? I'm not ready for this to be over."

"Darlin', this isn't over by a long shot."

She closed her eyes and prayed that it wasn't. "I'm so angry that . . . that man is intruding on my life this way."

"I know," he said. "Anything else?"

Her back to him, she looked out the window at the people outside. There were more of them now. "Damn," she said. "I guess we do have to be going. I don't want to answer anyone's questions, and I don't want my picture taken, or one of those cameras filming me for the evening news."

And then she put everything together. "Oh, God, Jack. I didn't even realize until just this minute, but—"

He was beside her in an instant. "What?"

"If I'm in all the papers . . . my name, my picture . . ."

"What?"

"Ray Williams got away yesterday. He knows now. He knows all about me. What if he decides to finish what he started?"

Chapter 16

Much as she hated to let him go, she did. While he made arrangements to get them out of the inn without A.J. having to walk past all those reporters, she hid behind the room's locked door.

Alone with her irrational fears about Ray Williams.

Jack promised that, once they got away from here, he wouldn't let her out of his sight until the man was caught, and she believed him. She also believed him when he said Ray Williams would have to kill him to get to her.

And yet, she was still afraid.

Her premonition that something terrible was going to happen was growing stronger. Ray Williams was loose now, and if he'd read any paper, seen any newscast, he knew who she was. If he wanted to find her, he could.

And the only way to get him off the streets was to give Jack the information needed to put Williams behind bars. And only she had that ability.

She wanted to be free to worry about nothing but herself and Jack and how they were going to spend the rest of their lives. She couldn't live in fear of her past any longer.

There was only one way she could get the information to help convict that man.

And she was afraid.

They ended up sneaking out the delivery entrance. The innkeeper was kind enough to loan Jack her car for a few hours as his was parked out front. They walked out the inn's back entrance and climbed into the woman's car without being seen. Luckily for them, the reporters hadn't yet grown into such a mob that they were covering all the exits to the building.

"Can we go back to the house today?" A.J. said. "Annie's house?"

"I don't see why not, as long as it's not surrounded. Did you remember something?"

"No, not yet. But there has to be something inside that house that I remember."

A few minutes later, they arrived at the house, happy to find it as deserted as the day before. Jack wanted his own car back, so that he would have his mobile phone, so they had stopped at the corner and made arrangements for the innkeeper to meet them at the McKay house to trade cars.

As a precaution, they parked in an alley behind the house and went to the back door.

"Did you hear anything about Ray Williams this morning?" she asked Jack as he unlocked the door.

"Nothing, but I haven't checked in with anyone in Chicago in the last hour and a half. I'll stay down here and watch for Mrs. Adams, and when she brings the car, I'll make my calls."

She nodded. Once inside, A.J. went upstairs and, without hesitation, walked into Annie's old room. She examined every item there carefully, picked up each of the stuffed animals on the bed, then went through the jewelry box, the clothes in the drawers, the shoes in the closet, everything.

And she found nothing.

Defeated, A.J. left the room and went into the one next door—Carolyn's old room, she guessed from the soft rose color on the walls and the white furnishings. Tired, frustrated, scared and angry, A.J. sat down on the bed.

Her gaze wandered around the room. Carolyn had said she'd left to go to college in Chicago, then taken a job there after graduation. So she'd never come back here to live. A.J. gathered that some sort of tension between Carolyn and her parents had developed when Grace took Billy to raise as her own son. She wasn't sure of all the details, and she hadn't asked about them. But now, as she sat here in Carolyn's old room, A.J. thought it was all so sad—the image of Grace McKay never changing her house, waiting for her two girls to come home.

A.J. looked around, noting that there were still a few girlish things in the room. She walked over to a bookshelf full of mementos, saw a worn-looking doll with long brown braids, a stuffed bear, a little ballerina figurine encased in a water-filled globe. Picking it up, A.J. turned it upside down and watched as the glitter floated down from the top, imitating falling snow. She found it fascinating. And the figure inside wasn't a ballerina, as she'd first thought. It was a skater on a pond.

"A.J. . . ." she heard Jack call.

"Upstairs," she said, turning the snowball over and finding a crank that she suspected made the figurine skate. She wound it and was surprised to hear music playing as well. She turned the globe right side up again, and the fake snow began to fall. The skater twirled around the surface and the music played—the "Starlight Waltz."

A.J. dropped the globe. It shattered as it hit the floor.

Starlight Waltz.

"A.J.?"

Suddenly Jack was there beside her, questioning her. She wasn't sure what he was saying, and she felt strange.

"I don't like that song," she told him, as if that explained everything.

"What song? What happened?"

Then she realized the song wasn't playing anymore.

"The 'Starlight Waltz,'" she said, feeling a little sick to her stomach. "I turned the crank on the bottom, and I thought it would make the skater skate, and she did. But it made the music play, too. And...I didn't like the song."

She bent down to pull the figurine from the mess on the floor, and scraped her hand on a piece of broken glass.

"Careful," Jack said.

Curiously, it didn't hurt at all, though she saw blood pooling on her finger.

"Let me see," Jack said, taking her hand. "You're trembling. Come and sit down, while I find something to put on that cut and something to clean up this mess."

He led her to the bed, and she sat. She was a little dizzy, a little disoriented.

"Jack?" she said, anxious all of a sudden.

"I'm here," he replied, back at her side. "The medicine cabinet was cleaned out, but I found some tissues in the bathroom."

She held out her hand to him, and felt a little better when he took it.

"It's just a scratch," he said. "Hold the tissue on it tight until it stops bleeding, okay?"

She nodded.

"A.J., tell me what happened."

"I didn't like the song," she told him again. If she could just figure out what that meant, surely everything would fall into place.

She was scaring him; she could tell by the way he was watching her, waiting.

"I'm going to clean up the glass. You stay put, okay?"

She nodded. That seemed the safest thing to do—stay there on the bed, stay quiet, try not to work too hard at figuring this whole thing out.

So she waited. It seemed as if she waited forever for Jack to return. Where was he? Why didn't he come back?

"Jack?" she called out.

"I'll be right there, as soon as I find the broom and the dustpan."

"It's beside the washer and dryer, in the closet under the steps."

And then she waited. Her finger hurt now, she noted curiously. It hadn't before. She took the tissue off for a second, but she was still bleeding. Replacing the tissue, she pinched her finger so tight it hurt.

"Jack?" She looked up to see him standing in the doorway, a broom in his hand and the oddest expression on his face.

He propped the broom against the doorframe, then made his way carefully around the glass on the floor until he reached the bed.

"My hand's almost stopped bleeding," she told him when he continued to look at her strangely. "What?"

He sat down beside her and drew her into his arms, pressing her face against his chest.

"What is it, Jack? Something's wrong. I know it is."

"Think about what you told me, A.J."

"About the song? It frightened me. I don't know why."

"No," he said. "After that. The broom. I looked all over the house for it, in three different closets."

"I don't—"

"You knew exactly where it was, darlin'. How did you know?"

"It's always been there," she said, as if that explained everything.

"How did you know, darlin'?"

"I just knew."

"How?"

"I don't know."

And then she felt him wiping the tears from her cheeks, felt him tuck her closer against him, felt his hands on her head, pressing it close enough that she could hear his heart beating beneath her ear.

A broom. After all this time, the first thing that had come back to her was the place where the broom was kept.

It had always been there in this house...in Annie's house...in her house.

She was finally starting to remember.

A.J. thought all her memories would come tumbling back to her right then and there, but it wasn't that easy. Nothing else in the house sparked a recollection, though she did find herself drawn to a photograph of Henry McKay.

"He died just last year, didn't he?" she asked Jack when he found her sitting in the living room holding the picture, which showed the man and his two daughters.

"Sometime in the spring."

"Carolyn said he was wonderful."

"Anything else?" he said, referring to her elusive memories.

She shook her head, then looked down at the man in the photograph, one girl on each knee. "I just missed seeing him again. It hasn't even been a year since he died."

"Do you remember him at all, A.J.?"

"No."

The house seemed a good place to hide out and wait, so they stayed there. At times, they saw cars with television station logos driving by slowly, but they must have been satisfied seeing the empty driveway, because no one came to the door.

Jack called Carolyn on his portable phone and learned that Hope House was surrounded by television reporters and photographers, all looking for the girl who'd seemingly come back from the dead. They were sure she would be the star witness against the man accused of kidnapping at least five little girls and suspected of murdering three of them.

There was nothing new on Ray Williams.

"Do we have to go back to Chicago?" A.J. said later.

"I think the people in my office could manage one more day without me," Jack replied. "Where do you want to go?"

"Anywhere but Chicago."

His beeper went off then. A.J. couldn't help but tense. What else could possibly happen today? How much more could she take?

She was still coming to terms with the fact that she knew where things were kept in this house, mundane things like the broom and the vacuum cleaner. And that snowball of Carolyn's, playing that song she couldn't stand. She was sure she wasn't supposed to touch that snowball—that the thirteen-year-old Annie hadn't been supposed to touch it. It must have been something Carolyn treasured. And the song . . . she couldn't begin to understand why that song affected her so.

Just thinking about it was enough to push her up off the couch and send her pacing around the living room. Annie McKay's memories were somewhere inside her head, where they'd been buried for nearly eleven years.

What could have happened to her that was so horrible, Annie had been totally wiped out of A.J.'s mind? The man had taken her, but he hadn't raped her. What else had he done? What was she so afraid of remembering?

It was tied up with that snowball, that simple little toy. Why else would she have such a reaction to it?

A.J. stopped pacing and turned as Jack walked back into the room. "Ray Williams?" she said.

"Maybe. We're searching the outskirts of the national forest, as best we can, and the police think they've found a couple of fishermen who might have seen him earlier to-day."

"Where?"

"A couple of hours southeast of here, somewhere in the woods. He's probably hiding out at that cabin of his, which we still haven't been able to find."

A couple of hours. Thank God he was that far away, at least. But the more she considered it in her mind, the more certain she was of what she had to do next.

"I want to go there," she said.

"No."

"What if I'm the only one who can take you there?"

"*I* don't even know where he is. That forest covers thousands of acres."

"We can go to the general area, at least. Maybe that's all it will take for me to remember."

"Darlin', I know you're scared of this man. I know you want him behind bars. Believe me, so do I. But don't put yourself through this. Coming back to this town was hard enough, but—"

"Coming here was what made me remember anything at all."

"Think about the way you reacted to that song, A.J. It was just a song. What if we do find this cabin of his, and it's the place where he took you? What do you think that's going to do to you?"

"I don't know." Her stomach was rolling, rebelling at the mere thought. But did she really have any options? "I've been so afraid of my past that I never even tried to find out who I was, Jack. I can't live like that anymore. I don't want to live like that."

"Are you sure you want to go there?"

"I want him caught. I want him behind bars. I don't think I'm going to feel safe until that happens."

* * *

The Hoosier National Forest was a sprawling area drifting south from Bloomington, Indiana, all the way to the Ohio River, the border with Kentucky. There were parks, lakes, rivers. It was full of tiny, sparsely populated areas, and a multitude of little roads seemingly leading to nowhere.

Ray Williams had gone down one of those little roads and disappeared. So had Annie McKay and three other unfortunate girls.

A.J. pulled Jack's map out of his briefcase. The land, so flat in much of the state, had finally given way to a few gently rolling hills.

She imagined herself disappearing into the trees, being swallowed up by them.

Except she had made it out of there. And she was going back now, of her own free will. She was stronger this time. She wasn't powerless, as a thirteen-year-old girl would have been against a grown man.

He would not hurt her this time. And he would never hurt anyone again, once Jack MacAlister got through with him in court.

"See anything on the map?" Jack said.

"No."

"Anything along the road that looks familiar?"

"Not yet."

"It's going to get dark soon. We'll have to stop for the night."

With Ray Williams nearby? She hated the idea. "We can look for another hour or so, can't we?"

"Sure."

They kept driving, but found nothing, heard nothing from the other people searching. They drove through a dozen little towns, then stopped for dinner at a rustic roadside café. The waitress was big, round and chatty. A.J. was only half listening to the woman as she and Jack were finishing their meal, when the woman asked if they were heading to the lake at the end of the road.

"There's a lake?" A.J. said. She was surprised she hadn't noticed the signs on the way in, but she'd been drifting off to sleep when they stopped.

"A beautiful lake," the woman said, "and a lodge, if the two of you are looking for a place to stay. The Starlight Lodge is the nicest one around here."

Starlight?

"What's the name of the lake?" she said, seeing the glitter-snow falling on the figure of the skater, hearing the music in her mind now.

"Starlight Lake, of course," the woman said.

Suddenly the room started to spin, and Jack picked her up in his arms and carried her out of there.

"What is it?" he said, when they got outside and he set her down on her feet by the parked car.

"I can't...breathe," she gasped.

Scooping her up, he placed her on the hood of the car, then pushed her head down between her legs and held her there so that she wouldn't fall. "I'm more worried about you passing out on me, at the moment."

She felt better in a little while, and tried to get up.

"Stay down," he said. "Give it another minute or two."

Somehow, she ended up with her arms around him, her head on his shoulder. "It's the lake."

"What about it, darlin'?"

"He took me to the lake. Starlight Lake. He told me it was a magical place, because the stars came down and danced on the surface of the water. And I would sit there staring at the water and thinking about Carolyn's snowball with the glitter inside it raining down on the little skater while the 'Starlight Waltz' played."

It came to her so clearly now, just that instant in time, nothing more. But for a moment, she felt it all, the emotions as strong and as frightening as if the whole thing had happened yesterday.

She'd been scared to death in that instant. And this was just the beginning, she told herself, just one moment out of endless frightening moments.

A.J. looked up into a cloudless sky filled with a million stars. He was here. Those same stars were shining down on him now, as well, and they had to find him.

She had to hold herself together and lead everyone to him. It was the only way she would be safe again.

"He took me to the lake," she said. "That's where he is now. That's where the cabin is, somewhere on Starlight Lake."

Chapter 17

Jack MacAlister was scared. A.J. was surprised to realize that, because it was so unlike him to be frightened of anything. He'd begged her to let him take her somewhere else while he came back to help find this man. She'd refused. She could be as stubborn as he was, and it was long past time, he realized that.

Then he'd said he'd come with her, stay with her until Ray Williams was located. It might be a while, because the lake had twelve miles of shoreline.

"He's destroying the evidence right now," A.J. told him. "You said that's what he'd do. That's why he came here, to get rid of anything linking him to the kidnappings."

"We'll find him, and we'll get what we need," Jack said. "He won't ever go free after this."

"I'll testify," she said, hating the thought. "I don't care what kind of evidence he destroys. I'll still be here, and I'll testify. That will be enough, won't it?"

"He's going away, A.J. I promise you that."

"He has to," she said, keeping a death grip on Jack's hand. "Because otherwise I couldn't stand it."

"Are you sure it's him? When you remembered the lake, could you see his face?"

She nodded. "I don't know how I ever forgot his face."

Jack called in every favor any law-enforcement agency in Indiana owed him. He called the local police and the state police, and Drew, to get the FBI involved. They set up roadblocks on the three routes leading to and from the lake, then started searching at four different points along the shoreline, with each team working its way clockwise around the shore. They were going to find Ray Williams.

A.J. sat in the car outside the Starlight Lodge, where a makeshift command post had been set up. Jack wanted her to try to sleep, but that would have been impossible. So she sat in the car, because it was quiet and she could be alone there. Because all those men knew all about her, and she didn't want them looking at her with that strange mixture of pity and curiosity anymore. She supposed she might as well get used to it, because she'd probably be seeing a lot of those looks in the future.

Things were coming back to her now, slowly, in brief snatches. She remembered Hope, Illinois, remembered a kitten she'd had when she was six or seven, remembered the elderly woman who'd lived next door and made the most incredible cakes from scratch, remembered her father in his fishing clothes. She cried a little remembering an afternoon spent sitting on the banks of the creek with her father.

If only she'd made it back a little sooner, she could have seen him again. He could have known that she was all right. She wondered if he knew now—prayed that he did.

She remembered her mother, remembered Carolyn, remembered the first time Carolyn had ever gone out with Drew, remembered that awful fight Carolyn and her parents had had the first time Drew Delaney came to the house.

All those years, she thought. So much she'd missed. How would they ever catch up on all of it?

MacAlister was swimming in paperwork from the county assessor's office. He was looking over deeds to the property here. Someone had to own the property where Ray Williams was staying, someone who paid taxes and whose name appeared on the tax rolls. If not Ray Williams, someone he knew, maybe someone related to him.

He would have liked to go out with one of the groups searching along the shoreline, but he hadn't talked A.J. into leaving yet, and until he did, he wasn't going to let her get more than twenty feet away from him—not while that bastard was still on the loose.

Williams had to be half-crazy by now, had to know that he was trapped here, that he was going to prison and never coming out again. A man like that was capable of anything.

MacAlister glanced out the front window of the room, to where his car was parked, to where A.J. was sitting.

He hadn't wanted to let her get that far away from him, but she'd insisted, and he'd picked up on the way everyone in the room was watching her. He knew she would hate that. He wished he could have done more to protect her from that sort of thing—hell, from everything, past and present.

He hadn't been there at all in the past, though he was going to help her deal with it as best he could. He would gladly have done anything to keep her out of this whole situation right now, but it had all blown up in his face. He should never have let her talk him into bringing her to Hope.

But then, she was one determined woman. Brave, strong, dedicated to her work, and extremely sexy. How had he ever gotten so lucky as to wind up following her out into the snow that night?

He looked out the window, had to wipe his hand along the pane to clear it of the fog, so that he could see the car, so that he could see . . .

Nothing.

Nothing but the empty car.

A.J. was gone.

He tore out of the room, opened up the car and searched it, even though he could easily see that she wasn't there. He walked around the lodge, walked down to the lake, and found nothing.

Then he screamed her name.

No answer, at least not from her. Men from inside the command center came barreling around the side of the lodge. He calmed down enough to tell them what had happened, then turned around and looked out over the water.

The sun was just coming up. It glinted off the surface of the water, blinding him for a minute.

He thought he saw something off to the right, maybe nothing more than a reflection, where something caught the sunlight at just the right angle, but that would have to be enough. It was all he had. He took off running.

He ran for about five miles; he judged the distance by how exhausted he was at the end. Normally, three was his limit, and that wasn't three miles running over leaves, roots, rocks and anything else that happened to be sticking out of the ground.

He must have passed her; she couldn't have come this far this fast. He took comfort in that, until he realized she could have covered the distance easily in a car, that she would have had no choice in the matter if someone forced her to get into a car.

Ray Williams wouldn't get away. The lake was surrounded; there were no roads out that the man could take and not get caught. He would not get away with A.J.

He had had her...for how long now? Forty minutes or so? More than enough time to do...whatever he wanted to with her.

Jack felt sick at the thought of that man getting his hands on her. He'd promised her Ray Williams would have to get through him to get to her, he'd told her he felt capable of killing Williams with his bare hands.

And he did.

Given the chance, he might well do that this morning, if that man did one more thing to hurt A.J.

Jack paced back and forth. He had to think. Thinking would get him through this.

Had she remembered something? If Ray Williams hadn't found her, had she found him? He didn't see what other explanation there could be for her disappearance.

And now that he was thinking a fraction more rationally than before, he knew there was no way Ray Williams would have come to the lodge, not when it was surrounded by law enforcement. He wouldn't have come into the parking lot and grabbed A.J. out of a parked car in front of their command center. It would be suicidal and absolutely impossible.

So, if he hadn't taken A.J., she must have left of her own free will. She must have remembered something.

He rubbed his forehead, looked out over the lake and wondered if she was staring at it now, again, as she had all those years ago.

I'm coming, he told her silently, praying that somehow she would hear. Hang on, because I'm coming.

And then he ran back toward the lodge.

Luckily, he met one of the search teams on his way back and caught a ride with them. When they arrived back at the lodge, no one there had found a trace of her.

"Mr. MacAlister?" a man in uniform standing in the doorway said.

"Yes?" He motioned the man over.

The man handed him a manila envelope. "You dropped these when you left."

It was the tax records showing who owned property at the lake. He had the urge to crumple them into a ball in his hands, but he resisted. Glancing down at the list of property owners, his gaze hit on one name.

Jennings.

According to the county tax commission, a Marvin Jennings owned property at the lake. He knew from digging into A.J.'s background that the man who raised her had been named Randall Jennings and that he and his wife had lived in a small town in Indiana called Norfolk before moving with her to Wisconsin.

Marvin Jennings had his tax bill sent to a Norfolk address. It couldn't be a coincidence.

"Where's that cabin?" MacAlister said to one of the local officers, pointing to the address listed next to Jennings's tax bill.

"Somewhere down this main road."

"Let's go."

They took the road, in hopes of finding some kind of marker on the turnoff to the Jennings place.

It seemed to take forever. Half of the cabins weren't designated by any name or number. MacAlister figured A.J. had been gone for about an hour before they finally found the place. At least they thought this was it. Two driveways back, they'd seen a sign for the Ryan cabin, and the tax rolls showed the Ryans two lots away from the Jennings cabin.

They walked down a path that barely seemed wide enough for a vehicle, through eerily silent woods. MacAlister, someone from the FBI and two local deputies walked into the clearing. There was no car, and no sign of life anywhere around the cabin. One of the deputies tried the door.

"Locked," he said.

"Break it down."

"Did you get a search warrant while I wasn't looking?"

He hadn't even considered it, and there was no way he was going to wait for one. To hell with the case. If the evidence in that cabin got thrown out of court because of what he was about to do, he didn't care. That man had A.J.

"Either break it down," he told the deputy, "or get out of my way while I break it down."

"Be my guest," the deputy said, stepping aside.

The door gave way easily, the wood splintering around the padlock, and clattered to the floor. There was no one inside the three-room cabin. He did find a mailing address on a fishing magazine that told him he was in the Jennings cabin. So where the hell was Ray Williams? And where was A.J.?

He went around to the back of the cabin, catching a glimpse of the lake through the woods, but there was no trace of A.J. or Williams.

Frustrated, and more frightened than he'd ever been in his life, he called out her name. Cupping his hands around his mouth, he did it again, and again, in every direction around the cabin.

"Jack?"

He turned to the left. Had the voice come from the left? Had she called his name? He called to her again, and he was sure this time that she answered him.

Once again, he took off through the woods, with the three other men trailing after him.

There was no path that he could find, nothing that he could see through the trees. The unraked leaves of the previous fall rustled at his feet as he ran, the tree branches scratching at his arms and his face when he couldn't push them out of the way fast enough.

He called her name again, and before she could answer him he broke through the trees into a small clearing, saw the remains of an old abandoned cabin.

This was Williams's place. It had to be. Why the hell couldn't he have found it weeks ago, before it ever came to this? Before A.J. had to see this place again? Before this monster of a man could get loose and make it back here?

"A.J.?" he called.

He went left, motioned for the two deputies to go right. The man from the FBI followed him. As they rounded the second corner of the cabin, he saw her. She had to be all right—she was standing on her own two feet.

And then he saw Ray Williams grab her from behind, lock his arm around her neck so that he was half choking her, then pull a huge hunting knife out of his pocket.

"Stay back," he warned them.

Jack's gaze locked on A.J.'s, willing her to stay calm, to be still, to let them get her out of this.

Steady, he told her silently, and told himself the same thing.

"Get back," Williams said as the four men tightened their circle around him. "She's mine, and you're not taking her from me this time."

"Drop the knife, Ray," Jack said, drawing the man's gaze, giving the deputies on the other side of him time to draw their guns and take aim. "There's no way out of here. If you don't let her go in the next five seconds, the deputies behind you are going to start shooting. Understand?"

Williams whirled around, knocking A.J. off-balance as he turned her with him, then saw the two deputies, guns drawn and pointed at him. He touched the tip of the knife to A.J.'s throat.

"Tell them to get back," he told her.

A.J. opened her mouth, then closed it again. He saw her grimace, saw the revulsion on her face.

Hang on, he told her. Just hang on. Then he forced his attention back to Williams.

"They know what you've done, Ray. They could shoot you right now, and still sleep like babies tonight. And they might be doing you a favor, because one way or another you're going to die. If not today, then after the judge and I get through with you.''

"You can't just shoot me,'' he said.

"Who's going to stop us?'' MacAlister said, wishing the man would give them an excuse. "Let her go. Let her go now.''

For a moment, he thought Williams was going to do just that. Then the man sank the tip of his knife into A.J.'s throat, drawing blood.

"Get back!'' Williams screamed.

Jack screamed, as well, and ran for the man, but A.J. was quicker. Williams was startled by the noise, by the confusion of the four men closing in on him, and A.J. took full advantage of that. Getting her hand free, she elbowed him in the stomach, then bit the arm he held around her neck.

The knife fell to the ground.

Ray Williams fell to his knees.

A.J. kicked him in the face and knocked him flat on the ground. "You bastard,'' she said, then kicked him again, this time in the groin.

Jack came up behind her and pulled her back, away from Williams. She fought him for a minute, screaming at the man, still trying to get to him.

He tried to turn her around, but she wouldn't let him. She refused to take her eyes off Ray Williams. She was shaking, full of nervous energy, all her attention focused on the man on the ground.

"It's all right, darlin',`` he said, waiting for the words to sink in.

The deputies pulled Ray Williams to his feet, none too gently. They searched him, read him his rights and handcuffed him.

"He kidnapped me,'' she said as she watched the deputies lead the now sobbing man away.

"I know." Jack slid his arm around her waist from behind and held on to her. Her neck was bleeding slightly. He kept telling himself it couldn't be much more than a superficial wound.

"He took pictures of me," she said, her voice filled with pain.

Jack knew exactly what she meant. And it didn't surprise him.

"He was trying to get rid of them," A.J. said. "He was getting rid of everything. He was burying everything in a hole back there."

Jack held her tighter, and put a hand over the cut on her neck. He had come so close to losing her today. Dear God, if he had lost her...

"We'll get all the evidence we need," he told her. "We've got him now, A.J. He's never going to hurt you again."

"I wasn't the only one," she said. "Those other little girls, he took them, too. He told me about them. And they didn't get away. I think they're back there. I think I saw one of their graves."

And then she started to cry.

He held her, and knew he might never be able to bring himself to let her go. If they hadn't found her, if that knife had gone in another half inch, if she hadn't been strong enough and smart enough to get away from that man...

Oblivious of anything else around them, he closed his eyes and locked his arms around her.

"It's all over," he told her, knowing that eventually she'd calm down enough for the words to sink in.

And maybe soon he'd calm down enough to understand that he had her back, that she was safe, that this whole nightmare was over.

He was going to take her away from here, take her back to that inn in Hope, to that room at the top of the old house,

the one with the big four-poster bed, and barricade the door.
There would be nothing and no one in the world but the two
of them.

Chapter 18

Two weeks later, the furor still hadn't died down.

A.J. had taken refuge in Jack's parents' house, if it could be called a house. It was more like a mansion, but that wasn't the most appealing thing about it for A.J. She loved it for the brick wall surrounding it, for the private security gate that kept the rest of the world out and kept her safe inside.

Sometimes she wished she could stay here forever. Jack's mother had been wonderful, even if A.J. did find her incredibly intimidating.

Mrs. MacAlister had been born to money, her grandfather having built half the city. She lived in a fifteen-room mansion on Chicago's Gold Coast, entertained the mayor, the governor and the richest men in the city on a regular basis, served on all the most important social committees.

A.J. had expected to have nothing in common with the woman, expected her to turn up her nose at A.J. and let her know in no uncertain terms that she was absolutely wrong for her son. But she hadn't.

She'd been kind, and quite considerate. The only fault that A.J. could find with her was that she was quite comfortable sticking her nose into everyone's business, especially Jack's. The woman desperately wanted grandchildren, and she seemed to think A.J. was going to give them to her. A.J. had no idea what to say to that. She certainly hadn't talked to Jack about the subject, and had no intention of bring it up.

After all, what could she say? Your mother is so desperate for grandchildren that she thinks I'd be acceptable as the mother of your babies?

She loved Jack MacAlister, of course, although she hadn't admitted that to his mother yet. She just stayed safe behind that brick wall, slept, soaked in the tub, avoided the television newscasts and the newspapers at all costs, refused to take phone calls from journalists, and from any number of people she really should talk to. Her mother, Carolyn, Nick...they kept calling, and A.J. had the housekeeper tell them she was resting. More often than not, it wasn't a lie.

She was vegetating in the lap of luxury. She planted herself in one of the chaise longues by the pool and stared at the sky, or curled up in the library with a book.

She didn't want to move or talk or see anyone. She wanted to think things through, to try to make sense of it all, to get ready to step back into her life and get on with things.

Why couldn't anyone understand that?

She remembered almost everything now. Her memories of the time at the cabin were still foggy, but they probably always would be, because she'd more than likely been drugged. At least that was what Jack thought. Nick tended to agree, from what she'd told him about her recollections. It seemed likely that Ray Williams drugged A.J. when he took her.

She remembered her feelings from that time—terror, bewilderment. She remembered Williams telling her that her parents were dead, that there was no one left to take care of her except him. And then he'd told her in great detail the things he planned to do to her.

And then something had happened. Someone had come to the cabin. The Jenningses, maybe? Ray Williams had known them somehow, having stayed at a man named Marvin Jennings's cabin at the lake.

But how had the Jenningses ended up with her? And why had they kept her? Why hadn't they given her back to her parents? They had to have known, at some point, that her parents and the FBI were looking for her. So why wouldn't they have taken her home?

A.J. heard a knock on the door and knew right away who it was. No one knocked on her door except the servants, and they never came this late. "Come in."

Jack walked in, his coat thrown over his shoulder, his tie hanging loose around his neck.

"Hi, darlin', I'm home," he said, like an old married man, then leaned over to kiss her softly on the lips.

She glanced at the clock; it was after ten. "You must be exhausted."

He'd been spending his days working on the Ray Williams case, and his nights with her. She'd protested at first— what would his parents think?

That I'm worried about you? he'd suggested. *That I'm obsessed with you? That I can't possibly be away from you for any length of time?*

And then he'd reminded her how big the house was, how far her bedroom was from his parents', and that there was nothing in the world that was going to keep him away from her now. So she'd given in. She needed him desperately, as well, even if he just held her in his arms while she slept.

"Miss me today?" he asked, kicking off his shoes. He threw his coat over the chair, and after removing his tie and unbuttoning his shirt, he situated himself on the bed beside her.

A.J. curled into his side. The world as she knew it settled into a wonderful, predictable order. He was back, with her, where she desperately needed him to be. "I may have given you a thought or two. How did it go?"

"I think we're going to take the plea. We can get him put away for life with no parole. He's willing to take that, because he's afraid of the death penalty. What would you think of that?"

She shivered and snuggled closer to him. "I'm not sure how I'd feel about it."

"It means no trial. None of the evidence would ever have to come out. No one would have to testify in open court."

"I know. Believe me, that part is tempting."

"It would be all over, A.J. Time to move on, instead of dwelling on the past until we could get it to trial and finish it. And the appeals in a death-penalty case can drag on for ten years or more."

"I know. Did you talk to the parents of the girls?"

They'd found two bodies buried near the cabin, but had found nothing regarding the third girl. There was no telling what had happened to her. Ray Williams wasn't talking about her, either.

"The parents are thinking it over right now. I'll let you know what they decide."

She nodded.

"I have some other news for you," he said.

"What?"

"I told you Ray Williams was using a cabin owned by a man named Marvin Jennings, and that he lived in Norfolk, Indiana."

"Yes."

"Marvin Jennings is Randall Jennings's uncle. Turns out Ray Williams is Marvin's illegitimate son."

"So they did know him," she said, stunned.

Jack nodded. "I found this." He held out a letter to her, one with her name on it in what she could have sworn was Randall Jennings's scrawl.

She was afraid to even touch it.

"Go ahead," he said. "I've already read it."

No doubt in an effort to protect her. "I don't understand. Where did you get it?"

"From Marvin. He was the Jenningses' closest living relative, and he inherited everything under the terms of the Jenningses' will. Said he hadn't heard from them in seven years at the time they died, and he never did understand why, until he was flipping through some of his nephew's private papers and found this letter."

"I don't want to read it."

"Of course you do. Marvin tried to find you, after he read it. But it was too late. You'd disappeared, and he had no idea where to find you."

"It's too late now."

"A.J., this is the last piece of the puzzle."

She eyed it as if it were a bottle of pure poison. What could Randall Jennings possibly have to say to her after all this time that would make any difference? They'd taken her. They'd kept her from her family. They'd filled her head with the memories of a little girl who'd drowned when she was thirteen years old. They had let her wonder all that time about the fear that was always in the back of her mind, the fear that she never quite understood.

Maybe she did need those answers after all.

She held out her hand for the letter. He rearranged some pillows against the headboard and leaned back against them, pulling her back against him. Once again, his big, strong arms encircled her. She could face any demon if she was within the circle of his arms.

She removed the letter from the envelope. The pages were obviously old and worn. She started to read.

My dearest Allison,

If you're reading this letter, then I must be gone. I can't imagine finding the courage to say these words to you myself, but I knew you'd find out the truth once your mother and I passed away and that I owed you an explanation.

I'm truly sorry that we kept you away from your real family all these years and that I was too selfish and too much of a coward to put things to rights long before this.

You see, we just loved you so much. We needed you so badly. Please, if you believe nothing else that I'm going to tell you, believe that. We loved you, Allison.

By now you know that there was another Allison before you, that we lost her that day by the docks. Nothing was ever the same after that. If I could have gone in her place, I would have gladly done so. And I thought about going with her, about taking my own life.

But I didn't know what would become of your mother. It seemed so selfish to leave her alone. She was never the same after our Allison died. Over the years, our family doctor told me she needed help, the kind he couldn't give her, that she might need to be put in some sort of institution. But I could never bring myself to do that to her.

We thought, after a couple of years, that it might be easier to live somewhere else, where the memories weren't so strong. Where we couldn't drive down the street and see the places we'd been and remember the things we'd done with our Allison. So we sold our house, I left my job, and we packed our things into the truck and headed for St. Louis, because I had cousins there who said they'd help me find work and help me take care of your mother.

We wanted to do one last thing in Indiana before we left. A picture frame was broken as we were packing, and it held the last photo ever taken of our Allison. The picture was scratched, and we couldn't stand the idea of losing it. But I knew who'd taken it—my uncle's boy, Ray.

I put off going to see him until the last minute, because I never liked Ray. By now, I'm sure you know why. I caught him once doing things he shouldn't be doing with another cousin of his, and to be honest about it, I didn't even know what he was doing at first. I didn't want to believe that I actually saw what I did, and when I tried to tell my uncle and the boy's mother, they didn't want to hear it.

I should have tried harder, right then and there, to make them believe me and to get some help for that boy. But I didn't, and I've had a terrible time trying to live with that all these years.

Anyway, we were ready to leave town, and we still hadn't managed to find Ray. We'd gone to the house several times and missed him, and finally his mother told us he'd gone to that old fishing cabin Marvin had on the lake. We went there on our way out of town to find him.

And that's when we found you.

I didn't know what to do. Marvin had told me years ago that Ray had a daughter somewhere, and I thought at first you were his little girl. And I knew he'd hurt you.

I beat him half to death that day, thinking I might knock some sense into that boy. I never went back to find out.

You tried to run away from Ray when we got there, and you fell and banged your head on one of the rocks. When you came to, you couldn't tell us anything. You were crying and clinging to my wife.

There was no way I was going to leave you with Ray. I didn't know what else to do. The boy was sick. Someone should have helped him. I should have made sure of that, but everything got so complicated later. And I couldn't stand the idea of losing you. But I'm getting ahead of myself.

We took you with us and left Ray there. Libby started talking crazy, like I'd never heard her before. She started calling you Allison, had you and her both convinced that you were our daughter. It scared me. I knew it was time for me to put her in an institution, and I didn't see how I'd go on without her. I told myself that as soon as we got settled in St. Louis, I'd call Marvin and find out where you belonged, that once Ray was taken care of and once I knew you'd be safe, we'd send you back home.

I didn't find work in St. Louis, and we ended up in Wisconsin instead. Months went by. I kept trying to tell Marvin what Ray had done, but he didn't believe me. And later I found out one of the reasons why. I was telling him that Ray had hurt his little girl, but you weren't his little girl. Marvin kept trying to tell me that, and I just didn't believe him. I thought he didn't want to hear the truth, that he was kidding himself, the way I kidded myself about what I saw Ray do to one of his cousins when he was younger.

Anyway, we'd had you for about six months when I saw your picture on the TV one night, when I realized that you weren't Ray's little girl, that you belonged to someone else. And I got scared. The FBI had all sorts of people looking for you. I thought they'd put me in prison, and again, I couldn't imagine what would happen to your mother.

She believed it when she told you that you were our Allison. It nearly killed her when we lost our daughter, and I knew she'd never make it through something like that again.

You were so sweet, so kind and gentle. We loved you so much. We needed you.

I started fooling myself, telling myself that those other people must not have been looking out for you the way they should have, to let Ray snatch you. I told myself that you needed us, just as much as we needed you, that no one could take care of you and love you the way we did.

I told myself sometimes that I'd give us one more week with you, one more month, that I'd find a way to turn myself in and explain everything so that somebody would believe me.

And I never did it. Weeks went by, months, years now. I couldn't bring myself to give you back.

It was selfish of me and cowardly. I know what I did to your other family, because I'd lost a daughter myself. I knew exactly what they were going through. I've suffered with my conscience all these years, and it's in God's hands now. He will be the one who decides how I'll pay for what I've done wrong.

I do have to ask one more thing of you, though I have no right to do that. Your mother. Allison, she believes in her heart that she is your mother, and if I'm gone, she'll have no one. Please, blame me, not her. Please don't make her suffer for things she simply can't understand. Please watch out for her and love her, the way she's loved you all these years.

And please, let me tell you one last time how much I loved you. That part was never a lie.

A tear fell from her cheek onto the paper, which was already stained with too many tears. And not all of them were hers. The ink had bled in places and smeared; he'd been crying himself when he wrote the letter.

She looked at the date, noting that it was a few short weeks before his death. A.J. wondered if he'd had some premonition about the train wreck that had taken his life and that of—her other mother.

"This is bizarre," she told Jack.

"I know, but I believe him. I think he walked into the middle of this mess someone else created, and didn't know how to get out of it. I think he loved you, A.J."

She looked back down at the letter. *That part was never a lie.*

She wanted to believe it. She needed to believe it. "They were good people. They were kind to me." Enough time had passed that she could admit that.

Jack held her close. "Does it help, a little, to know why they did it? How it all happened?"

"I'm glad you found the letter and that you brought it to me. I'm glad you're here, Jack. I don't know what I would have done without you these past few weeks."

He turned her face to his. "I don't know what I'd ever do without you. A.J., I—"

She put her fingers across his lips. "A little longer, please. Just give me a few more days."

"What are you so afraid of?" he said, working hard at controlling his frustration.

Loving him, losing him—that summed it all up quite nicely.

"Everything's happened so fast. Everything's changed, Jack. My whole life, and I...I need some time. Do you think we could talk about something else?"

He didn't like it, but he went along with it. "How's the pool? I hear you've turned lazy on me."

"I love the pool."

"How's my mother?"

"She's a trip. She tried out baby names on me today."

"Did you two come up with anything?"

"Baby names?" She couldn't believe she'd brought this up with him—and all because she was so intent on changing the subject.

"Well?" he said, sounding totally serious. "Babies have to have names."

"We're not having a baby," she said.

"I could make a liar out of you by morning."

That left her absolutely speechless.

"Hey." He took her by the chin and tilted her face up to his. "I've been patient, A.J. Give me that, at least. And tell me one thing. Why are you so scared of having this conversation with me?"

"About babies?"

"About us."

"We weren't talking about us, Jack, we were talking about what your mother wants to name the grandchildren she wants you to give her."

"Okay." He turned serious. "Let's talk about babies. Make my mother a happy woman, A.J. Be the mother of my children. Come and live with me. Love me. Grow old with me. We'll sit on the porch in our rockers together and laugh about the good old days, and I'll love you as much then as I do now."

She swallowed hard. Dammit, she hadn't been able to stop him before he went and said it.

"Hey," he said when she turned her face away to keep him from seeing the tears on her cheeks.

He wiped them away, the pads of his fingers caressing her cheeks as they followed the path of her tears. "I love you, darlin'. Surely I'm allowed to say that now."

She shook her head. The tears wouldn't stop falling.

"And I know you love me, too," he insisted. "Don't even try to deny it."

"You are the most arrogant man," she said.

"And you're stubborn as hell. What of it?"

She stopped to take a much-needed breath, then another. What was she going to do with him?

"I know you love me," he said. "You already told me so, but it's been too long since the first time. Tell me again."

"Is that some kind of an order?"

"If that's what it takes."

"Why should I tell you that I love you?" He already knew it, after all.

"Why should you tell me?" he repeated incredulously.

She nodded.

"Because I need to hear it."

"Jack—" She started to argue, then thought better of it. Could he really wonder about that? She thought she'd made it more than obvious to him that she would do anything in the world for him.

"Dammit, A.J., I almost lost you out there in the woods. That man had a knife at your throat." He ran his hands over the faint scar from the wound.

She'd almost forgotten that he'd had to watch her struggle. If she had to watch Ray Williams hold a knife to his throat . . .

"I thought I was going to go out of my mind when I walked out of the command center and found the car empty."

"I'm sorry," she said. "I never should have left the car. I just had to walk around for a few minutes. And then, all of a sudden, he was there and dragging me away. I'm sorry, Jack."

"That's not an issue anymore, darlin'. You keep trying to put distance between us and I can't let you. Whatever reason you have for pushing me away like this, you might as well give it up right now. Because it's not going to work. I'm not going anywhere. I'm not going to let you go, and since you're stuck with me, you might as well marry me."

She couldn't help but smile at that. It was the most out-landish reason she'd ever heard for getting married. "Jack, I had no idea you were such a romantic."

He scowled at her. "You want me on one knee?"

"On the bed?"

"You want candles, soft music, flowers—what? Name it. It's yours."

Just like that? She closed her eyes and counted to ten, before she just blurted out to him what was in her heart.

"I feel so... out of touch with reality," she said. "I feel like I've been caught up in a whirlwind, like my whole life has been turned upside down."

"It has, darlin'."

"Jack, I didn't even know you two months ago."

"Do you have any doubts about the way you feel about me now?"

"No." And she should have known better than to argue with him, because he always won. If, by some miracle, she got to spend the rest of her life with him, she'd have to go to law school to learn to fight with words the way he did. "Jack, it's not that."

"Then you must doubt me and the way I feel about you. Why is that?"

She tried to tell him, but couldn't. The words just wouldn't come out.

"A.J., whatever it is, just tell me. We'll work it out, I promise you."

"I do love you, Jack."

He grabbed her and crushed her to him, then covered her mouth with his and kissed her soundly. "Thank God for that."

A.J. held him tight. He was trembling, too, just as she was. Maybe he had needed the words just as much as she did.

"Now," he said, pulling back just a little. "What's the problem?"

The problem? Where did she start? "Everyone I've ever loved, I've lost."

"Okay, let's think about that for a minute. The McKays didn't leave you," he said. "They never stopped loving you, never stopped trying to get you back. You can't blame that on love."

"I don't."

"And the Jenningses died, A.J., but they did love you. Remember what he wrote—that part was never a lie."

She might even be able to accept that. "But I still lost them."

"You'll never lose me," he promised. "I'll never leave you. I won't hurt you, and I'll do my damnedest to see that no one else ever hurts you again."

That sounded even better to her than a marriage vow. She couldn't ask anything more of him than that. But...

"I'm still scared," she confessed.

"Hell, so am I."

"Jack, you're not scared of anything."

"I'm scared of the way I feel about you. Of how much I want you. How much I need you. When I think about coming here day after day to see you, about the way we can't talk about so many things because you're not ready to hear what I have to say...I imagine all these things that could be wrong.

"I think one day you're going to tell me you need some time alone, that you're going to walk out that door and never come back. I think maybe you're going to put your life back together and find that there's no room for me, or that you don't need me the way you thought you did or that you just don't want me anymore.

"A.J., it scares me to death."

She put her hand over her mouth and tried not to cry. "I didn't know. I had no idea..."

"The risk runs both ways, darlin'. You share in the risk, you share in the rewards. And you have to believe that loving someone doesn't have to mean hurting. It doesn't always end that way.''

She wanted to believe that. She wanted to live it.

''And right now,'' he said, ''you're keeping me on tenterhooks, because I just asked you to marry me and you still haven't said yes.''

She'd honestly never thought of it that way—that anyone in love assumed a degree of risks, that trust was essential in being able to love someone.

Sometimes she thought she and the kids at the shelter were the only people in the world scared to trust anyone, scared to depend on anyone.

Maybe everyone else was afraid, too. Even Jack.

''Do you trust me?'' he asked.

''Yes.'' Absolutely.

''And you love me?''

''Yes.''

''That's all we need. Those are the only assurances any two people ever have.''

She couldn't believe how he'd turned the argument around so neatly in his favor. Would she spend the rest of her life losing every argument they got into? ''Did they teach you this in law school?''

''How to propose?''

''How to talk anyone into anything.''

''Can I take that as a yes?''

He'd been teasing before, and she'd been trying to do the same, and then the conversation had taken on earth-shattering proportions.

He wanted to marry her. He meant it.

''Take my hand,'' he said.

She laid her palm across his, and held on for dear life.

''I won't let go, darlin'. I won't let you go. I won't stop loving you, and I won't stop begging you to marry me.''

''Jack MacAlister, you never begged for anything in your whole life.''

"You do want me on my knees, don't you?"

"No."

"Well, I want you—in my arms, in my bed, in my house. I want my babies growing inside you. You want that, too. I dare you to say that you don't."

"I do."

"What?"

"I said I do."

"Those are the magic words, darlin'. It's always a risk. And the only guarantees you'll have are that I love you and that you love me. What else do we need?"

She took a minute, just to make him squirm, then smiled. "I might want you on your knees."

He looked murderous, but down he went. He pulled her down with him and put his arms around her.

"Satisfied now?"

"I might want a ring."

"I'll buy you a rock, something other men can see a mile away."

"You're so kind."

"I've been trying to tell you that all along. I'm a damned nice guy."

"I love you, Jack."

Epilogue

Four months later...

A.J. was hiding upstairs in the bride's room at the back of the rapidly filling church. She still couldn't believe Jack's mother had talked them into a big church wedding with all the trimmings.

But the woman had put up a solid argument. She'd waited this long for her son to marry and, certain he would marry only once in his life, was determined they do it right. And they might as well put the female population of this city on notice that Jack MacAlister was off-limits.

A.J. couldn't argue with her future mother-in-law's reasoning.

"You're not nervous, are you?" Carolyn said from her seat in the corner.

A.J. hadn't sat down in hours. She had too much nervous energy to work off. "No, of course not," she lied. "Were you?"

Carolyn laughed. She and Drew had finally tied the knot two months ago, and the two of them were ecstatic. A.J. knew the only thing that could make her sister happier was if Billy knew the truth—that he was Drew and Carolyn's son.

And maybe he would, someday, when the time was right. For now, it was more than enough that the whole family was back together again.

A.J. looked at her watch. Thirty endless seconds had crept by since the last time she'd looked. She didn't even know why she was nervous, anyway—she loved Jack, and he loved her.

As he kept telling her, it didn't get any better than that. There were no guarantees in love. And maybe she'd stopped needing one, anyway. At first, this whole thing seemed so unreal to her. He seemed too good to be true. But the months had gone by, and he'd never wavered in his support for her, his understanding, his kindness. He said this would be forever, and she'd come to believe that.

She believed in him, in love, and in their future together.

Someone knocked on the door.

"Maybe they finally found the bride's bouquet," Carolyn said, and checked the door.

A.J. wasn't paying much attention, but she did look over when she heard Carolyn arguing with the person at the door. Then Carolyn gave in and said, "It's for you."

She'd barely opened the door two inches, and when A.J. looked through the opening she saw a dark-haired, masked man in a tux.

"Who're you, the Lone Ranger?" she said. "And what are you doing here? You're not supposed to see me before the ceremony. Didn't your mother explain any of this to you, Jack?"

"I can't see you," he said, grinning below the mask. "But she didn't say anything about kissing you."

He pushed his way through the door, closed it behind him and grabbed her. A.J. was laughing so hard, it was difficult to kiss him at first. "I don't think this is what they had in mind when they said the groom shouldn't see the bride before the ceremony."

"You want to go check with Miss Manners first, darlin', or do you want to kiss me quick, before my mother catches me in here?"

"If you two will excuse me for a moment, I'll guard the door," Carolyn said.

A.J. pretended to think about his offer for a moment, then found herself soundly kissed. Heedless of her gown, her veil and her makeup, he nearly crushed her, he held her so close. She felt that quick stab of desire that cut right to the heart of her every time he touched her.

He kissed her again and again, making her hungry for the night they had ahead of them.

He moaned—it was a deep, low sound of pleasure—and slowly pulled away from her.

"Still curls your toes, doesn't it?" he said smugly.

"What if it does?" she replied. "You are the most arrogant man."

"And you love me anyway."

"What are you doing here, Jack?"

"I came came to make sure you're going to walk down that aisle in fifteen minutes."

She liked the sound of that. "You're not worried, are you?"

He swore and yanked off the mask, then stood staring at her for the longest time.

She still hadn't gotten used to the way he saw her. He thought she was beautiful. He made her feel beautiful. He could curl her toes with just a look from those smoky brown eyes of his.

"You look incredible, Mrs. MacAlister. Don't you dare back out on me now."

"You are worried," she said, surprised as she always was when he voiced any of the same doubts she felt. There were still times when it all seemed too good to be true. Yet here she was, ready to walk down the aisle to him.

"You do look beautiful," he said.

"And don't you dare make me cry." She blinked back a few tears. "Now, what are you really doing here?"

"I thought I told you. No, I thought I showed you. I couldn't wait another minute to kiss the bride."

* * * * *

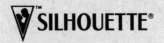

SILHOUETTE

SPECIAL EDITION ®

An invitation to three

Sweet Hope Weddings

from AMY FRAZIER

Marriages are made in Sweet Hope, Georgia—where the brides and grooms-to-be are the last to find out!

♥   ♥   ♥   ♥   ♥

NEW BRIDE IN TOWN
October 1996

WAITING AT THE ALTAR
November 1996

A GOOD GROOM IS HARD TO FIND
December 1996

♥   ♥   ♥   ♥   ♥

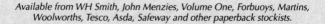

SILHOUETTE

Sensation

COMING NEXT MONTH

SERIOUS RISKS   Rachel Lee

Computer programmer Jessica Kilmer's life altered the moment she
realized classified documents had been stolen from her safe. But the
real change came when she notified the FBI and met Special Agent
Arlen Coulter. Arlen assured her that he would see her to safety, but
his sexy good looks awakened her heart to another danger altogether!

UNCERTAIN ANGELS   Kim Cates

Allison Crawford lived in a wonderland of mansions and private jets,
far from the gritty reality of the streets that Jesse Tyler James knew
too well. But from the moment the seductive renegade careened into
her privileged world, their fates were irrevocably entangled—and
they were heading straight for peril...

ONE GOOD MAN   Kathleen Creighton

Christine Thurmond needed a rescuer. But she'd long despaired of
finding one. Flat on his back with an uncertain future and an
unhealthy dose of bitterness, ex-marine Wood Brown was hardly in
shape to be anyone's saviour. But then Christine walked into his
room and his life—and he couldn't resist chipping off her ice-
princess façade, bit by beautiful bit...

CUTS BOTH WAYS   Dee Holmes

Years ago, Erin Kenyon had helped Ashe Seager through the darkest,
ugliest days of his life. But she'd been off-limits, engaged to marry
the man to whom he owed everything. Now Erin was back, widowed
and still off-limits, desperate to uncover the secrets behind her
husband's mysterious death. But Ashe knew some secrets were better
left untold...

COMING NEXT MONTH FROM

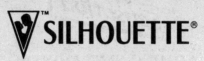

Intrigue

Danger, deception and desire

RECKLESS LOVER Carly Bishop
EXPOSÉ Saranne Dawson
MIDNIGHT COWBOY Adrianne Lee
BABY VS. THE BAR M.J. Rodgers

Special Edition

Satisfying romances packed with emotion

PART-TIME WIFE Susan Mallery
THE REBEL'S BRIDE Christine Flynn
MARRIAGE-TO-BE? Gail Link
WAITING AT THE ALTAR Amy Frazier
RESIST ME IF YOU CAN Janis Reams Hudson
LONESOME COWBOY Lois Faye Dyer

Desire

Provocative, sensual love stories for the woman of today

THE ACCIDENTAL BODYGUARD Ann Major
HARDEN Diana Palmer
FATHER OF THE BROOD Elizabeth Bevarly
THE GROOM, I PRESUME? Annette Broadrick
THE PRODIGAL GROOM Karen Leabo
FALCON'S LAIR Sara Orwig

To celebrate the **1000**th Desire™ title we're giving away a year's supply of Silhouette Desire® novels — absolutely *FREE!*

All you have to do is complete the puzzle below and send it to us by 31 December 1996.

The first 10 correct entries drawn from the bag will each win 12 month's free supply of seductive and breathtaking Silhouette Desire books (6 books every month—worth over £160). The second correct 10 entries drawn will each win a Silhouette music cassette.

S
E
N
S
U
O
U
S

Please turn over for entry details

Word	Letters
SENSUOUS	8
DESIRE	6
DARING	6
SEDUCTIVE	9
EMOTIONAL	9
COMPELLING	10
PASSIONATE	10
CAPTIVATING	11
ADVENTUROUS	11
PROVOCATIVE	11

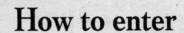

CELEBRATION 1000

How to enter

There are ten words listed overleaf, each of which fits into spaces in the grid according to their length. All you have to do is fit the correct word into the appropriate spaces that have been provided for its letters. We've even done the first one for you!

When you have completed the grid, don't forget to fill in your name and address in the space provided below and pop this page into an envelope (you don't even need a stamp) and post it today. Hurry—competition ends 31st December 1996.

Silhouette® Words of Love
FREEPOST
Croydon
Surrey
CR9 3WZ

Are you a Reader Service Subscriber?　　Yes ❏　　No ❏

Ms/Mrs/Miss/Mr _____

Address _____

_____

_____ Postcode _____

One application per household.

You may be mailed with other offers from other reputable companies as a result of this application. If you would prefer not to receive such offers, please tick box. ❏

mps
MAILING
PREFERENCE
SERVICE

OMA

SILC96